PENGUIN BOOKS

ICON
AND
INFERNO

BOOKS BY MARIE LU

The Legend Series
Legend
Prodigy
Champion
Rebel

The Young Elites Series
The Young Elites
The Rose Society
The Midnight Star

The Warcross Series
Warcross
Wildcard

Batman: Nightwalker

The Kingdom of Back

The Skyhunter Duology
Skyhunter
Steelstriker

The Stars and Smoke Series
Stars and Smoke
Icon and Inferno

ICON
and
INFERNO

A Stars and Smoke Novel

MARIE LU

PENGUIN BOOKS

PENGUIN BOOKS

UK | USA | Canada | Ireland | Australia
India | New Zealand | South Africa

Penguin Books is part of the Penguin Random House group of companies
whose addresses can be found at global.penguinrandomhouse.com

www.penguin.co.uk
www.puffin.co.uk
www.ladybird.co.uk

First published in the USA by Roaring Brook Press, a division of Holtzbrinck Publishing
Holdings Limited Partnership, and in Great Britain by Penguin Books 2024

001

Books design by Aurora Parlagreco
Logos designed by YY Liak
Printed and bound in Great Britain by Clays Ltd, Elcograf S.p.A.

The authorized representative in the EEA is Penguin Random House Ireland,
Morrison Chambers, 32 Nassau Street, Dublin D02 YH68

A CIP catalogue record for this book is available from the British Library

ISBN: 978–0–241–64652–6

All correspondence to:
Penguin Books
Penguin Random House Children's
One Embassy Gardens, 8 Viaduct Gardens, London SW11 7BW

To those seeking joy, and those who give it

CLAREMONT

MISSION LOG

AGENT A: "Do you want to reach out to ██████? Or should I?"

AGENT B: "Makes no difference to me, ma'am."

AGENT A: "I think it might."

AGENT B: "Are you afraid I'm going to scare the kid away?"

AGENT A: "I do think that's a possibility, yes."

AGENT B: "I'm a grumpy old man, not a rabid mongoose."

AGENT A: "Your expression scared the daylights out of our interns when you were tracking down those Orange Alerts we got last year. One of them cried because he thought you were mad at him."

AGENT B: "Look, I like ███████████ just fine. But I don't know how he'll react to a second mission with us. Pop stars aren't exactly easy to book, either. And then there's the issue of the Jackal."

AGENT A: "What's the issue?"

AGENT B: "She's . . . not exactly a fan."

AGENT A: "She said they made an effective enough team."

AGENT B: "I believe her exact words were, *I'd rather be incarcerated in a Moscow prison than have to work with* ███████████ *again.*"

AGENT A: "██████, my dear, when will you learn that asking the Jackal questions when she has the flu isn't going to get you accurate answers? If you haven't noticed, she has found a way to casually ask about him at least once a month since their London mission."

AGENT B: "That doesn't mean anything."

AGENT A: "Mm."

AGENT B: "What?"

AGENT A: "Nothing, I just think you're being a concerned father."

AGENT B: "I'm not her father."

AGENT A: "I know. But I also know why you're worried."

AGENT B: "Pray tell, why is that?"

AGENT A: "Because this is your last mission with ██████. Because that means you won't be here to watch over her anymore. And because you want to protect her, like you always have."

AGENT B: "She's a grown young lady. And a self-sufficient one at that. She doesn't need me to protect her, just like she doesn't need to babysit a spoiled pop star. Again."

AGENT A: "You know it's okay to be worried about her. And it's okay to be worried about retiring."

AGENT B: "I'm not worried. I'm looking forward to retirement."

AGENT A: "Are you?"

AGENT B: "Well, let's say, theoretically, that after I retire . . . I finally ask you out on a real date."

AGENT A: "Then let's say that I'd accept. Theoretically."

AGENT B: "Wait. Really?"

AGENT A: "*Theoretically*, ████. But . . . yes. I would."

AGENT B: "All right, then."

AGENT A: "You're adorable when you smile."

AGENT B: "You see? An adorable man wouldn't scare ██████ away. Shall I contact him, then? Or do you really insist on doing it yourself?"

AGENT A: "Let's have the Jackal do it. She was his partner. She should know how to get a yes out of him. Besides, she'll still startle him less than you will."

AGENT B: "I'm amused that you think so. Somehow, I doubt the Jackal is going to go easy on him."

AGENT A: "I don't think ████ would want it any other way."

AGENT B: "If that's true, then they're going to have a great time."

All Love Bears a Cost

Honolulu, Oahu
Hawaii

The forecast had called, as it often did in Honolulu, for scattered showers. But by midafternoon, luck had pushed the warm rains further up the island of Oahu, and instead the skies over Waikiki Beach were dappled with cotton clouds against the late summer blue. The winds were gentle and humid, the ocean changing colors under the shifting sunshine like a mercurial gemstone, from deep jade to a turquoise so searing that the water looked artificial.

It was the perfect day for the interview of the year, and the crowd that had gathered around the stage set up on the sand was frantic. Now and then, excited cheers pulsed through them, like ripples that originated with the boy seated at the center of the stage, his figure shaded under a translucent white canopy, one of his legs crossed casually over the other.

He was dressed in a pale collared shirt and shorts, and smelled like sunscreen, citrus, and salt wind. His hair was thick and messy, so pitch-black that it shone blue under the sun, and his eyes, dark and slender behind a pair of aviators, currently expressed a mixture of politeness and discomfort as he stared at his interviewer.

Winter Young, the most famous superstar in the world, had only agreed to this interview for the sake of his manager, Claire, who'd had to deal with star reporter Evelyn Dace for a year as she tried to nab Winter for a proper interview.

Now the reporter leaned forward from the chair opposite Winter, her green eyes fixed so intently on him that he felt like she could see into his very marrow. He kept his face calm, his own gaze steady and unwavering, a quiet challenge in return.

"Tell me," Evelyn began in a gentle yet patronizing tone. "Are you currently dating anyone?"

Claire had, as usual, given her a list of approved questions in addition to topics they were to avoid at all costs, but Evelyn had strayed from the list early on—first a pointed comment about Winter's diet (he didn't have one), then an off-the-cuff remark about his close relationships with his backup dancers. Now this. Winter could feel the heat rising at his collar, but he couldn't give her the satisfaction of a response.

So instead, he offered Evelyn a demure, practiced smile and pushed the sleeves of his shirt higher, exposing more of the tattoos decorating his forearms. "Not right now," he said. "I've been too busy with the new album to date."

Instead of taking his hint to steer the conversation back to the album, the reporter just looked down at her notes slyly, as if she knew there was more Winter wasn't letting on. "Come now, Winter. You've been dropping hints in all your new tracks."

He shrugged. "Every artist is inspired by life. And love is one of life's greatest inspirations," he said, and scattered shrieks came from the crowd.

Evelyn smiled at that, nodding at the career highlights reel playing on the screen behind them. Winter watched the footage of himself as a fourteen-year-old boy, long and lanky like an unsteady colt, newly famous and petrified of crowds, stepping out onto the stage of an arena for the first time.

Sometimes he forgot how young he was when he began this wild journey. Years later, he still found it strange to look back.

"This is my very first concert," the past version of himself said shyly in the video, offering the crowd his famous, secret smile. And the audience went wild.

Winter glanced away from the screen and back at Evelyn, who had crossed her arms. "Some people say that you've reached a renaissance in your work," she said. "Bolder melodies and complex lyrics hinting at new secrets."

"Are you some people?"

"Sure. Let's say I am."

He took the opportunity to steer the topic back to his album. "Then thank you," he replied. "There are a lot of tracks I'm excited to share. I hope others can relate—"

The reporter interrupted him. "It seems fairly obvious your growth isn't just random. You really expect us to believe you don't have some new passion—new *love*—inspiring you?" She was not letting him go easily. "What really changed—or better yet, who changed you?"

Sydney Cossette.

Her name sprang unbidden to Winter's mind, and he had to force himself to keep his expression neutral.

Sometimes Winter forgot that, for a month, he had been an actual secret agent.

Sometimes, what happened last year—that he'd been recruited to work undercover for an intelligence agency called the Panacea Group to help take down a billionaire tycoon—still seemed like a fever dream. Sometimes he forgot that the girl who'd posed as his bodyguard back then was really a secret agent assigned to be his partner.

Sydney Cossette.

If only they'd given in to being so much more.

They'd hated each other at first, and then they'd become allies. And then . . . well, they'd had a moment with each other that went beyond friendship. And now it didn't matter, because they'd probably never see each other again.

His thoughts about her had been hourly for the first few weeks after he left London to recuperate fully at home, sometimes so overpowering that he could barely bring himself to get out of bed. But now they had faded to something manageable, the image of her small, fierce face framed with blond hair pushed inevitably aside for the crowd of concerts and parties and banquets and galas and interviews that all came back with regular force once he returned to his work.

Sometimes he forgot entirely, and that strange world felt so distant that he wondered if perhaps he had imagined the whole thing.

But sometimes he would walk past a cobblestone street or a quiet, hedged garden. Sometimes he would see an elegant bridge or a particular frame of airplane. Sometimes he would see a messy blond bob in the crowd. And those thoughts would return to his mind.

She would return.

He coped the only way he knew how: by writing. For the past half year, he'd written music like a boy possessed, gotten out some of the best songs of his life, filled an entire stack of little notebooks that sat teetering on his work desk at home. It felt like a guiding light had switched on in his mind, and all he had to do was follow it and the notes would come pouring out of him.

He snapped back to the present, waving at the crowd by way of answering the reporter's question. Cheers momentarily drowned out anything and everything.

He smiled at them again before turning back to the reporter. "I've just been grateful lately," he said. "Any romance in my new lyrics is inspired by that, by gratitude for what my fans have given me. That's it."

Evelyn's jaw tightened slightly, a flicker of annoyance crossing her face. Winter's eyes darted for a moment to Claire, who was standing at the edge of the stage with her arms crossed, her lips flattened into a line. Their eyes met, and she gave him a near-imperceptible shake of her head.

Hang in there, she seemed to say. *Time's almost up.*

"That's a lovely statement," Evelyn said, her gentle smile so professional that it grated on Winter's nerves. "There's been a real sense of joy in your recent music, nevertheless. Perhaps you've been able to put aside some of the tragedies in your past. Would you say that's true?"

Winter stiffened, holding back a sigh of frustration. She was really going there. "What do you mean?" he said.

"Tell me about your brother," she said. "It's common knowledge that his death has always loomed large in your life, yes?"

Artie.

Off in the corner, Winter could hear the unmistakable hiss of Claire taking a sharp breath. He didn't need to look at her to know she was furious at this question.

"Yes," he answered curtly. "Of course."

"Have you found a way to move on from that loss?"

Had he? For a moment, Winter imagined that he wasn't sitting in this interminable interview, but wandering along the edge of the ocean in Santa Monica beside his older brother, twelve years apart in age, fathered by different men but united by the same mother.

Look, Artie had said on that misty morning. *An unbroken shell.*

He leaned down to pick up a pristine, pink-tinted clamshell, then washed it in the tide before handing it to Winter. *Toss it back in the ocean and make a wish,* he'd said.

Is that a thing? Winter had replied.

Artie had laughed and mussed up Winter's hair. *You can make it a thing.*

So Winter had tossed it into the sea and wished to be famous, to be loved by his mother, to be remembered by somebody.

He should have wished instead for Artie to stay alive.

The memory faded. "You don't ever move on from a death," Winter answered calmly. "You just find better ways of coping."

"You've managed to replace the grief in your past with love, then."

"Grief *is* love. It's the price we pay for the gift of someone meaningful in our lives." They should be nearly at the hour mark. Almost done.

The reporter seemed to hear something in her earpiece. She paused, listening.

Then her eyes darted to Winter, and a look of what Winter could only describe as gleeful anticipation came across her face. She nodded. "Now, my sources say that a major publisher has just announced a tell-all book about you, to be released in the fall of this year. Any comment?"

Winter's polite smile faltered at the same time the crowd let out a chorus of confused murmurs, then gasps. He must have heard her wrong. Behind Evelyn, he saw Claire staring down at her phone with an expression of growing horror. The news must have broken right in the middle of his interview.

Evelyn seemed to catch the crack in his façade, because a gleam came into her eyes. "This is a surprise to you, I see."

A tell-all. Who would write an unauthorized tell-all about him?

Say something, he told himself harshly. "That rumor's new to me," he answered out loud.

She nodded with false sympathy and leaned toward him, her guise of concern still on her face. "I'm sorry to catch you off guard, as I thought you were already aware of it. No one has announced the author of the book yet. Perhaps you know?"

"I don't," he heard himself say stiffly, but the words sounded like they came from someone else. His eyes darted to Claire, who was now arguing with one of the producers. When the man shook his head at her, a look of fury crossed her face.

"Could it be someone you know well? A family member?" the reporter pressed.

"I don't know," Winter repeated.

"Winter," the woman said in a gentle, coaxing voice. "Tell me about your mother."

His mother?

"Are you implying that she wrote this?" he said.

"Absolutely not." Evelyn lifted her hands in innocence. "But the nature of the book feels like an inside source. Perhaps someone close, familial. I've heard you've had a rather contentious relationship with your mother. Is that true?"

"I'm not going to answer that," he said, his voice tight. "And nothing anyone has to say in a book about me will be a surprise to the public."

But Evelyn's words had already planted seeds of doubt in his mind. *Could* it be his mother? Had some company called her, talked her into doing it? Had she neglected to tell him? She *had* done unauthorized magazine interviews that had approached her, had once given away one of his school notebooks for an auction without telling him, the contents of which were then spread everywhere online. The thought was too much to handle, at least in a setting like this, with thousands of eyes fixed on him and the shine of a Hawaiian afternoon suddenly much too warm.

He needed to get off this stage. He needed to escape.

The reporter's sweet, sympathetic expression soured to a grimace. "You once considered ending your career early in your first year in order to take care of your mother while she suffered a mental health crisis. Isn't that right?"

At that, Winter snapped. He moved as if through a dream, suddenly rising from his chair and stripping the microphone from his collar, yanking the device's wire out of his clothes. The clip fell from his side and onto the wooden stage with a hollow clank.

Down in the sand at the side of the stage, Claire nodded at him and made a circular motion with her finger.

Let's go, she mouthed at him.

The audience stirred, murmuring at the commotion. The reporter's smile wavered. She'd pushed him too far, and her demeanor quickly changed again, turning naïve and bewildered. "Mr. Young," she said, "we are happy to move on to a different topic if that's more comfortable for you—"

"Sorry." It took the last of Winter's media training to utter the simple apology to her. Then he looked straight at the camera and said it again, this time sincerely. "I'm sorry, everyone." Then he walked off the stage.

The beach around him was a blur. On the sand, fans shrieked and reached for him, eagerly snapping photos as he strolled past, and he managed a smile and a wave for them before he reached Claire. She looped a hand through his arm as bodyguards moved into formation around them, guiding them along the path that led back to the main walkway where his car was waiting. Behind them, the producer tried to call them back to the stage, but Claire just lifted a middle finger over her head without looking back. Already, clusters of onlookers had started to shift toward his car, waves of excited screams accompanying them.

"I'll take care of it," Claire whispered as they climbed into the car. "I promise. Don't waste your time worrying."

He looked at her. His jaw clenched, his entire body still tingling with anger from Evelyn's final question. "But is the rumor true?" he asked quietly.

Claire gave him a rare, pitying look. He knew that could only mean one thing.

"We'll talk about it later. This is an invasion of privacy on a gross scale. We'll sue everyone for all they're worth, and we'll win. Evelyn. The publisher. The author, whoever it is."

Winter nodded numbly without believing her, felt his heart sink as the car pulled away. So, the book news was true. He hated to admit it, but all he could think about was the only suspect: his mother. And the possibility that she might have, once again, but as always, wounded him deeply. Likely without even realizing it.

Because it didn't matter that millions of people around the world knew Winter's name, that they followed his every move, that they said they loved him. No one did so for free. To everyone, even his own mother, he wasn't a real person—just a product to be used.

And products were easily discarded.

Getting back to his hotel felt like an eternal voyage. The crowd along the beach had been roused into a frenzy at his sudden departure, fans intermixed with paparazzi all crowding around the car, their questions muffled by the window glass into an incoherent mess. Winter hid behind his shades and gave them all a tense wave as his driver inched and honked his way through the crowd. At last, they reached the barricades lining the road, and the commotion fell away into the rhythmic sound of tires against pavement.

"We're never returning to that show," Claire hissed beside him as she typed madly into her phone. "I'm sorry I ever arranged it."

"It's Evelyn Dace," Winter replied tiredly. "Of course we were going to say yes."

She tensed her jaw, teeth grinding. "Do you know what that producer said to me when I told them to cut the interview? *'Think of all the headlines after this airs.'* The audacity. Like we're the ones who need headlines. And after that mistreatment?" She cut off, her eyes flashing. "I'll take care of it," she vowed again.

In spite of everything, Winter couldn't help smiling a little at her fury. No one did revenge like Claire. "Don't go after her entire family, now."

"Oh, I'm sparing nothing and nobody. I'm already emailing the head of the network and now I'm texting Stevenson over at Hearst to tear Evelyn a new one. She'll be lucky to keep her position after I'm done with her."

"She was just doing her job."

"And I'm doing mine." Claire looked up at him briefly over her phone. "Believe me, the publisher is going to get a very strongly worded letter from our lawyers. If they don't want to get themselves caught in legal hell, they're going to think twice about releasing this book. Oh, and I'm also sending Evelyn a very special gift basket."

Winter closed his eyes and groaned. "Claire."

"Don't worry. It'll have her favorite sugared almonds with a card that plays an excruciatingly loud song when opened and has a battery that's impossible to remove. And glitter. A gallon of glitter."

Winter laughed and shook his head at her, then closed his eyes. "Thank you," he said quietly.

"I'm really sorry, Winter," Claire said, her voice quieter now.

"It's okay." He didn't even feel angry anymore, or nauseous, or anxious. He was just tired, and all he wanted was room service and the cold comfort of an unfamiliar hotel bed. Outside his tinted window, he could still see clusters of fans on the occasional street corner, framed before the majestic green slope of Diamond Head in the background, cheering as his entourage passed by.

His phone continued to buzz nonstop. He glanced at it wearily and caught a glimpse of the messages from his friends Dameon and Leo, who had been texting him in their group chat before the broadcast even began.

r u ok

Leo's icon was that of a brown-skinned boy with a grin almost too large for the rest of his features, his light brown curls a wild frame around his face.

Of course he's not okay, do you need to ask

Dameon's icon was entirely opposite in mood—a side profile of a Black boy with long dreads and a serious expression, looking out at a cityscape from a hiking trail.

just asking. that was awful
not you, the interview lady. you just looked unhappy
Leo wow stop

stopping

anyway Winter I'm at Bloom later tonight, come grab drinks and forget this mess

yall are going to Bloom?

Best club in the city with food

i'm jealous, sigh. drink an extra shot for me

Wish you were here, Leo

Their texts went on and on. Winter could almost hear them in his head, bickering as they always did during their rehearsals since they began as his backup dancers at the beginning of his career. Technically, they were still with him because he paid their salaries, but they had also become like his brothers, his second family and closest friends.

But only Dameon was here in Honolulu with him this time. After what had happened in London last year, Leo had taken a sabbatical to rest at home with his family. The memory still triggered Winter's guilt. Leo wouldn't have been in that situation, had it not been for Winter. And Leo deserved to recover, although Winter missed his friend sorely.

But at least Dameon was still here. Maybe Winter could use some company tonight, could vent about the day with him and laugh over a few drinks.

I'm ok, he texted back. *Heading back now.*

Then he put his phone down and closed his eyes. He should try to call his mother, ask her about the book directly. But right now, he didn't have the strength. All he wanted to do was shut down.

He turned his phone over idly and nudged a finger under the rubber case, touching the edge of a business card he always kept tucked inside.

It was a card for the Claremont Hotel in Saint Paul, Minnesota, one of the finest luxury stays in the city. But Winter knew what the business card was really for, that inside the hotel hid the headquarters of the Panacea Group, the place where he first met Sydney. As they often did, he found his thoughts wandering back to her. What she might be doing.

Where in the world she might be. What dangerous mission she might be on without him.

If you're ever in need of help, Sydney had said to him, *call us.*

He'd memorized the number, even though he'd never used it. For the past year, he had been searching for every excuse in the world to dial that number and get patched through to Panacea, hoping for another chance to dip his toe back into that secret world, fantasizing that the person who picked up on the other end would be Sydney.

Laughable, of course. Why would they ever need him again? He was nothing but an entertainer. The mission he'd been sent on had been an unusual, once-in-a-blue-moon kind of situation. He would probably never see Sydney again. Panacea would never contact him again. That was just the way it would be, and the sooner he accepted that, the better.

By the time they arrived at the hotel, the sun had lowered enough to touch the water, and the entire sky was a rainbow of setting colors against gathering clouds, foreshadowing warm rains later in the night. Winter could feel himself crashing, his emotions turning ever inward.

"I'll have some tea sent to your room," Claire said as the elevator stopped on his floor. "Jasmine, decaf, no sugar, two kettles of water. You just get some rest, okay?"

Winter nodded as the elevator doors slid open. He stepped out.

"Good night, Claire," he said over his shoulder.

"Good night, Winter," she answered, already back on her phone.

He walked down the hall toward his suite. After the chaos at the beach, he should have been happier about being left alone—but as he went, he felt the empty air close in around him, thick and suffocating. He couldn't muster the energy to hang out with Dameon right now, and yet he didn't know where to put the anxiety that now thrummed within him.

Sure, Dameon and Claire could listen to his woes, could sympathize, but no one could truly understand the strange path he walked, or feel the same fears that now swirled inside him.

Wasn't all this what he wanted? Wasn't he so lucky? Hadn't he once been poor and forgotten, hungering for affection every day of his life? A hunger so deep that even a stadium filled with fans couldn't sate it? Didn't he crave the attention?

No, it wasn't the attention he needed. It was the love. He just wanted to create something and know that it mattered to someone, that *he* mattered. That maybe someone, somewhere was listening to his work, nodding along to the words, feeling something real. He just wanted to make things that made people happier, wanted to close his eyes in a stadium and hear the voices of fifty thousand souls all singing along. But he didn't know how to get that without also getting this—the salacious rumors, the invasive questions, the cruel articles full of false information, the microphones shoved in his face.

No one knew what it was like to keep an entire life bottled up for fear of it getting out to the public, what it was like to sit on the floor of a hotel room and hesitate to call his own mother, just in case she might leak his words to the press.

No, that wasn't entirely true. Sydney knew. Sydney would understand that.

When she was in his life, he'd felt like, finally, someone understood the most misunderstood parts of him, without him ever saying any of it aloud. Someone had been with him and seen him for who he truly was. And then she had vanished without a trace.

Maybe it was for the best. While he was here, doing trivial interviews about nothingness, she was out saving the world, without a single person applauding her. Maybe he didn't deserve her, anyway.

His mind was still on Sydney when he turned the corner and saw a girl standing outside the door to his penthouse suite.

His heart jumped.

Sydney? Could it be?

But then the silhouette turned, and he recognized the figure with a sinking feeling. How did *she* get up here past the security?

She must have just come from a party—under her trench coat glittered a silver dress that winked at him as she moved. Her hair was pinned up in pretty brown waves, a loose tendril grazing the side of her face. And those eyes—just like how he remembered them. She looked as lovely as she had the final time he put his arms around her waist and she whispered his name the way only she knew how.

That was before their tumultuous breakup. Before she broke his heart for the dozenth time.

She was the last person he needed to see right now.

At the sight of him standing there, frozen, she smiled, pushed away from the wall, and sauntered over to him.

"Well, Winter," said Gavi Ginsburg. "You've certainly looked better."

The Calm Before the Reunion

Sydney Cossette was the kind of girl nobody noticed.

She could enter a room without a single glance turning her way. A stranger would strike up a conversation with her only until they spotted someone more interesting. She supposed that she was pretty, with dark blue eyes and blond hair chopped in messy waves to her chin—but unremarkably so. She could meet the same person over and over and they would never remember her name. She could drift from place to place without anyone realizing she was there, flitting along the periphery as a tolerable presence but never the center of attention.

Niall, her mentor, told her that it was her natural talent. When people don't notice you, they tend to entrust to you their secrets, sharing weaknesses and vices, failing to recall that they'd ever given them away. Sydney saved those crumbs in her vast memory, as Panacea had trained her to do, archiving them until they became useful. When she needed them again, she'd lay them all out in a neat row. Confessions. Fears. Sins.

Or, in this case, confirmation of the location of Winter Young's rehearsal studio.

Sydney leaned against the driver's window of the parked white van, adjusted her earpiece, and pretended to be bored as a pair of security guards outside Winter's hotel argued within earshot.

"We can't keep his car idling around the back."

"Claire said it had to be here for him first thing in the morning."

"But Queen Street will be blocked off until four A.M."

"That's fine. He always practices early."

Queen Street. That meant the Waikiki Dance Studio, the only spot with the right facilities in the area. Sydney smiled a little as the two men argued, keeping them at the edge of her vision. Half an hour earlier, one of them had rapped on her window, asking her how long her equipment van was going to be parked here. She'd just given him an innocent shake of her head.

Claire told me five minutes, she'd said, holding up one hand with all her fingers outstretched. The man had shrugged and walked off, thinking Sydney was part of Winter's team, and then promptly forgotten all about her.

"Jackal?"

"Ouais chef?" she replied distractedly to Niall's gruff voice in her ear. This was her habit when talking to her mentor, greeting him in one of the twenty-seven languages she knew.

He grunted, as he always did, and she smiled.

"Syd, this isn't a game," he said.

"Fine, stopping."

"You're waiting in the van until dawn?"

"Unless you want me to knock on Winter's door. I could grab a bell-hop uniform," she offered.

"No. Fine. Whatever works best," Niall said. "Just letting you know we only have that van rented out until ten in the morning."

"Ten's all I'll need."

"You sound so sure he'll agree."

"Because I am sure." Sydney glanced up at the hotel. "After that nightmare of an interview, Winter's mood will be much better when he wakes up tomorrow. And I'd prefer him at his happiest if I'm going to be asking him to risk his life. Again."

"Just try to keep the insults to a minimum."

"Me?" Sydney feigned shock. "But I'm always nice."

Niall laughed, warm and genuine, and Sydney smiled again. "Just be careful. That area's crawling with security. Don't get yourself a black eye from one of his guards."

Sydney raised an eyebrow. "Are you telling me, the agent you once sent to infiltrate a Swiss bank, that you're worried I can't handle a superstar's security detail?"

"I don't know, you can tell me later which is worse. Our intel says Winter's detail has gotten much more serious since last year."

"Have you forgotten that you promoted me to full operative? I'll be okay, Dad."

He sighed. "I've told you to stop calling me that."

"But it's our last mission together, *Dad*. When will I ever get to call you Dad again?"

Niall snorted, but didn't argue the point, and a pained silence cut through their conversation. Sydney felt her chest seize, even though her lungs felt fine.

"What are you going to do," she asked, keeping her voice light, "once you're officially retired from Panacea?"

"Take a vacation, maybe. Go to Bora-Bora. I hear the water's very nice."

"Is Quinn excited to see you?"

Another pause, followed by Niall clearing his throat. He never seemed comfortable talking about Quinn, but Sydney was always fascinated by Niall's biological daughter. His *real* daughter. "I haven't told her anything yet," he said at last.

"Are you nervous?"

"I'll be fine."

But behind Niall's deep growl, Sydney could hear a hint of fear. She recognized it from their own conversations—she heard it each time she had a brush with death on a mission or pushed her lungs too hard or missed a rendezvous. Sydney recalled the day he'd shown up at her high school in her decrepit, dying town, a secret agent disguised as a recruiter from a local factory. He had been touring the West, looking for promising agents to join Panacea's training program, and she had been a fifteen-year-old girl who spent her days cutting class, who shoplifted as a coping mechanism, a girl still grieving her mother's death from the same illness she had. A girl searching for a way out. Niall had caught her breaking into the school's locked gym, had noticed her penchant for acquiring languages, and offered her a job. She wouldn't find out until weeks later what Panacea was—or who she was about to become.

Niall never talked about Quinn, but his silence said more than anything. Sydney knew it must have been hard to have a relationship with a daughter who never saw you, whose childhood you missed but could never explain why.

"She'll talk to you," Sydney said gently.

Niall didn't answer right away. "Here's hoping, right?" he finally replied, and Sydney felt a pang of envy.

It was stupid, of course, to be jealous of Quinn. She'd never met the woman, and Niall wasn't Sydney's father. Hers was an alcoholic who hit her whenever he had a bad day at work, would taunt her for wanting to see the world beyond their small, suffocating town. Her father had let her mother die alone at the hospital because he was too much of a coward to be at her bedside.

Her father was not a good man, and Sydney had turned her back on him long ago.

She shoved the memories aside and stared up at the hotel. She knew the truth behind her pain—she was grieving Niall's retirement as if he were giving her up along with Panacea. After this mission, he would be gone, off to make amends with his estranged daughter, the one that really mattered. Per the agency's strict rules, he would never make contact with Sydney again. She would be truly alone.

She still had Sauda, Panacea's director and her advisor of sorts, but Niall was the one who worked directly with Sydney on each and every one of her missions, had trained her from the start, had vouched for her when her thieving habits returned, when Sauda wanted her kicked out of Panacea for good.

Served her right, Sydney supposed, for letting herself get attached to someone. Hadn't that been one of her first lessons at Panacea?

Loyalty to a secret, above all else.

Above emotions, above human bonds, above love. Loyalty to duty, to making the world a safer place.

"Just get the van back before ten." Niall was still talking, and Sydney's mind snapped back to the present, to the task at hand. A humid drizzle had begun dotting the van's windows.

"I'll have it back to you with a bow on top," she replied.

"Leave off the bow, please."

"You're no fun at all," she said, and he hung up.

Sydney put her phone away and slumped in her seat. At least Winter was a welcome distraction.

How long had it been since she'd seen him, anyway? A year?

Before she met him, Sydney—like the rest of the world—had her own assumptions about the superstar. Too aware of his good looks, too aware of his charisma, too aware of what he could do.

But then she'd learned that the truth was much worse. He was too aware of *her*. Sydney Cossette was good at being the girl no one noticed— better yet, she enjoyed it. But Winter had seen her immediately, in a way that made her feel exposed, in a way that unsettled and excited her.

She and Winter had had their fair share of arguments during their first mission together, and had gotten a bit . . . carried away with each other during a rather heated tryst in an indoor swimming pool. It all came flooding back, her cheeks starting to warm at the memories.

Maybe their reunion would be a painfully awkward one. But she still found herself looking forward to seeing him. She might walk through this world alone, but when she was with Winter, she had someone to walk with. And on this night, when she was feeling particularly vulnerable, the thought was comforting.

Unless . . . he didn't want to see her again. Maybe he remembered their time together differently—maybe he didn't remember it at all.

"Only one way to find out," she murmured to herself, her eyes gazing up at the window to his room. The rain was picking up. With a sigh, she settled deeper into the van's seat, trying to get comfortable for a few hours of sleep. Changing someone's life at four in the morning was going to require getting some rest.

Old Flames, New Fires

Winter took one look at Gavi and immediately pulled out his phone.

She crossed her arms and pouted—her signature look. "Oh, come on. Don't bother Claire at this hour. You're not even going to let me rest in your room for a sec before kicking me out? After the night I had, I'm positively exhausted . . ." she said, wagging one of her lacy Ferragamo stilettos.

He lifted an eyebrow. "How did you even get up here?" he asked.

She ignored his question. "It's pouring buckets outside, and my hotel's on the other side of town. Just thought I'd stop here for a bit. Aren't you happy to see me?"

Winter sighed. He knew her games too well. He and Gavi had been on and off for years, though the last time they spoke was over a year ago, several months before his mission with Panacea. But every time he thought they'd broken up for good, Gavi would show up on his doorstep. Somehow, she always knew where he'd be—and when his defenses would be down.

It was his own fault. No one was forcing him back to her, and yet he always went.

"Go back to your own hotel," he said as he swiped his keycard. "I'll book you a car, if you need me to."

"No chivalry at all," she said, shaking her head at him, jeweled earrings flashing. "I just escaped my date at a movie premiere, and I don't feel like rushing back to sit in my room all alone."

"Who, Rory?" he asked incredulously. "I thought you two were head over heels for each other."

"You of all people should know better than to believe the tabloids, Winter." She looked down at her heels, letting her perfect highlights fall softly against her face. "Turns out the fairy-tale romance has been a little one-sided."

Winter felt a pang of guilt—she was right. He should know better. With Gavi, things were never as they seemed. Now he vaguely remembered the big movie premiere in town this week, and if there was a lavish event, Gavi would be there. As an It Girl on the social scene, even a five-minute appearance from Gavi could boost an event's publicity tenfold. The world couldn't get enough of her. But apparently her current fling could.

Or so she said. If there's one thing Winter knew, it was to take Gavi's words with a healthy dose of skepticism.

"I'm sorry," he said politely, without asking for more details.

She looked up at him, her doe eyes soft but hungry. "Judging by the news spreading online, I'm guessing you're not having the best night either."

Winter entered the open doorway, put his hands in his pockets, and leaned back into the frame. He had worked so hard to distance himself after their last epic breakup, had done so well staying away.

You need to say no, warned the voice in his head. *Right now.*

But he knew he was weak tonight, and when he looked back into Gavi's upturned eyes, he couldn't help himself. So instead of saying *no,* he uttered a different word. "And?"

"Figured you needed the company as much as I did," she answered, a sly smile playing on her lips.

In spite of their history, Winter felt himself waver. His relationship with Gavi had been completely different from the one he'd had with Sydney; he and Sydney had loathed each other at first sight, a tension that turned into something he'd call friendship, maybe more. But Gavi—he had fallen for Gavi too quickly. They'd found each other irresistible and funny and fascinating before they both realized that they were awful for each other.

And yet here he was, about to make that mistake again. Even now, Gavi drew him in, lulled him into the feeling that perhaps, with one more try, they could work out.

Gavi was still studying him with a coy look that he knew he couldn't refuse.

"Well?" she said. Her eyes turned down. "Don't make me beg."

He sighed. Looked into his suite. Looked back at her.

"Just until the rain lets up," he said, recognizing the lie before the words even left his lips.

"That's all I was hoping for," she replied with a shrug.

He stepped aside and held a hand toward his suite. "Claire's sending some tea. Should I ask her to make it for two?"

Gavi walked past him, the dangerous smell of jasmine and vetiver trailing behind her. "Tea sounds perfect."

By the time their tea arrived, sheets of rain were slanting down across the nightscape outside his window.

Gavi took her cup and went to stand by the glass, her gaze fixed on the palm trees swaying against an ink-black ocean.

"So," Winter said, coming to stand beside her with his own mug. His eyes stayed on the scene outside, too. "How bad was the premiere?"

She shrugged. "About as bad as finding out some mystery person is going to reveal your darkest secrets in an unauthorized tell-all."

He snorted. "I'd much prefer a terrible movie to my reality."

Gavi laughed, in that easy way of hers, and pulled her lustrous hair over one shoulder. "So, you don't know who's behind it?"

He shook his head. "Whoever it is, Claire probably already has our lawyers drafting up a lawsuit."

Gavi smiled, then leaned sideways to bump her hip lightly against his. "Too bad. Should have been me."

"Drafting the lawsuit?"

"Writing that tell-all. You know I have lots of interesting stories."

"Please don't," he replied dryly.

"What? I wouldn't embarrass you." She reached up to rub his shoulder lightly, and his skin tingled. "I'd tell only the good stuff."

"That would be impossible, because every good thing in our relationship was poison."

"Oh, don't be so dramatic."

"We were nothing *but* dramatic, Gavi. Drama defined our entire relationship."

"Not the *entire* relationship."

"You seriously don't remember the headlines? *'Drama Defines Winter and Gavi's Entire Relationship.'* Ring a bell?"

"Fine. Maybe. But we had fun too, didn't we?" she said, smiling into her mug.

He knew she was baiting him, so he didn't answer.

She turned to face him, biting her lip. "Mm," she said. "Of course, my stories about you would need a content warning."

He raised an eyebrow. "Would they?"

"Like our first time?"

Baiting him. Winter's jaw tightened, even as her words beckoned the memory back. A party hosted by a mutual friend, followed by a series of increasingly rowdy games. Gavi had gone, giggling, into the bathroom where Winter was washing his hands, and when he'd tried to go around her, she'd stumbled right into him and knocked them both against the sink. Gavi had blurted out a ridiculous swear that caught Winter off guard and made him laugh so hard he cried. They'd teased each other about it all evening, had gotten touchy. They'd gone back to her place, and Winter could only remember the rest of that night in pieces—their clothes in a pile by the door, a lamp knocked off her nightstand, her legs straddling him and his hands gripping her bare hips, her labored breathing hot against his neck as she gasped his name, the shudders that racked his body in response.

It would be so easy to fall back in, he thought as he looked down at her. Too easy to relapse.

"What are you really doing here, Gavi?" he asked her.

"Same reason you let me in," she replied. "Can't we just let it be that?"

"Be what, exactly?"

"Selfish for a night." She shifted her weight to one hip so that she brushed against him again. "No strings attached."

He laughed humorlessly. "There are always strings attached with you."

"The undatable Winter Young," she whispered. "Always so wary."

"Am I wrong?"

"Are you afraid people are going to find out we hooked up again?"

"I'd prefer not dealing with a fresh round of headlines about us getting back together, if that's what you mean," he said tiredly. "Today's interview was enough."

She smiled and touched his cheek. "You care too much what other people think."

"So do you."

"Wrong." She tucked her hair behind her ear. "I don't care at all, as long as people are talking about me."

"Oh, I know."

"Come on, Winter. Let yourself relax for once."

"I wouldn't call you relaxing."

She leaned up toward him, and now her lips were so close to his that he could feel the warmth of her breath against his skin. "Call me whatever you want, then," she murmured, and Winter shivered, remembering all the times she'd ever whispered in his ear. His body leaned toward her, as if drawn purely by muscle memory.

There was no reason, really, for him not to sleep with her. Maybe she was right. Maybe a one-night stand would be a good distraction. Maybe this time, there really wouldn't be any strings attached. They knew each other well, knew how to make a touch turn into much more, and they also knew how to go their separate ways—at least until the next time.

But instead of giving in, Winter hovered there, refusing to close the gap between them. Gavi's eyes flickered over his face, and a small smile of satisfaction touched the edge of her mouth at the way he tensed.

Winter forced himself to pull away and look back outside. "Rain's not letting up anytime soon," he said, nodding at the blanket of dark clouds that stretched across the horizon. "Take the bed, if you want. I've been using the couch, anyway."

Gavi sighed. "Fine, have it your way." As she walked toward the bedroom, she peered at him over her shoulder. "But I can think of better ways to strain your back than sleeping on that thing." She turned and started unzipping her dress, letting it fall to the floor in a heap of sequins before she was fully out of sight. "If you change your mind, come join me. You can have your usual side."

Then, without asking, she grabbed one of the shirts from his suitcase and disappeared into the bathroom.

Shortly before four A.M., a noise woke Winter on the couch.

Immediately, he winced. His back did hurt from the hard cushions, just as Gavi had teased. He sat up gingerly, massaging the sore spots with both hands, and looked over to the bed.

Gavi was still asleep, breathing evenly, dressed in nothing but her underwear and his shirt, one bare leg curled up over the blankets. The rain had stopped some time ago, and the night had just barely begun to transition from pitch-black to muted grays, the weak light outlining the curves of her body.

In sleep, she looked like the girl he'd once fallen for—stunningly pretty, serene, and a little amused, a girl secure in her identity. He could still remember waking up beside her the morning after their first time together, staring down at that face, and thinking she was still asleep. Then she'd opened one eye and grinned at him, and he'd laughed, daring to think that maybe, just maybe, he had found someone he could wake up next to for the rest of his life.

Then he'd discovered that she'd leaked their story to the tabloids, and by lunchtime, their tryst had been on every news outlet.

It was an accident, she'd told him with a cute laugh, and he'd believed it. Even worse, he had forgiven her.

That had been followed by months of exhausting social games—bringing him to events just to be photographed together, intimate conversations suspiciously reported by "anonymous sources," and an endless parade of lies, lies, lies, lies. About things that didn't even need to be lies: what brand her shoes were or where she grew up or what her favorite meal was, so that she could mutter later on that a gift from him wasn't what she had in mind. She'd once told him she was allergic to shellfish after a decadent, uni-filled omakase. He'd rushed her to the hospital and stayed with her for hours, fended off news reporters at the entrance, only to find out later that she wasn't allergic after all. Another time, she'd locked him out of his own house as a game and let the media assume that he'd been kicked out for upsetting her.

Winter would show up haggard and defeated at rehearsal, and Dameon would just shake his head.

Why do you like that girl? he'd ask.

All Winter could do was put his hands up in despair. *I know, I know,* he would reply. And then the whole thing started all over again.

Because. Gavi . . . She was an addiction. She could start a conversation with anyone, could become the life of a party just by showing up. She was the kind of person who always left an impression, who always found reserves of energy, no matter how late in the day it was, who could convince anyone to fall for her with just a wink and a gentle touch. Gavi craved attention in the same way Winter craved love, would seek it to the ends of the earth, and she was unapologetic about it.

Something about that drew him to her. Maybe he envied her, thought that life was easier for people like her. Maybe he was just vulnerable to her bold flirtations, admired how direct she was about getting what she wanted. But most likely, maybe he thought they were similar, that she was what he deserved, that she represented a world that he understood. Sure, she used him. But he used her, too.

And, well, they had fun in bed. A lot of fun. That didn't hurt, either.

A buzzing phone knocked his thoughts back to the present. That was what had woken him up. He grabbed for the glowing screen on the coffee table, wondering for a moment if Claire was texting him and if he'd forgotten about some early morning interview.

But when his eyes fell on the screen, he saw that it wasn't his phone at all, but Gavi's. The screen lit up, and despite how quickly he looked away, he still caught enough of the messages waiting there.

Here now. Take ur time.

Babe u still coming?

Babe where r u? U missed the red carpet?

The name of the sender was Rory Jones. Gavi's terrible date.

Now her agent was texting her. *Rory said you never showed?*

Apparently Gavi stood up her date, spending the night with Winter instead. Not the story she'd told him, of course. Her words came back to him.

Turns out the fairy-tale romance has been a little one-sided.

She'd conveniently left out that it'd been one-sided . . . for Rory. The poor guy didn't know what the hell he'd gotten himself into.

Winter shook his head and laughed a little. Gavi knew every trick in the book, every way to use her private life to advance her public one. This, she had always been honest about. She had never promised him the kind of honest relationship he seemed to want, had always warned him that they needed different things.

I'm not here to be your emotional support, she'd told him early on. *I just think we could be fun together. That's why you like me too, isn't it?* She'd leaned toward him. *You know I'm fun.*

Even last night, she'd warned him.

Selfish for a night, no strings attached?

She'd told him exactly what to expect. By now, he should know this better than anyone.

Still, he felt a familiar ache as he glanced across the room at her once more. Then he got up and went to his suitcase, pulling on a fresh pair of briefs and sweats. He left a note for Gavi on the dresser.

Gone to practice. Order whatever you want.

Without a sound, he pulled on his shoes and left the room—the smell of jasmine following him into the hallway.

Just Another Job

By the time Sydney stirred out of her half sleep and drove the van along Queen Street to the entrance of the dance studio, she knew Winter was already inside.

For one, the lights were on, which meant it was already open at this ungodly time, five hours before its normal schedule. Second, she recognized the black car parked outside as the same one she'd seen behind the hotel last night—bodyguards, ever watchful for fans who might have caught on to Winter's whereabouts and could attempt to get into the studio.

Sydney jogged past the back door, as if out on a casual four A.M. run. The humidity in the air irritated her weak lungs, and they reacted accordingly, an uncomfortable ache stirring in her chest each time she breathed. She forced herself to slow down.

As she went, she took a good look at the two bodyguards inside the car. Their eyes were trained on the building, but not on her, watchful only of the studio's entrance. She did a lap, then came back around from the other end of the street, where they would be less likely to see her, stopping at the back of the building where the garbage bins were all lined up in a row.

The door was locked, but she went right up to it anyway and took out a small pin from her pocket. As she worked on the lock, she glanced up, searching for security cameras. There were two in the front, but none back here, not by the garbage bins. *Amateur hour*, she thought, ever grateful for lazy security.

She twisted the pin once more and was rewarded with the sound of a light click. *Bingo,* she thought as the door handle turned all the way. She slipped inside.

Inside, the studio was quiet and muffled, but Sydney could hear the beat of music. As she followed it down the hall, she heard the squeak of shoes against a polished dance floor.

It had been a year since she'd been this close to Winter, and the sound of those shoes made her heart jump. Even without seeing him, she could tell from the rhythm of the noise what he was doing—spinning, arching backward, the thud of his shoes against the floor in perfect sync with the music. If she closed her eyes, she would be able to see him moving in her mind, in her memories—gliding across a floor bathed in moonlight, his shirt translucent like a ghost.

She shook her head and clenched one of her fists at her side, and for a moment, she slowed in her steps, as if she might abandon the meeting. What did she expect, anyway? Even if he was happy to see her, even if he wanted to do the mission, there couldn't be anything more between them. Sydney had watched Niall and Sauda as they spent the last decade circling each other, never allowed to be together because of Panacea's strict rules, yet never able to move on because of their deep feelings for each other.

Not that that was the case with Winter. He was a superstar. People falling at his feet at every turn. Chances were that he'd forgotten all about her.

Maybe it had been a mistake for Sauda to send her to fetch Winter. *C'mon, Sydney*, she thought to herself, shaking her head. Two years ago, when she was tasked with making contact with the world's most dangerous drug lord in Antwerp, did she hesitate? No. And here she was, getting cold feet before asking a freaking pop star whether or not he wanted to join her on another mission. Ridiculous.

Sydney turned the corner and found herself standing before the doors of the practice room, staring at a boy stretching on the floor. Her rambling mind cut off abruptly, and all she could do was take in the sight of him.

There was something strange about seeing someone in the flesh whom she usually, like everyone else, saw filtered through a screen. Sharper, more angular, human in that extraordinary way that only famous people tended to be, in possession of an intangible quality that made it impossible to look away.

All right, she told herself forcefully. *Back to business.*

Sydney's mind snapped to attention again. She moved silently, opening and closing the practice room door and posing herself against the wall, her eyes fixed on Winter's back. She was so quiet that he hadn't noticed her enter the room—his head stayed tilted down toward the floor as he stretched his legs, his brows furrowed in the mirror, his lips murmuring to the music blaring through the speakers. For a while, she just watched him. She remembered everything about him so vividly, but what she remembered best were these little moments, like when he'd look skyward to enjoy the rain or dance alone in a room, when he was so absorbed in something that he forgot entirely about the world around him. If spies and artists had anything in common, it must be this: an all-consuming focus on their work, missions by a different name.

She wondered what he was thinking about. Music, most likely. A dance routine, perhaps. Selfishly, foolishly, she wondered if perhaps he was thinking about her.

Long minutes passed before he finally finished his stretch, rubbed his neck with his towel, and pushed himself to his feet. His gaze went to the mirror instantly. And at last, his eyes jumped to her.

Their gazes met and he froze.

Sydney felt the lock of his eyes on her own as if he'd physically touched her. Maybe she remembered everything about him, but she had forgotten this—how his attention could feel like the sear of the sun.

He blinked once, as if he couldn't quite believe what he was seeing, as if she were an apparition. Then he spun to face her directly, and a surprised smile spread on his face.

And in spite of everything, she felt her own lips answering with a smile, felt her entire body warm with the glow of his presence.

"I hope you remember me, Mr. Young," she said.

Ten minutes later, they had settled into a private booth at the back of a nearby café. Sydney snuggled deep into her seat across from Winter and regarded him with what she hoped was a neutral expression.

"No black car this time? Where are Niall and Sauda?" Winter said in a low voice as he looked curiously around the empty shop.

"Just me this time, I'm afraid," she replied. "Panacea bought out this coffee shop for the day, so depending on your answers, we'll see about sending out a black car."

"Ah." Winter's smile tightened. "I'm guessing the barista is an operative, too?"

She nodded. "And aware that we're meeting in private here. You won't see any patrons coming in this morning. Or any paparazzi."

Winter snorted at that. "Of course not," he muttered in understanding. "I hope you're compensating this place handsomely."

"More than they'd make in a week," she answered. "So don't worry."

His slender fingers tapped against the porcelain of his mug. She found herself studying them before his voice drew her gaze back up to his face. He was taking in her face with care, as if savoring her, which made her heart twist.

"You look . . ." he began, then trailed off as he idly brushed a few strands of hair from his eyes. "The same," he finished. "Exactly the same."

"I don't know how to feel about that," she answered.

He gave her a secret smile before taking a sip of his tea. "It was a compliment," he said.

Her heart twisted again. She couldn't tell if she liked the feeling or not.

"I see your compliments haven't improved," she replied archly.

"Neither has your ability to take one."

"Clearly nothing has changed between us."

"Nothing?" He made a *tsk* sound with his tongue. "Then we're in trouble, Ms. Cossette."

Usually, she could engage someone in a flattering conversation, taking the opportunity to study them while they got carried away talking about themselves. Usually, they never noticed her playing this game, too caught up in their own ego to see they were being played.

But Winter saw through her, and to her annoyance, she could feel her cheeks turning warm.

"Congratulations on your new album," she said, switching the topic to distract herself. "I didn't even know they could be Multi-Diamond. New world record?"

His nod in return looked blank, telling her immediately that something else was on his mind. *The tell-all book,* she remembered, picturing yesterday's headlines—as well as the footage of him walking out in the middle of the biggest interview of his career. It didn't take a spy to know that it'd be best to avoid the topic.

"That's what they say," he answered with a shrug. "Have you listened to it?"

"No," she lied.

"Good," he said. "I don't want to know what you think."

She laughed a little. "Good," she replied. "Because I wouldn't tell you."

The truth was that she'd listened to his album on repeat for the last three weeks—in preparation for their mission, of course. She replayed it until she could hear the bars in her sleep, had memorized every lyric and every space where he took a breath. In those private moments, she'd closed her eyes and let his voice fill her mind, allowed herself to miss him. Most of all, she had hoped in vain for a specific track, one titled "You Are My Meditation." It was a song he'd started writing during their last mission together.

Who is it about? she'd asked him then.

You, he'd answered.

But it wasn't on the album. Maybe he'd never finished it. She'd thought back and forth about it, caught somewhere between relief and what she would have to force herself to describe as disappointment. That was foolish, though. It would be best for her cover if the song never saw the light of day.

She'd managed to push him from her mind since they said their farewells after their last mission. And she'd been successful—mostly. Sydney had been in and out of flings before, both with other agents and random operatives she'd met overseas. If there was one thing she was good at, it was walking away from a relationship.

But then she'd watched him through the dance studio's window this morning—and felt the snare close around her again.

Damn it all.

"Tell me what's up, then," he said, folding his arms. "Unless you just wanted an autograph."

Sydney composed herself, pulled her phone out of her pocket, and placed it on the table between them. The screen lit up—and seconds later, a hologram appeared between them, a video clip showing a black car parked on a dark street.

As they looked on, a grainy figure stepped out of the car and glanced surreptitiously over their shoulder before looking away. The video paused, then repeated once, before Sydney closed the clip and pocketed her phone again.

"Who was that?" Winter asked.

"I know almost as little about him as you do," Sydney explained. "All I know is he's one of ours—a Panacea agent sent to an overseas division called the Sapphire Cross."

"The Sapphire Cross." Winter frowned. "Isn't that an international charity?"

She smiled at him. "As much as the Panacea Group is a luxury hotel."

"Curiouser and curiouser," he murmured.

"The agent was supposed to rendezvous with me two weeks ago in Washington, DC, to deliver some intel that he's been gathering for the past three months. He never showed."

"Maybe he just stood you up?"

Sydney studied her nails and refused to react to his tease. "Maybe," she said. "Or maybe he's in danger and needs our help. We don't know, because we've been unable to make contact ever since, and in our experience, that's never a good sign."

"So what's the mission?"

"An extraction. I'm going in to rescue him and bring him back home. Niall will be on the ground, as he'll be coordinating with the CIA on it. And I'm in need of a partner."

"A partner." Winter regarded her carefully. "Me?"

"Glad you're catching on."

"Why me?"

Sydney took a sip of her coffee. "He's stationed in Singapore."

She saw Winter's eyes light up in a flash of understanding.

"First stop on my Asia tour," Winter said.

"Exactly." Sydney pointed a finger at him in approval. "You're scheduled to headline the Warcross Championship opening ceremony in Singapore, yes?"

He shrugged. "What, is the agent a fan of the Warcross games or me?"

"The intel's vague, but I'm guessing he's not there for your slick dance moves. We all know how huge that annual ceremony is, not to mention the gala. CEO Emika Chen is going to be there in person this year, and the event has a guest list that's being vetted by Singapore's prime minister himself."

"But Panacea got your guy in without any problems."

"We did, although now he's missing in action. It will be a challenge to get another operative into that gala in time. To build up another iron-clad cover will take months, time we don't have."

He folded his arms against the tabletop. "Except now you have me."

She tilted her head at him and smiled. "Care to rehire me as a body-guard?"

"I don't know. You're not very good at it," he scoffed, leaning back in his chair. Somehow, even this simple gesture looked graceful on him. "I seem to recall barely making it out alive last time."

She lifted an eyebrow. "Maybe I'd try harder if you gave me bene-fits."

His smile turned mischievous. "I thought I was the benefit."

"Not a very useful one."

"That's not what you said in the pool that night."

A tidal wave of emotions hit her. In an instant, she was overcome by the memory of his soft lips against hers, the sloshing of the pool around them, the cling of soaked clothes against their bodies.

"I don't think I said anything at all, to be honest," she replied qui-etly, and now it was his turn to look flustered, a faint flush rising on his neck.

The tension between them buzzed underneath her skin like an electric current. What was wrong with her? A make-out session wasn't a big deal. She'd had her fair share of hookups and done plenty more with them.

"So," he said, clearing his throat. As if they'd rehearsed it, they simultaneously straightened in their seats and blinked the moment from their eyes. "When do we start? I'm in the middle of preparing for my tour. If you need me for training, you're going to have to schedule around Claire to do it."

He's agreeing. Sydney couldn't suppress the small thrill that shot through her. She crossed her arms and kept her words calm. "Sauda wants us at headquarters tomorrow. Can you do that?"

Winter thought for a moment. "I'm scheduled to head back home for a month, starting today."

She nodded. "Yes, we figured."

"Of course you knew that." He nodded. "I'll tell Claire I'm visiting friends. Not a lie, really."

"We like to make sure we know as much as possible," she replied. "Any chance we can pass by your hotel room later? There's a set of instructions I need to give you before you arrive at headquarters, and I'd rather we not do that here, as much as we have this shop to ourselves."

"Oh, um." He hesitated, and Sydney saw a new, mysterious expression flit across his face. "There's, ah, someone in my room right now. I'll find another private place for us to talk."

Someone else in his room.

All of the tension between them at this table, all of their playful swipes and reminiscing, evaporated into thin air.

Of course, there was someone else.

A rush of embarrassment hit her. Why had she just assumed he would be alone, that he wasn't seeing anyone? Why had their intel missed this? She bit her cheek and pushed down the spark of jealousy. Had she forgotten who he was? Did she think that a little flirting meant anything to him, that he wasn't sleeping around with every starlet in sight?

She mustered every bit of her training to keep her face straight, her mask intact even in the face of shocking news. Not that this was that shocking, of course. That was hearing that her passport had been blacklisted at the airport two hours before she was scheduled to fly out of Cairo. Learning that her contact in Jakarta had been detained and she would need to face Indonesian authorities on her own.

Shocking news was *not* that Winter Young had slept with someone last night, that this person was still in his hotel room.

"She's really—" Winter began.

"Not a problem," Sydney heard herself interrupt, her voice dismissive and nonchalant. Hurt flashed in Winter's eyes, but she didn't linger on it. "It'd actually be easier if you already have a date ready to bring with you to the gala."

At that, Winter seemed to still. "I have to bring a date with me to Singapore?"

Sydney looked down at her mug and sipped her drink before she dared to reply. "Yes," she said. "It'd be out of the ordinary for you to arrive unattached to a fancy event like this one, so it'd be best if you had a plus one. We'd talked about assigning you a date, but if you're already seeing someone, then that makes for a better cover. Less paperwork for us."

He shook his head. "It's complicated," he muttered.

"Doesn't have to be the person in your hotel room," Sydney said with a cold shrug, "if she was *that* disappointed with your performance last night."

Winter lifted an eyebrow. "She wasn't."

Sydney hated how his retort stung even more. She forced herself to smile. "Good for you. So bring her. We're just trying to distract the reporters."

"Can't I just go solo? With you as my bodyguard?"

"What, can't catch a date?"

He frowned at her irritated tone, his body stiff now. "Does it bother you that much?"

Sydney could just let it slide. Why was she being such a jerk? "Doesn't bother me at all. Just didn't realize you had such a hard time finding a date. I thought people were throwing themselves at you."

Winter narrowed his eyes, studying her face. But this time, there was no warmth in his gaze. Somehow, it just increased her annoyance. "Well?" she said. "Can you find a date or not? Should Panacea get me another partner? I don't have all morning."

"Fine." His expression had darkened, and the small smile that touched the edge of his lips looked more like a grimace. "I'll ask her. Happy?"

Sydney swallowed the last of her own feelings. Did she really go into this thinking their meet would have ended any other way? Hoping that maybe there was something to rekindle between them? How foolish. Winter was off-limits. He would always be off-limits, as far as she was concerned, and the sooner she got that through her head, the better off she'd be.

Loyalty to a secret, above all else.

"Good. Then forget the instructions," she said. Her voice sounded too lighthearted. "I'll reach out to you via encrypted message with what you need to know before we head to Saint Paul."

Winter was still studying her, she could tell, searching her face for a reaction. He'd sensed something from her, but whatever it was, it must have disappointed him. His hands curled stiffly around his coffee cup.

And when he spoke, he just said, "Great."

Sydney rose from her seat and cast him a cool glance. "Well?" she said. "Are you planning on nursing that cup forever, or are you ready to head out?"

Whatever moment they'd had was over. Winter looked warily at her before rising, too, a new distance in his gaze. They stared at each other before he nodded, his hands finding his pockets. "I'm always ready," he said. "What, no tip?"

Sydney slapped a twenty on the table before walking to the door, holding it open with a flourish. "Here's a tip, Winter. We don't like to be kept waiting, so hurry along back to your room and break the happy news to your date about your romantic getaway with her." She tore her gaze away from him. "And tell your manager you're bringing me back on as your bodyguard. I'm sure Claire's going to be delighted to deal with me again."

Hidden Floors and Secrets

To those unaware of the Panacea Group's existence, the Claremont Hotel in Saint Paul, Minnesota, looked and operated like any standard luxury resort, its Grecian columns and domed roof reminiscent of a historic European cathedral. Guests entered the property's wrought-iron gates and checked in at its marbled registration counter, took photos at Christmastime in front of the lobby's grand, forty-foot-tall holiday tree, and enjoyed dinner in its Michelin-starred restaurant, Food for the Gods.

Winter had once been one of those people.

The last time he'd arrived, he'd come without any idea that hidden within the kitchens of that restaurant was the entrance to a secret agency—that situated a mile beneath the hotel was an entire labyrinth of experimental laboratories, floors filled with training facilities, of secret weapon arsenals and war rooms.

Now, as his car pulled up to the hotel's private side entrance behind a set of security gates, Winter glanced up at the imposing building. The sky overhead churned in a palette of charcoal, promising a storm that the news had been warning about for days. It matched his mood well.

His phone dinged, and he looked down to see a text from Gavi.

What are you up to today? she asked.

Seeing a friend, he typed back.

No one I know?

He hesitated. *Not yet.*

Ooh. Sounds intriguing. You know I love an adventure.

Believe me, it's just business.

I love business. Especially when it's your business.

He put his phone down and looked out the window as the car came to a stop. He'd regretted agreeing to take Gavi to Singapore almost immediately, but he wasn't about to back out now—no matter how much he wished he could. But now here he was, preparing for a mission he'd been dreaming about for a year, with an impossible ex-girlfriend on one arm and an irresistible secret agent on the other—one who might or might not hate him, depending on the day.

He sighed and rubbed a hand across his face, wishing he'd been able to get more sleep the night before. After an evening of trying in vain to reach his mother, she'd finally called him back at one A.M., from what sounded like a loud party.

Winter, she'd said, *is this an emergency?*

It was how she always greeted him—as if she couldn't wait to get off the phone again, as if she could barely stand to speak to him.

Winter had swallowed the familiar ache in his heart. *Where are you?* he'd asked.

At a friend's birthday! She shouted above the din.

Have you heard the news about the book? He'd asked, the dread settling in.

What book?

Someone is releasing an unauthorized tell-all book about me. Rumors say it's you. I figured I should check in.

Me? His mother had laughed, and in it, Winter could hear the origins of his own voice—warm, melodic. *Why would I write a tell-all about you?*

Remember that interview, Mom? The one you thought was "off the record."

Oh, that. He could almost see her waving her hand flippantly. *Am I not allowed to talk about you?*

That interview had dogged Winter for months—based on the answers his mother had given, reporters were suddenly digging for more about his private life growing up, about Artie's death, about his absent father, about his struggles with depression.

Did anyone approach you with a book deal? Winter pressed. *Did you agree to anything? Sign anything, maybe without reading it?*

Of course not, his mother had scoffed.

Winter didn't believe her, not entirely—ever since Artie's death, she'd had a tendency to absentmindedly agree to things and then promptly forget about them. It went hand in hand with her habit of constantly mixing up memories of him and his brother—who liked what, who went to what school in which year, who lived where—just as she constantly forgot her keys, her wallet, her money.

Winter had gotten used to her state after his brother's death. But with the book news, he felt the tension between them come roaring back.

Ma, he said over the phone. *You promise you didn't do the deal?*

I have to go, Winter, she called back, and it was clear that she hadn't heard him. *We'll talk later!*

Then she'd hung up.

Winter had spent the rest of the night tossing and turning, trying to guess whether his mother had just forgotten, or whether she had nothing to do with the book at all. Those restless thoughts quickly bled into dreams of being a small child in his old home, trying to hide from the horrible stench of cigar smoke. A foul smell that only meant one thing: his father was visiting. He'd woken up disoriented and bleary-eyed, head pounding, with the phantom odor of cigar smoke still stinging his nose.

An attendant opened the car door for Winter and he stepped out, rubbing his temples. He hurried in through a door held open for him by another attendant dressed all in black.

The second attendant gave him a respectful nod as he passed by. "Welcome, Mr. Young," he said as he closed the glass door behind them. "Ms. Cossette is already waiting for you. Please follow me."

Last time, Winter had arrived on a warm day into the sun-dappled dome of the hotel's Michelin-starred restaurant, the crystal chandelier dominating the ceiling casting a million sparks of light against the walls. Today, that interior looked different with the dark skies overhead, the chandelier dull and unlit, the grayness permeating the space and turning the pastoral European scenes painted on the round walls ominous.

He followed the associate, noting the restaurant's name etched into the stone columns.

FOOD FOR THE GODS

There, at the end of the hallway, right in front of the security check, was Sydney, her blond bob messy with waves, dressed in her usual black bomber jacket and a pair of black and gray striped trousers.

"On time, for once," she said archly before waving for security to let him through.

"I'm always on time," he replied. "Everyone else is just early."

She didn't answer, nor did she give him a second glance as they walked.

Now that he had a chance to steal looks at her without her staring back, Winter noticed that there *were* a few things different about her compared to when they last worked together. Her hair had grown longer, the tips of her strands ending in a slight wave that curved right against the tops of her shoulders. There was a faint, inch-long scar near where her jaw connected with her ear, as if she'd gotten nicked in a fight. He wanted to tuck her hair back and get a better look at it, ask her what had happened.

It took Winter a second to realize that his body language was mimicking Sydney's—hands in pockets, stride in sync. Their bodies still seemed attuned to each other, the way they were during Winter's training. What a strange pas de deux between them; he instinctively tilted his head whenever she did, and she always seemed to turn exactly when he did. But now there was also an almost awkward distance between them, something he'd felt when they'd exited the café in Honolulu.

Sydney led them through a set of double doors and into the restaurant's kitchen, where they walked through a veil of steam and smoke. The rich scent of garlic and bay leaves filled the air, and Winter breathed in deeply as restaurant staff hurried past them. Now and then, one of them would recognize his face and their eyes would settle on him momentarily. But no one stopped him, no one gasped or screamed in delight. The lack of attention felt unfamiliar. Uncomfortable. Unpleasant.

They're all Panacea staff, Winter reminded himself. Still, it was a strange sensation, walking among so many people as a nobody. People who weren't what they seemed.

They stopped in front of a line of refrigerators. Sydney pulled the second one open—but instead of revealing chilled compartments of food, it gave way to a long, secret corridor, the carpet thick and dark gray.

Winter had done this before, but it didn't matter. It was hard to get accustomed to using a fridge as a secret entrance. He suspected this was a thrill that would never fade.

When they stepped inside an elevator at the end of the corridor, Winter reached out to push the buttons heading down—but Sydney covered them before he could. Her cool fingers wrapped around his wrist, and a shiver ran through him.

"Not this time," she said.

"I thought we were going to Panacea?" he asked.

"We are." She hit the button for the seventh floor, then glanced upward. "We're just heading up today."

He looked at her. "I thought the labs were a mile under the hotel."

"We're heading to wardrobe today," Sydney replied as the elevator rose. "Sauda and Niall are waiting for us there."

It hadn't occurred to Winter that the hotel's upper floors weren't all regular suites, that Panacea operated out of the Claremont's rooms themselves as well as the space excavated far below. He recalled the way his stomach had leapt during his last trip, when the elevator descended for several minutes and then opened into an extraordinary underground bunker.

They traveled in silence for a minute. Then the elevator came to a serene stop, and the doors slid open to reveal a single, massive floor that stretched to every wall.

At first glance, it reminded Winter of a fashion house's headquarters—dozens of color-coded clothing racks were arranged in neat rows against one wall, while elegant outfits on display inside glass cases lined the others, as if they were part of a curated gallery at the Met. In the center of the room was a cylindrical structure, its surface smooth and reflective.

They passed through one last set of security right in front of the elevator.

"Sorry, this gate's new," Sydney said. "We had several added after some Orange Alerts last year." Then she nodded in the direction of the clothing on display. "Welcome to the House of Panacea. Here, our highly specialized tailors create everything we need to wear on each of our expeditions."

Winter looked around incredulously, then toward the windows lining the walls. Through them, he could see the rain starting to come down outside.

"No one has ever asked questions about a mysterious fashion house located inside a luxury hotel?" he asked.

"Not when they can't see it," Sydney told him as they went. "Those aren't windows. They're double-sided screens."

Winter blinked at her. "Screens?"

"We commissioned them from Henka Games." Sydney led him over to the windows, then ran her finger against what appeared to be a windowpane. "Embedded in the wall right above each window is a near-microscopic camera that sends a live video feed of the outside world to this screen. It makes it look like you're staring out at the street, but you're actually watching a video stream. From the outside, people looking in through what they think are windows are seeing live video from a staged floor we have set up at the top of the building. To them, this floor looks like the interiors of hotel suites. It's more challenging than it looks, as it needs to adjust the scenery for depth, depending on where you're standing." She grinned at him in a way that made his heart leap. "But it fooled you, didn't it?"

"It absolutely did," he murmured, admiring the screen. Even this close to it, even knowing what he did, he couldn't make out the pixels. The resolution must have been so high that he couldn't discern the difference. A shiver of fear and delight ran down his spine. Maybe it wouldn't matter how many times he visited Panacea. They would find a way to surprise him every time.

"Well. Look who the Jackal dragged in."

Sydney and Winter turned their heads in unison at a woman dressed in a buttery yellow hijab and a vest suit with trousers.

Sauda Nazari, Winter thought immediately, one of Panacea's mission directors. She was tall and dark and willowy, almost delicate, but when she reached them and shook Winter's hand, her grip belied her strength.

"Let me cut to the chase—I didn't expect to ever call you again after London," Sauda continued. "But here we are."

Winter couldn't help smiling at the sight of her. "Didn't think I caused enough trouble last time, Ms. Nazari?"

Sauda raised an eyebrow at him, but a smile twitched at the corner of her mouth. "I suppose we concluded that your help is worth the potential damage," she answered. She released his hand and waved him forward.

"Come. Niall is already complaining about being pulled away from one of his projects for our meeting today."

As they followed in her wake, Sydney walked closer to Winter and nudged him gently with her shoulder. "Not a word about his beard."

They passed the rows of clothing on display before they reached the cylindrical structure in the center of the room. Sauda pressed her hand against its side.

The curved wall rotated, and a door slid open, revealing an interior that looked like a polished fitting room. A series of suits hung on a rack against one end of the space, while the other had an elevated dais surrounded by mirrors.

Inside stood a big, burly man in a burgundy-colored suit, his brows thick and furrowed as if he were ready to start an argument. The man looked over at them from where he was busy arranging several of the outfits hanging on the rack.

"Finally," he grumbled, his voice matching the low, grating sound of thunder coming from outside. "Welcome back, Mr. Young."

Winter's eyes went straight to the man's broad, smooth chin. "You're . . . clean-shaven," he commented instinctively.

At that, the man's brows pushed even lower, until they seemed like they might swallow his eyes whole. "Against my will," he growled, his gaze darting to Sauda.

Sauda crossed her arms. "Oh, come now," she said. "You look tidy." She nodded at Winter. "He's retiring in two weeks, right after your mission. Just wanted him to look his best for his farewell tour."

Winter thought he looked a bit like an enormous baby without his facial hair, but a sharp elbow to his ribs from Sydney jolted him out of his thoughts. He winced and glared at her.

"What part of 'not a word' did you not understand?" she whispered.

Winter rubbed his chest and nodded at Niall. "Retiring? Congratulations, sir."

"Don't congratulate me yet." Niall scowled and rubbed absently at the smooth skin on his chin. "I'm coordinating your mission on-site with the CIA, and apparently some think I look too sloppy with my beard."

"That's not exactly what I said," Sauda replied.

"Sloppy and messy are synonyms," he argued back.

Sydney leaned toward Winter and whispered, "Once he retires, he'll be visiting his daughter for the first time in a decade. He's a little anxious. Go easy on him."

Winter stared at her, noting the way her shoulders tensed as she spoke. "You seem a little anxious, too," he said in a low voice.

She shrugged him off, but her posture remained unchanged.

Niall's attention finally returned to Winter. "Good to see you again, kid."

"Glad to be invited back."

The man shrugged. "You weren't my first choice."

"One can't hear *that* enough," Winter said.

"Be nice, Niall," Sauda scolded, and the man rubbed his round chin again.

"Are we fitting him first?" Sydney asked as they stopped before the central dais.

"Might as well do it now, since he's here," Sauda replied. She nodded at Winter and gestured at the dais. "Please."

Winter stepped up onto the round platform and found himself staring at three long mirrors reflecting three angles of himself. At least this felt familiar—over the years, he had been fitted a thousand times for a thousand different outfits.

Sauda raised her voice slightly and spoke to no one in particular. "Avalon—his measurements, please."

Avalon. Winter had almost forgotten about the AI that ran throughout the entire building. Last time he was here, Avalon had scanned every single one of his personal details and displayed them on the meeting room wall, from his social security number to the last order he'd placed at a restaurant.

This time, a pleasant voice came on the room's speakers.

"*Winter Young,*" it said, "*please hold out your arms to either side.*"

Winter obeyed. As he did, clusters of numbers and text drifted onto the mirrors facing him on the dais, appearing in the appropriate places around his reflection.

Arm length to shoulder: 36 inches
Shoulder width: 51 inches
Waist size: 29 inches
Inseam: 33 inches

"The gala you'll both be attending after the Warcross ceremony is a rather grand affair," Sauda told him as the numbers went on. "And that means looking the part, but in your own way, given who you are. So we wanted to make sure we dressed you in something you'd actually wear."

Winter's attention shifted from the floating numbers on the mirror to the line of clothes hanging on the racks. His gaze settled on a suit closest to him that had been carefully separated from the others.

"This one?" he asked.

"We'll tailor it to fit you like a glove," Sauda said. "But yes."

It was an Alexander McQueen design, he could tell immediately, with its skull-shaped cuffs and unique detailing along the seams, a scarlet kerchief folded into the breast pocket. It was the most beautiful suit he'd ever seen. He would have ordered this, had he seen it on a runway.

"I'm guessing the House of McQueen isn't in on this caper," he said.

"Of course not," Sauda answered. "We just had it altered a bit."

"Altered how?"

Niall stepped forward. "Keep your arm extended."

Winter obeyed. As he did, Niall removed the suit jacket from the rack and pulled its left sleeve, then right, onto Winter's arms. The fabric slid on, cold and sleek. Niall smoothed the lapels, took a step back, and reached into his jacket.

"Stand absolutely still, please," Niall added.

Winter nodded.

Niall pulled out a gun and pointed it at Winter's arm.

Winter's eyes popped open. He started to protest—but Niall had already pulled the trigger.

The bullet rocketed out of the gun and into his sleeved arm. A violent jolt of pain shot through him, and he flinched, his body swinging to one side from the impact. Then he heard the bullet clink to the floor.

"Ow!" Winter managed to yell. "What the hell?"

No one else reacted. Sydney nodded at her mentor. "You got the design to muffle the sound, too?" she asked.

"By thirty percent," Niall said with a nod as he bent to pick up the bullet case.

Sydney made an impressed sound. "I can tell."

Niall held the bullet case up to Winter—and Winter found himself staring at a bit of metal that looked like it had slammed into a steel wall. Well, *this* was new. He'd never been shot at a fitting before.

"What makes this suit special," Niall said to Winter, "is that the fabric isn't made out of fabric at all, but a synthetic diamond mesh engineered to feel like linen but strong enough to be impenetrable by bullets. The technology of the mesh's molecular structure combined with the technique of the weave also absorbs a great deal of the impact." He looked at Winter. "How does your arm feel?"

"Sore," he complained, rubbing at the spot where the bullet had hit.

"But unharmed, yes?" Niall suggested.

Winter nodded begrudgingly as he ran his fingers along the suit's sleeve. The material felt slightly heavier than the suits he was accustomed to wearing—and when he peered closer at where the bullet had struck, he noticed with astonishment that the sleeve looked almost untouched, with just a trace of gunpowder dotting the surface. He brushed it off, and the jacket was as good as new.

"Those skull cuffs also aren't just cuffs," Niall added as he touched the metal studs.

"Listening devices?" Winter suggested, remembering the chips that his jewelry had been embedded with during his last mission.

Niall shook his head. "Tap the left cuff three times in rapid succession with your thumb, then twist it sideways. It's designed to respond only to your fingerprint, and only to this pattern of touch."

Winter followed the directions—and the cuff popped off, then flashed a blinking red light. Startled, he dropped it.

"Is that a bomb?" he said incredulously.

"Of sorts." Niall picked it up and tapped it twice, shutting it off. "Only you can activate yours, although anyone can turn it off. Not a massive explosive, but it'll cause a bit of damage."

"Right, sure," Winter muttered, gingerly pressing it again so that the cuff snapped back onto his sleeve.

"Of course, try to use it sparingly," Niall said, patting the pocket beside the front lapel of the suit. When he removed his hand, Winter saw a gleaming silver pen tucked into it. "You've got a pen flare here that will work just fine as a distraction. Shield your eyes." To demonstrate, he took it out and clicked it twice.

A blindingly bright flare burst from the tip of the pen, drenching the room in light.

"You'll each get one," Niall said, twisting the pen, and the light shut off again. "Keep this on you at all times." He tucked the pen back into the pocket with a pat.

Winter blinked, still seeing a few spots from the flash. "I could have used a suit like this during the last mission," he muttered.

"Our apologies," Sauda replied. "You were only supposed to attend a party last time and get a recording for us. We didn't think you'd need this."

Her words sent a ripple of unease through Winter. He turned to look at her. "But I will this time?"

"I'm sure Sydney gave you a brief introduction to what your mission will be," Sauda said.

Winter glanced at Sydney. "She mentioned this was a rescue."

"Yes, an extraction. Given the high-profile politicians at this event and the level of security, I think we'd best play it safe and fit you for one of these."

Best play it safe. Winter turned his eyes back down to the suit and concentrated on the feel of it, not wanting to dwell on Sauda's words. Safety precautions weren't new to him, of course—someone had once stabbed him with a knife as a crowd mobbed him outside an after-party, someone had once grabbed his hair and thrown him to the ground, someone had once broken into his home while he was asleep. Over time, Claire had nearly perfected the art of keeping him safe, everything from placing the right number of bodyguards in a location to getting him in and out of buildings with top speed and secrecy.

But compared to this, his usual security tactics seemed like child's play. Keeping someone from grabbing his hair was a far cry from fitting him into a literal suit of armor and sending him into the middle of a political battlefield.

"You okay?" Sydney asked, peering at him.

He frowned. "I'm doing so great. Please tell me more about the imminent and immediate danger we're heading into face-first."

Sydney folded her arms, unbothered, and turned to Sauda. "Might be a good time to enlighten us both," she said to the director. "I don't even know the name of the operative we're rescuing."

Sauda exchanged a look with Niall, who gave her a subtle nod.

Sydney frowned. "What?" she asked.

Niall shrugged. "Just tell her," he said. "Get it over with. Then we'll move onto everything else."

Sauda looked at Winter through the mirror, then at Sydney. "Very well," she said with a sigh. "The agent's code name is the Arsonist."

It meant nothing to Winter, but he saw Sydney stiffen.

"You're kidding," she murmured.

"I'm not." Sauda narrowed her eyes at her young ward. "You'll be extracting Tems Bourton."

Sydney didn't say anything more. Instead, her blue eyes darkened into a storm. She pushed away from the curved wall of the fitting room, her eyes flickering briefly to Winter before she stalked out of the space, slamming the door behind her.

"Give her a second," Sauda said to Niall.

"I know," Niall answered.

The unease Winter felt quickly congealed into dread. He turned around on the dais and gave Sauda a curious frown. "Why'd she do that?" he asked.

Sauda looked in the direction Sydney had gone. "You would, too," she replied, "if you were just ordered to rescue your ex."

Bad Diplomacy

The Arsonist.

The name echoed in Sydney's mind as she marched out of the room. She had been the one to suggest it for Tems, back when they'd graduated from Panacea's training program and he'd completed his first mission. It had been an escapade that ended with him setting alight an entire freight train in the middle of a midnight field, an inferno so bright that the snaking flames could be seen from space.

You should name him the Arsonist, she'd said sarcastically to Sauda. *He follows orders about as well as a wildfire does.*

It had stuck. And then Sydney hadn't seen him again until three years later, when they were both stationed briefly in Stockholm, Sweden, and Niall had assigned her as his partner.

They'd ended up getting snowed into their hotel for two days—days they spent in bed together.

She cringed at the memory of their affair. He'd been a good kisser—good at a lot more than that, actually—but he had also stranded her in the country by stealing her passport and altering it to use himself.

Sorry, sweetheart. Just business.

She could still remember his scrawled note, signed at the bottom with a knife through a heart.

What an asshole. She still hadn't forgiven him for it. Still, she sometimes wondered idly what Panacea had him up to. Rumors swirled about his insubordinance—that Niall had him shipped overseas for it, although the analyst never mentioned him. She'd only pieced it together after she spotted Tems in a photo on the Sapphire Cross's site, broad smile on his face as he handed out supplies at the charity's outpost in Greece. But when Sydney was in London last year with Winter, Tems had been the one who'd left a parcel for her in the Alexandra Palace's bathroom, the only evidence of his identity being that same signature.

She would have been fine with that being the only contact she had to endure from him for the rest of her life. But now here she was with orders to rescue him from his own mission.

No wonder they had kept his identity a secret from her until now. She was going to kill Sauda for this.

As if on cue, she heard Sauda's voice calling her. "Come back, Syd," the woman said in her calm, unconcerned voice. "And meet us in Sim A."

"You could have told me," Sydney snapped over her shoulder.

"Why?" Sauda called back with a shrug. "So you could throw this tantrum sooner?"

"So I could tell you to pick someone else for this mission."

"There's always a reason we choose you for your missions. It's possible your refusal could trigger a global war." She nodded once at Sydney. "And cost Tems his life."

Sydney hissed a swear under her breath and looked away at the false windows. Sauda's words burned in her mind. *Global war.* God damn it all. She could have been a tour guide instead—or any other job that required knowing multiple languages and where the world's salvation didn't hang on her every task.

"He nearly cost me mine once," she snapped. "We'd be even."

"Look, I get it," Sauda said. "Tems is a bit . . . unruly. We've had our own frustrations with him." She turned in the direction of the glass rooms lining the end of the floor. "But he's also one of our best. If you're still upset about it later, just say the word. We'll send Winter home, and try to avert global disaster. But don't begrudge our commitment to protecting our agents. We'd do the same for you—and we need him as much as we need you. So just hear me out. Are we clear?"

Sydney stood where she was for a second longer, trying to push her annoyance down. Behind Sauda, she saw Winter emerge from the dais with his hands in his pockets, his eyes cautiously fixed on her.

Then she started walking back. "Crystal," she muttered. "But this better be good. And give me several backup passports this time."

Sauda just turned coolly away and started leading them to the offices. As Sydney caught up to Winter, he fell into step beside her.

"An ex, huh?" he murmured.

His words sounded light, almost teasing, but she noticed the tightness of his jaw, the stiffness of his posture. It made her tense, too.

"Ex is too strong a word," she said coldly, without looking at him. "We had a two-day affair while on assignment. An overrated fling."

"Mm," he answered. "This mission's getting more fun by the minute."

They stepped into the first of the glass offices and entered what appeared to be an empty room. The blank door had several words etched on it.

SIMULATION ROOM A

Winter paused, as if wondering where the chairs and tables were.

"Just stand still," Sydney told him. "The room's recording your dimensions."

Niall closed the door behind them and turned to Sauda. "You do the honors," he said.

Sauda twisted her wrist in midair. A hologram suddenly appeared between them all, a map of Southeast Asia hovering in the air like a glowing lantern. She gestured at a small dot on the map. "Avalon," she said, "zoom in on Singapore."

The dot expanded all around them until a three-dimensional simulation of Singapore filled the entire room. Suddenly, they were standing in a busy intersection in the middle of a city. The sound of motorbikes and cars filled the room. When Sydney looked to her side, she saw street stalls lining open-air buildings, the vendors tossing pan-fried noodles in woks and turning skewers of meat behind curtains of steam, luxury skyscrapers and jungle foliage filling in the scene behind them. It was such a realistic simulation that she could almost feel the humidity in the air.

"I transferred Tems here three months ago," Niall said.

"Sightseeing?" Sydney suggested, her eyes following the traffic.

"Recon," Niall answered, "on an alleged plot to assassinate the US president."

At this, Sydney's head whipped sharply to Niall. "Rosen's under threat?"

"Mr. Rosen, yes. His dissenters have always had dangerous intentions, but their actions have escalated lately."

Sydney turned back to the simulation. Her hands were gripping her elbows hard enough now to leave white marks fading against her skin. She'd met the president once, at a private White House security event. She knew to distrust politicians, had too much intel on too many of them not to, but Rosen was different. He was the kind of person who inspired loyalty, who had a way of speaking that made you love him—believe in him, even. His campaign promises may have been lofty, but somehow, he made it seem possible, and more importantly, like he meant what he said. She remembered the way he'd shaken her hand at the event and the kind smile he'd given her, how he'd taken the time to quietly thank her for her work in taking down a homegrown terrorist group in Montana.

Suddenly, she understood the delicate nature of their mission. Rosen was the most beloved president they'd had in decades. If he was assassinated, the streets would explode with riots. It would be a murder of John F. Kennedy–level proportions. It would destabilize the entire globe.

"We've been tracking the threats closely alongside the CIA," Niall continued.

"Now, Mr. Rosen is scheduled to attend the Warcross gala as a celebration of how the global economy has come together over technology. Earlier this year, our analysts sniffed out a plot by a rebel group to assassinate Mr. Rosen at that gala."

The world around them shifted again, and this time they found themselves standing outside what looked like a neo-Palladian palace in the middle of the city, surrounded by lush lawns and tropical trees. Banners in the colors of the Singaporean flag fluttered on either side of the entrance steps.

Sydney shook her head. "Why target Rosen right now?"

"The rebels plan to pin the blame on China. They're hoping to trigger a war between China and the United States, with Singapore trapped in the middle as the proxy country. We believe they have an arms deal with China that is motivating them to do this." Sauda tapped the air, and the simulation shifted again. Now they were standing in the marble lobby of the gala building, the sound of other people's footsteps and voices echoing around them.

"We'd sent Tems to gather information on this rumor, which he would then pass to the US authorities arriving for the gala in order to stop the assassination attempt—without any of this information going public, of course."

"You mentioned the CIA's involved?" Sydney asked.

"Yes." Sauda made a swiping motion in midair, and the scene around them shifted to another part of the gala building—a hallway down which now walked several people in suits. The simulation suddenly froze on this scene. "Niall will be on a separate flight. Once he arrives, he'll head to the CIA's setup there to coordinate their work with our agents at the Sapphire Cross."

Sydney's stomach sank at the familiar, bejeweled cross pins glittering on the trio's suit jackets. "Can't President Rosen just say he's unable to go?" she said. "Broke a finger? Caught the flu?"

"Bad diplomacy," Niall replied. "The president won't be cowed by a mere rumored threat. Besides, the culprits will simply postpone their plans for another time. The CIA wants them arrested as soon as possible, as you can imagine. It's not much of a choice." The man gave her a dry scowl. "A bit like how we need you to rescue Tems."

Sydney wanted to snort. Bad diplomacy, indeed.

"So, what happened to your agent?" Winter asked.

"Last week, Tems was supposed to reach out to us and deliver preliminary intel he'd gathered on the assassination ahead of the gala. He never showed."

Sydney swallowed, but her throat felt like it had a rock lodged in it.

Niall nodded. "We believe he might have had his cover blown, or has someone on his trail that's making it difficult for him to communicate with us, or is in some similar trouble. He told us in his last message that he will still be present at the gala. So we've arranged secret transportation for him out of the country on that night, possibly the only place with enough security for him to be safely present. We think if you can find him at the gala, we can smuggle him out from there. But he can't get out alone. He'll need new identification and another agent to help him."

"That's where we come in, I'm guessing," Sydney said.

Sauda pursed her lips, then eyed her and Winter. "Your mission," she concluded, "is to go to the gala and get the Arsonist out of there without causing a scene. We'll tell you when and where to meet him."

Sydney took a slow, deep breath in, but her lungs were already reacting to the thought of being in the middle of a political crisis.

Beside her, Winter nodded. "So all you need from me is to get Sydney in?"

Niall leaned his elbows against the table. "You'll be putting on the biggest concert in Singapore's history a day before the gala. We can easily get you onto the gala's guest list, and you'll get Sydney in as your bodyguard."

"You mentioned you had a date ready?" Sauda asked.

"Yes," Winter answered, his voice clipped.

"Good. Name?"

"Gavi Ginsburg." Winter looked away and focused instead on the simulation around them.

Sydney tried to look nonchalant, but her mind was already spinning. So, this was the girl who had been in Winter's hotel room. Sydney knew the name, had seen it in his file and the occasional article: Gavi Ginsburg, New York socialite. She had a long, on-and-off relationship with Winter, according to the tabloids. And apparently, they were on again. She shifted her stance, folding her hands together behind her back. Niall glanced briefly at her, but she pretended not to notice.

Sauda nodded. "I ask because the gala will require her information as soon as possible. They'll do a background check on her."

Winter shrugged. "They'll find plenty in a public search."

"You won't need to do anything once you're in," Niall added. "It shouldn't even disrupt your tour schedule. Let us handle getting to Tems and ushering him out. All we need you for, Winter, is access."

"What about the president?" Sydney asked. "What about the plot to assassinate him?"

"Let me be clear. That is not your mission," Sauda replied. "Let me worry about that with the Sapphire Cross and the CIA. You worry about getting our guy safely back home." She tilted her head at Winter, then nodded at Sydney. "That is, if you're both willing to accept this."

Sydney glanced over to Winter, a thoughtful expression on his face. She recognized the look from her early days as an agent—questioning whether she'd make it out alive, whether the mission was worth doing, why she bothered throwing herself into these sorts of situations over and over. Another dangerous game in a foreign country. Another brush with shadowy groups and those hell-bent on bringing chaos into the world. Singapore was one of the wealthiest countries in Asia—and a gala in the city-state meant encounters with the world's elite. The most insufferable people on the planet—but also the most powerful. They weren't just rescuing a fellow agent. This was a political dance that could remake nations.

Winter spoke first. "As long as it doesn't interfere with my tour," he muttered. "I don't like lying to Claire, so I don't want to have a hard time explaining it all to her."

"We'll make it work seamlessly with your schedule and your performance," Sauda answered.

"That's what you said last time," Winter replied.

Sauda shrugged, offering him a grave smile. "You know there are only so many guarantees in this business. We will do our utmost, as long as you do, too." Then she glanced at Sydney. "And you?"

Sydney sighed and unfolded her arms. Her eyes wandered around the paused simulation, still stuck on the scene of the Sapphire Cross agents making their way through the gala building. There were a million pieces of this rescue mission that could go wrong—she could sense it, could feel the chaos building. Niall had to coordinate successfully with the CIA; she had to be able to make contact with Tems at the gala; the assassination attempt had to be thwarted; they had to be able to get out in time.

There's always a reason why we choose you for your missions. Sauda's words came back to her. It was why she was still here, why she put her trust in Panacea, why she had taken their oath when she was first recruited. Panacea always had their reasons, and they almost always involved the security of their agents.

Sydney nodded. "I'm in."

Sauda smiled. "Then let's get started," she said.

By the time Sydney escorted Winter back to the side entrance of the hotel, the worst of the storm had passed, but the slanting rain was still pouring a waterfall onto the glass awning over the door. The sky was pitch-black, even though it was only midafternoon.

"We can put you on a later flight," Sydney offered as Winter flipped the collar of his coat up and stared out at the rain. "Yours isn't canceled, but it won't be a fun ride home in this."

Winter shook his head. "Can't. I have a date."

As if on cue, his phone buzzed in his pocket, but he didn't bother answering it.

Sydney folded her arms and tried to ignore the way her heart recoiled at his words. "Well, the sooner you confirm your date for the gala, the better," she decided to say. "If she refuses, we'll need time to resubmit your date's info to the Singaporean authorities."

Winter shot her a sidelong look. "Her name's Gavi."

"Oh, I know."

He stared at her a beat longer, as if he were trying to discern the reason for her dismissive answer. As if he knew it bothered her. Her annoyance only deepened.

"Besides, how do you know she's the date I'm talking about now?"

She shrugged. "You're a creature of habit, Winter," she replied. "I just assumed it was the same person."

Winter looked at her for another moment, then turned back to the rain. His phone buzzed again in his pocket. "Well, what about you?" he said.

For a second, his question confused her—it sounded a little like he was asking whether she could be his date. She frowned at him, her heart suddenly racing. "What about me?"

"Tems. Your ex. Or fling. Whatever you want to call him." Winter nodded at the curtain of water covering the glass. "Aren't you the reason Sauda chose us for this mission? Because you have the best chance of luring him out?"

"I'm not luring him out. He's in trouble."

"Then why send you in particular?"

She put her hands up. "The hell if I know. Ask Sauda."

"You must know him well."

She snorted, ready to give a sarcastic reply. But there was an edge to Winter, and suddenly she had the urge to annoy him further. "Well enough," she answered instead. "He is . . . very talented."

She glanced at him from the corner of her eye. To her satisfaction, Winter's lips tightened, but he didn't betray more than that.

"Hope he's nice," he muttered instead.

"I only date nice guys," she said sweetly.

He raised an eyebrow. "Then I must have been a mistake."

She smiled at him. "Didn't think that counted as dating."

He smiled back. "Fair enough."

The buzz of Winter's phone cut the rising tension between them. This time, he sighed and reached into his pocket. "Claire probably wants to confirm our interviews tomorrow," he muttered.

But when he looked at his phone, Sydney saw his demeanor change. His skin paled, and his eyes darted over the same section of the screen—something had his immediate attention.

"What is it?" she asked.

Winter didn't say a word. Instead, he just tilted his phone so that she could see the white text on the screen.

CLAIRE: *Winter, it's urgent. Part of the book was leaked to the press. Get ready for the headlines.*

Impressions and Suspicions

EXCLUSIVE: Leaked Chapters from Winter Young's Tell-All!
Excerpts Reveal Winter Young's Past Struggle with Depression, Drugs . . .

WINTER STORM: Does the World's Favorite Pop Star Have a Rage Problem?
New Book Details!

The avalanche of media that followed the book leak was overwhelming and unavoidable. Despite Claire's best efforts to steer them clear of the headlines as they headed to their waiting plane, Winter still caught glimpses of magazines all over the VIP terminal of the airport, lies from the upcoming book printed in bold on the cover pages.

"I don't want you reading the full excerpts," Claire told him in a low voice as they walked down the terminal hall, their entourage ahead of them. "But I know you've seen enough. Do you recognize the stories? Are they all lies?"

"Mostly lies," Winter muttered.

"Then I'll pass that along to the lawyers and release a statement confirming the stories are fake." Claire frowned. "Some of it is true, though?"

Winter didn't answer right away. Only when they reached the end of the hall and stepped out onto the tarmac, the summer sun turning their waiting jet searingly bright, did he say, "Some of it."

"Do you recognize anything about the excerpts? The writing style? A turn of phrase?" Claire asked quietly. "Do the stories match up with any particular person in your life?"

Winter thought of one excerpt he read that morning, detailing his past depression and drug use. It was exaggerated, but not entirely false. He thought back to the time right after Artie had died, when his mother faded into a still figure on her bed, curtains drawn, body curled up, for days at a time. Winter had been twelve and did his best to fend for himself. But he found himself lost in a fog of darkness, too, and although he didn't know what it was at the time, he'd started sneaking pills out of the bottles that were always sitting open on his mother's dresser. Antidepressants, anti-anxiety meds. She never noticed, of course, never commented on his behavior. Not when he seemed to wander around the house in a daze, or when he'd suddenly wake from the fog, only to lie in bed at night, shivering, withdrawing from whatever he took. On those nights, everything about his senses would be heightened—he could feel every stitch in his blanket, could smell the awful stench of the smoke from cigars in the fibers of the carpet.

"No," he said, and shook his head. Claire nodded, her lips tight with disappointment.

"We'll get to the bottom of it," she said. "I promise."

Winter stayed quiet as he walked behind his entourage and up the jet's steps. As they entered the interior, Gavi took one of the seats in the front row, while Dameon slumped onto the couch lining the back and held up a paper with their full schedule.

"Rehearsals are on the same day we land?" he groaned.

"We only have two full days before the opening ceremony," said Winter as he settled down beside Gavi. "I don't think we have much of a choice."

Dameon looked at him. "You'll be there for both, right?"

Winter nodded. "Unless Claire calls me away for some last-minute thing."

"It's fine. Sleep is overrated." Dameon's eyes skipped to Gavi. "Besides," he said, staring warily at her. "I think I'd prefer to sleep through this entire flight, anyway. I'll be plenty rested."

"Oh, cheer up, Dame. I make a great flight companion," Gavi said, and from her voice, Sydney could tell that they must have known each other for a while.

Dameon tightened his lips at her. "Won't know. I'll be asleep."

Gavi gave him a sweet smile, then winked at Sydney, who sat in the row behind her. "Ashley here likes me just fine."

Ashley Miller. The name for Sydney's cover. Winter tensed as Sydney regarded Gavi politely. "I don't have opinions on my client's acquaintances, ma'am," she answered.

Gavi made an O with her lips. "So, you're a discreet one," she said, tilting her head at Sydney. "Thank god. Last thing I need is the security detail to have an opinion."

"She's here to protect us, Gav," Winter said with a sigh.

Gavi crossed her arms and regarded Sydney carefully. "You know, Winter, I was surprised you invited me along, after what happened the last time we were in Singapore. She might have her work cut out for her," she said with a wicked grin. "Well, girl, try not to mess with my vibe too much."

"I won't, ma'am," Sydney said, her professional tone completely unfussed. "Not if I can help it."

Gavi's lips twitched at her answer. Winter gave Sydney a raised eyebrow and an expression that said, *Please keep the peace in here, for my sake.*

Sydney just smiled a little and looked away, but Winter could read the dislike on her face.

Gavi looked at Winter. "You can spare me your rehearsals," she said. "I'm just here for your date nights at the gala. Don't worry. I'll find ways to keep myself busy. Maybe Ashley here can join me. Right, Ash? You seem fun." She grinned at Sydney.

Sydney looked back at her without reaction. "I'm just here to protect Mr. Young, ma'am."

"I bet you are," Gavi said with a cold smile.

Across from him, Winter saw Dameon's eyes shift to his. The boy's gaze was calm, as serene as it always was, but to Winter, it felt searing enough that he got up from his seat and headed to the back of the jet. Sydney looked at him, as if asking whether or not he wanted her to follow him, but he just shook his head subtly at her and opened a door, revealing an elegant bedroom with a queen-sized bed.

He turned around with a sigh, eager to lie down and close his eyes.

"Winter."

Dameon had followed in his wake, those serene eyes locked on him.

Winter shrugged and stepped away so that his friend could enter. When they were alone, he turned and gave Winter a quizzical frown.

"You gonna tell me why Gavi's here?" he asked. "You guys can't really be back together again?"

Winter ran a hand through his hair and slumped on the edge of the bed. "It's a long story," he said. "Claire told me I needed a date for the ceremony, and Gavi was just . . . there."

Dameon frowned at him. "You could have just asked me."

Winter laughed a little. "Aren't you seeing that baseball guy?"

He shrugged. "It's casual. I'm just telling you that I would have suffered through a night as your plus one if just to spare us all a trip with Gavi."

"Sorry," he muttered. "But I promise, we're not back together. It's just a business thing."

Dameon looked at him skeptically, then turned to nod at the closed door. "And Ashley . . . Why's she back?" he asked quietly.

"She did a decent job last year in London. We needed extra security, so I had Claire reach out to her again." Winter lifted an eyebrow at him. "What, you've got a problem with her, too?"

He shook his head. "No, I liked her last time. This time, too."

"Then what?"

"I don't know." Dameon folded his arms as he stood before Winter. "You tell me."

The carefully crafted story that Winter had told himself began to fall apart under the steadiness of Dameon's stare. But the truth—that he was Sydney's partner in another dangerous mission, that the president was in danger, that Panacea's agent might be missing or dead, that he couldn't tell anyone. Not even one of his best friends.

"I don't know what you want me to say," he replied. "I'll be fine. Gavi's going back to the States after we leave Singapore for our next stop. And Ashley's an asset to the team. She's good."

"Is that why you treat her differently from your other guards?"

Winter crossed his arms. "What's with your fixation on her?"

"Just seems odd you only hire her for overseas jobs. Why didn't you keep her on after we came back from London?"

"Because we didn't need her." He rubbed his temples. "She's too expensive, and we don't use her to her full potential. You know she's got experience with presidents, right?" Not exactly a lie.

"Yeah, when we were boarding, I overheard her speaking fluent Mandarin to the flight attendant."

"Are you saying she's overqualified to be my bodyguard? Because I'd have to agree."

Dameon hesitated. "I'm just saying. When she *is* here, she never leaves your side. Never. Does she go to the bathroom with you, too?"

"Dameon, she stays in the adjoining room. Just like every other one of my personal bodyguards. There's nothing weird going on here. I promise." The lie stung and Winter braced for impact.

But even though Dameon didn't look like he believed Winter, not fully anyway, he gave him a nod and let it go. "Sorry," he said after a moment. "Maybe I'm reading too much into this trip."

Winter smiled a little. "Well, you may be right about that."

A beat of silence hung between them before Dameon finally nodded again. "See you back out there," he said.

"I'll be out in a few minutes," Winter replied. "I just need to close my eyes for a bit."

Before he left, Dameon leaned closer to Winter.

"And be careful with Gavi," he whispered.

"You always say this," Winter began. "I didn't think you cared who I dated anymore."

"I don't. It's been years since we—" He paused and threw his hands up in frustration. "Look, I mean it," he went on in a low voice. "I know you invited her, but she always has an ulterior motive. So you might want to ask yourself why she's really here."

He scowled. "We've only dated for three years. I'm aware of who she is, Dame. I've got it under control."

Dameon studied him, then turned away. Winter looked on at the swing of his friend's dreadlocks as he shut the door behind him. A current of fear hummed under his skin, the unspoken glances and tension telling him what he didn't want to admit to himself—that Dameon suspected something. Dameon was better at reading him than most, perhaps because of their past; he'd always been able to sense changes in Winter's mood. And maybe he couldn't put his finger on it, maybe he would never be able to give voice to what it was, but Winter knew he could feel it, could sense his friend's unease stirring.

If Dameon found out, it could endanger his life. That had happened with Leo in London. And it could put Sydney at risk even more.

Winter had to get better at hiding everything, even if he didn't know how.

He flopped backward onto the bed and stared up at the ceiling, felt the disorientation of being suspended in a tin can forty thousand feet in the air. Maybe this would be the last time his friend suspected anything.

Maybe, years later, when he and Sydney had long put this behind them, Dameon would ask if he'd ever had a fling with Ashley or if anything strange had happened between them, and Winter would lie and laugh along, and everything would be fine.

You are going to become a professional liar, Winter Young, Sauda had once told him. *Your deception to your loved ones will protect their lives.*

He was doing a good thing. Winter repeated it to himself several times, letting the thought cling to him. And although he couldn't quite convince himself, at least he had sixteen hours on this flight to try. So he lay there, his mind whirling, until the flight finally lulled him into a light sleep.

Enemies in Plain Sight

From the sky, Singapore looked like an expanse of emerald and blue—swaths of thick jungle interrupted by sprawling squares of farmland or terraced hills of rice paddies, the greenery turning patchier the closer they drew to the center of the city, until the plane banked and the entire city came into view, a massive metropolitan expanse of futuristic skyscrapers and bridges arching over snaking rivers.

Sydney stared at the enormous electronic ads playing against the sides of the skyscrapers as they came in for a landing, her eyes locking now and then on landmarks—twin needle towers joined by a dozen walkways, an illuminated skyscraper that looked like a spiraling fractal, a building in the shape of a giant fan.

As they touched down and the others shuffled around for their bags, Claire snapped her fingers in Winter's direction.

"We have a situation at the airport," Claire muttered.

Sydney turned away from the window as Winter came from his side of the plane to lean over their row, his attention turned down at Claire's phone. "What situation?" he asked.

His voice still sounded a little hoarse from sleep, and his hair was fluffed up in a mess that looked like someone should run a hand through it. Sydney averted her eyes and focused on Claire.

"Security's having issues with the crowd," Claire now said. "I'd warned them—it's been a while since you performed in Singapore, after all—but they aren't authorized to run us through any special customs gate. So we've got to go through their main terminal, and their doubled shift doesn't seem like enough."

"Are we going to be okay getting through?" he asked.

Claire nodded and folded her phone away with a decisive snap, although she didn't look convinced. "We'll make it quick," she said. "We've been through worse. Ashley?"

Sydney nodded. "Ma'am?"

"I'm telling the other guards to focus on shoving people away," she said, "but you keep an eye out for alternate routes. Stay close to me and follow my instructions, do you hear me?"

Sydney's eyes went briefly to Winter, and this time, he was staring back. His face looked relaxed, but she could recognize the telltale hint of stubbornness in his eyes.

I'll be fine, the expression told her. *Just get out in one piece.*

She gave him an imperceptible nod and smiled at Claire. "My best class during training," she replied with a shrug. "I'll get him out."

Soon, they were ready to step out, and a flight attendant pushed open the door. Sydney took in a breath of warm, humid air as she walked down the metal steps toward the tarmac. The air was sticky with the feel of late spring in a tropical place, something she tended to associate with being on the hunt. At least, that was how all her past missions near the equator had gone.

They were ushered into a private sedan at the bottom of the steps, then driven to the main terminal. Winter craned his neck as he sat beside Sydney, and the movement pressed his arm against hers.

"It seems fine in there," he mused, his eyes fixed on the building they were approaching.

"You always say that," Dameon said. "And you're never right."

"I don't see a crowd, do you?" he replied.

His friend crossed his arms over his chest. "I think the main entries are all on the west side."

"So what if there's a crowd?" Gavi said. "You've been through this a thousand times. You wouldn't want no one to show up, would you?"

Winter shot her a sidelong look. "I still want to live through it."

"You will." She pointed a manicured finger at him. "And you're going to love it, too."

Winter snorted at her words, and Sydney felt the tickle of jealousy well up under her skin again. She looked away from them and back out the window.

For a while, she thought that maybe Winter was right, that they would be fine—that the reports of issues at the terminal were exaggerated.

Then they turned a corner to reveal the huge indoor waterfall encased in a steel glass dome at the heart of the airport—and saw the massive crowd past it that had gathered in a sea around the bottom of the escalators.

The instant they rounded the bend, the sea of fans let out a round of screams. She could see the airport's security buzzing exhaustedly around the pack of people, struggling to keep them from spilling into the corridor meant only for arriving passengers.

Sydney had seen the mayhem Winter's presence could cause during their mission in London, but this would be a different sort of challenge. Beside her, Claire was walking backward and giving their entourage a pep talk, her heels clicking efficiently against the floor.

"Deep breaths, everyone," she was saying. "We've run this gauntlet plenty of times before." She glanced at the four security guards that had already moved into position around Winter. "Don't ever leave his side, and don't be afraid to shove people out of the way." She looked at Dameon. "Stay in front of Winter. If you lag behind him, you're going to get swallowed whole by that crowd, and we're going to have to fish you out. Every second of delay makes this harder." She nodded at Gavi. "Miss Ginsburg, you cling to Winter's arm like your life depends on it."

Gavi shrugged. "I've done it before."

Claire's eyes locked on Sydney. "You walk beside me," she said. "Scout our way to the door. You see it, right?"

Sydney had long noted the entrances lining the side of the airport. A part of her wanted to answer with *Considering I've waded through stampedes in active war zones, this is going to be a piece of cake.* But aloud, she just said, "Yes, ma'am."

"You look like you can dart between the crowd pretty easily," Claire went on. "Follow my instructions at all times. Don't ever lose track of where Winter is. Believe me, it's harder than it sounds." She clapped her hands together. "Are we ready?"

Winter nodded.

Claire spun back around. "Our cars are waiting outside at the front entrance. Let's go."

The crowd had started pooling at the bottom of the escalators from where they were coming down. The instant they reached the bottom, Claire pulled Winter behind her in a single, smooth gesture, and his four bodyguards formed a tight square around him, shoving bodily through the crowd as Winter walked as quickly as he could within their secured space. Around them, people swarmed in a ripple of motion.

Sydney melted immediately into the crowd, sliding between bodies until she'd put herself slightly ahead of Winter. A frantic hand shot out from the throngs to grapple at Winter's jacket. He seemed to steel himself and picked up his pace. There was nothing but a serene calm on his face, but she could read the fear in every line of his body, the way he seemed to be bracing himself to run but with no path to take.

Sydney shoved the hand away from him, then pushed back against a never-ending sea of arms all reaching for him. Paparazzi rushed around the edges of the crowd, their cameras hoisted high. They hurried through the terminal's lobby and down a path lined with airport security.

Sydney cast another look toward their exit. The airport's security seemed to be struggling to contain the crowd around it. One sweep was all it took for Sydney to realize that there was no way they'd get through without going down in a sea of people. *Dammit*, she thought. Things were always more complicated with Winter than they seemed.

On Winter's other side, Claire hugged closer to him and waved at the other bodyguards. Her gaze locked briefly on Sydney, and there, she could see the older woman's skepticism. In a crowd like this, Sydney could barely be seen—let alone protect Winter.

She looked around, searching for an alternative path.

In the airport's shopping atrium, Winter stumbled. It was all it took for a line of fans to squeeze in between him and his security, and for a split second, he was cut off from them. Sydney whirled around to see him disappear into the sea.

She snaked through the crowd in a flash. A second later, she found him, then looped her arm firmly through his.

"This way," she snapped.

He glanced backward. Claire had been pushed a few people away, and the rest of his bodyguards were shoving their way roughly forward. She glimpsed Gavi cutting sideways through the crowd in an attempt to reach Winter. Reuniting Winter with her would take too long, though, and she was causing her own stir as the crowd recognized her.

Sydney caught sight of a small, nondescript freight elevator door opening in a corner, and an airport staff member stepping off with an ID card looped around a lanyard on his neck.

She pivoted.

"The team—" Winter started to say.

"Follow me," she snapped.

One of his other bodyguards growled at her as they fought to rejoin Winter. "Orders are to take him to the entrance," he barked.

"Does that look possible to you?" Sydney replied without looking at him. "We're taking him this way."

"You're not my boss."

Sydney just ignored him. Before he could stop her, she steered Winter toward the elevator. "We're heading up into departures," she said in a low voice.

"Why?"

"Because if you want to be in one piece by the time we get to the car, you'll listen to me."

They reached the elevator right as the airport staff member froze there, staring numbly at the wave of people before him.

In one move, Sydney snatched the ID off of his lanyard and swiped the keypad for the elevator door. The staff member turned to her with a startled shout—but she had already stepped on board with Winter.

"Sorry!" she shouted over her shoulder.

The bewildered attendee saw the elevator door close in front of him with Sydney and Winter alone inside. Then the elevator sealed shut, and the chaos cut off into blissful silence.

Sydney's ears were still ringing from the chaos as Winter turned to her.

"What the hell are you doing?" he rasped at Sydney. "No one else knows where I am now."

"That's the point," Sydney said.

Then the elevator stopped, and they were stepping off into a corridor of luxury stores.

"They're going to figure out our new route," she muttered, then pushed him lightly as they reached the door at the end of the hall.

This opened back into the airport, across from a small gate with a smattering of people waiting in front of it. None of the people around them looked up right away—but down the concourse, Sydney could already see a couple of startled passengers recognize him, their fingers pointing in his direction.

"Now what?" Winter grumbled.

"Now we're going to set off an alarm and possibly get you banned from this airport." Sydney glanced at him. "Ready?"

"No," Winter said, but she had already grabbed his hand and walked right past the ticket counter at the small gate across from them.

A lady in a starched shirt behind the counter blinked at the sight of them. "You can't go through there!" she shouted—then abruptly stopped talking when she recognized Winter's face. Sydney just gritted her teeth and kept walking.

"Stop," Winter told her. "*Stop*. We're going to get this entire airport locked down."

"Claire's problem," Sydney replied.

"Ours too, if we get arrested and kicked out of the country."

"You're not going to get arrested for this," Sydney said as she cast him a knowing side-eye. "They'll want you out of this airport as soon as possible."

"You don't think causing this much of a scene is going to blow our cover?"

She just lifted an eyebrow. "Do you want people to believe I'm a competent bodyguard or not? At least there'll be footage of me doing my hypothetical job."

And before Winter could say anything else, she pushed open a heavy door leading right out onto the tarmac that was marked EMERGENCY.

An alarm blared on, followed by a rush of air. Suddenly they were outside, a hot, humid wind hitting Sydney in the face. Around the bend was the row of Winter's private caravan waiting for him and his team, black-suited men standing at the ready in front of each car.

Then she saw him.

She wouldn't have noticed the man approaching if it hadn't been for her training. He looked like a typical traveler at the airport, T-shirt a little rumpled, step a little hurried, one hand dragging a bag stacked on top of a suitcase—maybe someone perplexed by the commotion who just wanted to get to his flight. As they rushed toward the waiting cars, the man headed toward the entrance nearest to them.

Sydney caught the slight shift of the man's eyes, and the way they settled for a heartbeat not on Winter—but on her. She memorized his face in a flash.

As if in slow motion, she saw his free hand disappear into his coat pocket.

Her instincts kicked in before her mind could. Before she even saw the glint of a knife cutting through the air, her body was moving—shifting sideways out of reach, her hands seizing Winter and pulling him to her other side, her head tilting backward in defense.

The man swung at her at the same time as she moved. The attack lasted barely a second—a lunge that Sydney barely managed to dodge.

When she caught a glimpse of his face, she could see the surprise in his eyes. He tried striking a second time. His movement was so fast that Winter didn't even react—so distracted was he still by the crowd that was starting to cluster again around them.

Sydney whirled to look at Winter, making sure he was out of harm's way. When she looked back in the direction of their attacker, he had vanished into the throng.

Her eyes searched the masses frantically. She had trailed plenty of people before—she was good at tracking, and her memory had preserved the man's face as if in amber, his every feature clear and distinct in her mind. But he had disappeared into the crowd as if he had never existed. She looked in vain for his frumpy hair, his bag and suitcase, a figure facing away from them while everyone else was turned in their direction.

Winter had noticed her expression by now. He frowned, but there was no time to stop, no time to ask questions. Sydney just shook her head and motioned for them to keep moving toward the cars.

They were the first to arrive. Sydney kept searching the crowd as their door slid closed, sealing them in and offering them a temporary respite from the noise. At last, they saw Claire cutting through the crowd toward the second car, followed by Dameon and Gavi. As if on cue, Sydney's and Winter's phones buzzed with texts from Claire almost simultaneously.

Don't ever do that again, she messaged to Sydney. But even through the text, Sydney could sense the gratitude.

"What happened back there?" Winter said as their car began to pull away.

Sydney shook her head and let out a sigh. "Sorry. Couldn't help going a different route. There's no way you could have made it through the direct path. You saw the crowd."

Winter let out his breath. "Claire's furious."

"Tell her I was just doing my job."

He shot her a pointed look. "You tell her."

But in his expression, Sydney saw a different question. *What* really *happened?* she knew he was asking. He knew something had gone terribly wrong, something that had nothing to do with his frantic fans.

Sydney leaned toward him until she felt the warmth of his arm pressed against hers, then typed something rapidly on her phone and held the device out. To the driver glancing at them through the rearview mirror, it must have looked as if she were showing him Claire's text.

But she had spelled out a message completely different from what she'd just told him. Winter said nothing as he read it, but she noticed the way he paled, the way his arm muscles tightened against her skin.

Someone just tried to kill me.

An Unexpected Guest

To Winter's credit, he stilled his face into a picture of calm at the sight of her words. Still, she caught the clench of his jaw as he leaned his head close to her, the way his face drained of color, the way his eyes jumped to hers. To her surprise, it sent a wave of unease through her that cut through her fear.

He was afraid for her.

"I thought no one knew we were coming," he whispered, his voice so quiet that she could barely make out his words. "Except for Panacea."

Her eyes darted to the vehicle behind them—even from here, with only the silhouette of Claire visible in the other car's passenger seat, she could see the manager twisted around in her chair to talk animatedly to the rest in the car, as if she were checking to make sure they'd all made it in one piece.

Sydney turned back, trying not to meet his eyes so that she didn't see his fear there. "Guess someone does," she responded. There was always a point in every mission where the danger became a reality, the point when Sydney would come crashing back down to earth. She just hadn't expected it to come so soon this time.

Winter narrowed his eyes. "Did you recognize him?" he murmured.

Sydney shook her head. "I'll give Niall the details. He might ID him for us."

"Maybe there's footage." Winter's eyes darkened. "There were plenty of cameras out there. Someone was bound to have caught something."

"Maybe it was an attack intended for you," she replied. "Wouldn't be the first time you've been targeted."

Winter shook his head imperceptibly. "If they'd wanted me, we'd know."

He was right. The man had looked directly at her as he'd passed, had intentionally turned his body and his weapon toward her instead of angling it toward Winter. He'd been there for her.

The question, of course, was *why*. Who'd want Sydney dead now? The rebel groups plotting the assassination? If so, how would they know about her? No matter what, news of the failed attack would have already been relayed to whoever had ordered it.

Beside her, Winter picked up his phone. Sydney could hear Claire's voice from the other side the instant he accepted the call.

"I'm okay," he said.

"Good." Claire breathed out a sigh of relief. "Once we arrive at the hotel, Dameon will come fetch you for your rehearsal. I'll have food sent."

"Okay," he said again.

As they talked, Sydney typed up a rapid report for Niall, giving him as thorough of a description of her attacker as she could.

Seconds later, Niall sent a message back to her.

On it, he said.

here yet? she asked.

With the CIA now. Stay safe.

At least he had arrived now, too. His message—along with Sydney's report—deleted automatically from her phone an instant later.

Stay safe. His two-word message of concern sent a twinge of comfort through her, and she let herself take a breath, forced herself to relax her shoulders a bit. Niall was here, the CIA was here—they had their allies on the ground. She would be okay. This was far from the most dangerous thing that had ever happened to her.

But the attack still remained vivid and sharp in her mind. Niall himself had drilled her in self-defense against a knife, had gone over and over it until she was fending off assailants in her dreams.

What causes death? he'd asked her during the lesson. *In every scenario?*

Hypoxia, Sydney had replied.

Hypoxia, Niall had confirmed with a grim nod. He'd held out a knife to her and demonstrated the lethal points on a mannequin. *Every attack is designed to cut the flow of oxygen to your body's cells. You can lose fifteen percent of your blood before you start hitting the danger zone.* He had given her a sober look. *Keep your wits about you during a knife attack, Cossette. A split second could cost you your life.*

Had Sydney not trained for such attacks, her assailant at the airport would have plunged his knife deep between her second and third ribs, all the way through her liver. A fatal blow. She would have bled out in seconds.

Whoever he had been, he knew what he was doing.

As Winter finished his call with Claire, they fell into a tense silence, watching the scenery go by. Avenues lined with broad-leaved tropical trees changed gradually into skyscrapers filled on the street level with brightly colored food stalls. Trucks rumbled past them with foreign license plates, the sound of their honking strange and unfamiliar. Now and then, someone on a motorbike would peer curiously at their tinted windows, as if trying to see what important person might be inside.

Sydney instinctively leaned back from the windows so that her face couldn't be seen through the glass panes. To her relief, Winter did the same. She had been attacked in a car before, when a motorbike had stopped beside her at a traffic light in Sacramento and fired two shots at her windowpane before speeding off. The bullets had shattered the glass and missed hitting her by mere centimeters.

Sydney replayed the moment at the airport in her mind. She could still see the man with his knife drawn, the glint unmistakable in the light, stumbling toward her in a lunge. She didn't shudder, but her free hand curled together tightly at her side, her fingers tapping nonstop against her knuckles until they finally reached the hotel where they would be staying.

She had seen pictures of this hotel before, as had everyone in the world: the Marina Bay Sands, a trio of pillars connected by a boat-shaped rooftop with trails of flowers and lush foliage. Its sides were lit up with lines of light that ran along each building's edges, giving it the appearance of a futuristic docking station.

No clusters of fans were here to greet them this time as they exited the vehicle. Instead, they were immediately ushered across a courtyard and into a lobby that had been blocked off with velvet ropes. As she went, Sydney noted the security gate that they'd driven through in order to get to the back entrance of the building. It was electrified from the inside; she could tell by the blinking green dot on either side of the fence posts. That was good, at least.

Gavi and Dameon met them in the hotel lobby. Dameon's eyes were round, and as Winter approached him, he started shaking his head.

"What was that?" he said, nudging his friend on the shoulder. "Forget adding more security detail. We should have flown you into a small regional airport in another country and then smuggled you across the border."

"I'm sure the airport staff would agree," Sydney added dryly.

"That wasn't so bad," Gavi said, looping her arm through Winter's as they walked through the lobby, which was already lined with security anticipating his arrival.

Sydney looked away as the girl leaned up to say something in Winter's ear, but not before she caught Winter leaning back to listen to her, his arm pressed against hers. Her heart sped up—she forced it back into calmness. Now that they had arrived, she needed to focus on the business at hand—which meant it was just as well that Gavi would keep Winter occupied when she didn't need him. The girl was doing her a favor.

She repeated this over and over to herself as she caught up with Claire.

Claire glared at her, and Sydney pushed aside all the dread in her stomach from her brush with death to give the woman an apologetic smile. "I'm sorry," she said, holding her hands up. "But you know I had to do it."

The woman pressed her lips together, but Sydney could see on her face that she didn't have a counterargument. Instead, she said, "I'll deal with the airport's complaints. They didn't give us much of a choice, after all." She nodded at the elevators. "We've booked out the entire top floor. Your room is adjoining Winter's, as expected, while the rest of our staff will be staying in the other suites."

Her room was probably separated by nothing more than a suite door. Sydney nodded and held back her wince. That meant she'd be adjacent to where Winter and Gavi would be sharing the main suite. An awkward situation, if she had ever been in one.

"Sounds convenient," she said instead.

Fifty-six stories later, Sydney could feel her ears popping from the ascent. By the time they stepped out of the elevators, she was rubbing the sides of her head in discomfort. Several other security guards stopped before Winter's suite.

"See you in an hour?" Dameon called to Winter over his shoulder. Sydney watched as Winter nodded at him. Dameon's gaze lingered for a second longer on him, then on Sydney, before he turned back around.

Sydney noted Dameon's stare. Perhaps he'd sensed something off about the dynamics of this trip—he'd always been an observant one, had been paying attention in London, too. She turned back to where Winter and Gavi had stopped in front of their suite door, then sucked in her breath.

"Well, Winter," Gavi said, casting him a wry smile. "This can't go any worse than our trip to Italy two years ago, can it?"

"Don't jinx it," he replied as he swiped the door open. As he did, Gavi caught Sydney's gaze and winked.

Sydney thought of Dameon's skeptical stare and forced herself to give Gavi nothing more than a polite smile back. Her heart folded carefully in on itself. It was time to take her relationship with Winter seriously—and by relationship, she meant their brief partnership during this mission. So she said nothing as they stepped inside—into the most breathtaking hotel suite she'd ever seen in her life.

The same glass walls lined the interior of their space, and thick plush carpets covered a floor decked out in teakwood. Near the wall was a grand piano that must have been brought in specifically for Winter, as well as a canopied bed piled high with thick pillows. Another door against a side wall seemed to lead into the adjoining suite, where Sydney would stay. A crystal chandelier hung from the ceiling, casting a kaleidoscope of colors around the room.

But the incredible luxury of the space wasn't what caught Sydney's attention.

She was instead staring at the person that was already in the room, lounging easily in one of the chairs near the glass wall, his arms folded and his eyes locked on them in amusement.

Even though it'd been several years, she recognized him right away.

It was Tems.

Change of Plans

Sydney must have tensed visibly at the sight of him, because Winter moved instinctively closer, his body turned protectively toward hers. When she looked up at him, she saw his gaze fixed on the young man, as if ready for him to attack. Again, she felt that uneasy flutter in her stomach. No partner had ever protected her like this—usually, they didn't even work in the same physical location. His nearness felt strange.

"A friend of yours?" Gavi said, lifting a questioning eyebrow at the newcomer before looking at Winter. "I wasn't expecting company."

Before Winter could answer, Tems gave them a wide, disarming smile and spread his arms.

"Mr. Young!" he exclaimed, giving him a deep bow of his head. "I'm terribly sorry for the intrusion. Unfortunately, one of your passcodes here leaked, and a cluster of fans have been using it to access unauthorized floors. We've already switched the codes for the rooms, but I'm doing a routine check of your suite to make sure everything is properly updated."

A good impromptu story, Sydney thought. Her fists had clenched so hard at her sides that her nails were about to draw blood against her palms. He smiled at her, but in his eyes, she could see the recognition. What the hell was he doing here?

"This isn't the first time this has happened to us," Winter said, and Sydney looked sharply at him.

Tems nodded. "Is that so, Mr. Young?"

A good follow-up, Sydney thought, and felt a twinge of admiration for Winter. Sauda was right about his lying skills.

"A tour stop in Nashville," Winter said with a sigh as he sat down, as if this was all part of the job. "We had all our hotel details exposed by a staff member. My manager spent the better part of a day figuring out an entirely new routine for how to get us in and out." He looked at Tems. "Are we going to need to do that here?"

"We'll need to discuss it, yes," Tems replied. "I apologize for this inconvenience. It hasn't happened here before. Then again, this is the first time we've had you as a guest, Mr. Young."

Sydney had to force herself not to roll her eyes at Tems's buttery voice.

This was the hint for Gavi to leave the room, and when Sydney looked at her, the girl seemed ready.

"How long is this going to take?" Gavi said as she folded her arms.

"Many apologies for the inconvenience, Ms. Ginsburg," Tems said with a bow of his head. "We should be done in an hour, and the room will be ready for you to settle in. May I suggest the shops downstairs or a session by the rooftop pool? They have been closed to outside visitors for the duration of your stay."

"I'll figure it out myself," Gavi said, giving him a winsome smile. She patted Winter sympathetically on the arm. "Have fun figuring this mess out. I need to go buy a local SIM card anyway. Want one?"

Winter shook his head. "No, I'm good. Thanks, though."

"Then I'll catch up with you later at dinner."

Winter nodded. She leaned forward to give him a kiss on the cheek, and he tensed, but didn't stop her. Then she turned on her heel and headed out of the room. The door shut behind her with a click.

As soon as she left, Tems's polite subservience vanished, and he walked over to sit down in a chair across from the couch. "Well," he said, giving Winter a sly grin. "You clearly have some skills in the improvisation department. Commendable."

Winter frowned. "And I'm guessing you're not hotel staff," he answered.

"What a smart one," Tems said. "And I'm guessing you didn't take your girlfriend's offer because your phone's a Panacea one. Or do they even bother equipping pseudo-agents?"

Sydney came over to stand beside Winter. She waved a disgusted hand. "This is Tems Bourton," she told him. "The Arsonist."

Winter's eyes went to Tems. "So it's you."

"A pleasure." Tems unfolded his arms, put his hands in his pockets, and gave Sydney a wink. "You look good, Syd."

"What the hell are you doing here?" she demanded.

Tems shrugged, his eyes staying on her. "I thought you knew."

"Did Niall send you here? Because we certainly weren't expecting you."

"Ah, is our former mentor joining us?" He nodded at the door. "Did he come with you?"

"He's with the CIA." Sydney frowned. "Shall I tell him to come see you himself so he can give you a proper piece of his mind?"

Tems shook his head. "I think Niall has given me enough lectures for a lifetime. We can hold off on one more."

"What happened during our original rendezvous?" She glanced around the room. "Why'd you go dark?"

"The government here is watching me." He glanced at the windows. "It was hard enough getting up here unnoticed. Their security has been wiretapping me for two weeks now."

Perhaps it was the very real threat on her life that had just happened—perhaps it was the long flight—but everything felt surreal now, like she was swimming through a dream. "Why? For what?" she asked.

"It's a long story."

"Well, we flew halfway around the world to hear it. And you're supposed to meet us at the gala, not here. How did you even get in?"

He grinned slyly at the expression on her face, then shook his head in regret. "Sauda shouldn't have sent you."

"Why not?" she snapped.

"Oh, come on. I bet you had the same thought when she debriefed you. Sauda probably chose you because she thinks I've got a thing for you." He tilted his head in that infuriatingly mocking way she remembered so well. "Maybe I do."

Beside her, Winter's posture had turned to stone.

Tems pushed himself casually up from the chair and wandered over to the suite's bar, where he began pushing buttons on the espresso machine. "Anyone want a coffee?" he asked.

Winter frowned at him. "I'm sorry, I must have thought that this was my room."

"Thank you, by the way, for letting me borrow your bar," Tems answered over his shoulder. "You might notice a few things missing." He pulled down two mugs, then swapped them out for martini glasses. "Actually, after the conversation we're about to have, you may need something stronger. Please. Have a seat."

As if he owned the whole damn place. Winter shot Sydney a look, and Sydney gave him a helpless shrug. Then she settled onto a spot at one end of the couch while Winter took a seat at the other end.

"Why are you here?" Sydney asked again. "Why now?"

"That happy to see me, are you?" Tems replied. "Maybe I should have joined you earlier at the airport—although I did hear that turned a little messy."

Even though Winter was sitting on the opposite end of the couch, Sydney could feel the subtle shift of the couch's fabric as he draped one leg over the other and glared at Tems in annoyance. She scowled at Tems and started to snap back—but he filled a cocktail shaker, and for a few seconds, the clacking ice drowned everything out.

When it stopped, Tems came back into the living room and handed each of them a glass, garnished with an olive. "I know we were supposed to meet at the gala," he said, "but I didn't think that would be enough time for us to go over everything. So here I am."

"To go over what? Does anyone else know about this?"

He went back for his own mug, then settled on the couch facing them. "Nope," he answered. "Just the three of us." He nodded at Winter. "And I'd really prefer if we kept it that way."

Sydney frowned. "Why haven't you told Sauda and Niall you're meeting us?"

"Because the entire reason you've been sent to Singapore," he said with a nod, "is to escort me home. Correct?"

She nodded. "To extract you safely."

At that, Tems gave a dry laugh. "I tell Niall I need more time, and he sends an associate to drag me back. Typical."

"Agent," Sydney corrected him shortly.

"Oh, a promotion? Well, a big congratulations, then." He glanced at Winter. "And what about a proper introduction to your new friend?"

"Don't think I need one," Winter answered.

Tems gave him a dismissive once-over, refusing to talk to him directly. "Are we in the business of hiring pop stars now?"

"Booming business, apparently," Winter replied coldly.

"Winter has a personal invite to the prime minister's gala," Sydney said.

"Ah, I see. He's just your golden ticket." Tems eyed him up and down.

"Lose something?" Winter offered, following his gaze.

"A little respect, yes," Tems replied.

"Leave him alone," Sydney said.

He smiled at her. "So protective of your new partner. I don't remember you being this nice to me."

"Hate to pierce your heart, but you were never my partner."

"What a shame." Tems took a sip of his drink. "Well, I'm not going anywhere."

"I don't think Niall said it was your choice, to be honest."

He leaned forward to rest his elbows on his knees. "I'm not going anywhere," he repeated, "and I'm going to tell you why."

"Why, then?"

"What we knew about the assassination plot against President Rosen is no longer accurate. The rebel group isn't acting alone. They're being sponsored by someone higher."

At that, Sydney blinked. "How do you know?"

"The rebel suspect I was trailing for months was killed recently in an ambush. But a parcel he was meant to deliver still somehow went through, and I suspect that it went through successfully because it was given to a very specific patron."

"Who?"

"Ethan Seah, Minister for Foreign Affairs. The same person seated next to President Rosen on the gala's seating chart."

A shiver traveled down Sydney's spine at his words, and she paled. "The suspect is in Singapore's own government?" she said.

"Wait—" Winter interjected. "Singapore is sponsoring the murder of the US president?"

Tems nodded. "Yes, although I doubt the entire government is aware of it. What I need is evidence, but that's a bit difficult when I'm being watched all the time." He shook his head. "You see why I can't leave. If I go now, my trail goes cold, and we leave President Rosen vulnerable to the assassination at the gala."

"So what do you want from us? To report it for you?"

Tems shook his head. "I need you to disobey Sauda and Niall."

"What?"

"Help me stop the assassination at the gala."

Sydney's heart began to beat quicker. "Sauda warned us to steer clear of it."

Tems's voice had turned low and urgent now. "I can't just call for the arrest of one of Singapore's cabinet members without giving a good reason. I need to hand the CIA something that solidly points to Mr. Seah before the gala. And that means I need someone who can get proof—a recording—anything—that can prove to the CIA that Mr. Seah is the culprit. If we can do that, the CIA can ensure that Rosen is absent from the gala at the last moment, and we can have Seah arrested there instead."

"Why can't we tell Sauda and Niall?" Winter asked. "Niall's here with the CIA."

"Because you know what he'll say. Niall wants the CIA to handle it and drag me home because my cover will be compromised."

"And why is that bad?" Winter pressed.

"Because I'm not about to put Rosen's life in the CIA's hands. They don't know how precarious the situation is."

"Stopping the assassination isn't our mission, Tems," Sydney said.

He gave her an arch look. "Technically, that's true," he replied. "But I know you'll do it anyway."

His look annoyed her. Tems had a knack for getting her in trouble with Panacea—not that she needed the help. Sauda and Niall still hadn't forgiven her and Winter yet for their transgressions on their last mission.

"Niall's meeting me tomorrow morning," Sydney said. "If I keep you a secret from him, I'm breaking my oath for this mission. For *you.*"

Tems grinned. "So do me a favor, sweetheart. For old time's sake?"

A memory bloomed in her mind, some long dormant seed opening to reveal a winter day in Stockholm as she waited in a lonely little hotel that already had its lamps lit because it was dark at two in the afternoon. She could still remember looking down from the balcony at the stray pedestrians, wondering which one would be the asset she'd been assigned to meet, squinting occasionally at the dark sky roiling with the first hints of a snowstorm. She could still hear the clack of wet boots against the wooden floor of her room as he came in, could still see him shaking snow from his coat, one of her keycards in his hand.

Do me a favor, sweetheart, he'd said as he hung his hat on the back of the door. *And turn up the heat a bit in this room. Aren't you freezing?*

She recalled how she gave him the intel Panacea had sent her to collect, crucial details on an arms ring stationed in the city, how they'd lingered a little longer than they needed to over plates of steak and preserved fish in the restaurant. How he'd handed over a package for her in his hotel room—only for both of them to be snowed in together by the onset of the snowstorm.

And then . . . well, they had to find some way of passing the time together. The third morning of their tryst, Sydney had woken up to an empty bed and a scrawled note from Tems, signed with his dagger through a heart.

Sorry, sweetheart. Just business.

Five minutes later, she'd discovered her missing passport.

Sydney felt her face flush at the memory, even though she couldn't tell if it was because she recalled what Tems did or because Winter was right here, witnessing this entire exchange. At least he couldn't see into her mind.

"You're asking me to risk my job," she said in a low voice.

"Is that all? We risk our jobs on the daily."

"You know what I mean. I've dealt with enough shit from you."

"And yet you're not refusing, are you?"

Niall was going to kill them for this. She sighed inwardly, wondering if she would ever get a mission where everything went according to plan. She pictured Niall sitting across from her tonight, grumpy eyes under thick brows, and imagined lying to him about Tems's plans. It made her wince.

"Look, I understand what I'm asking," Tems added. "I know you, and I know what our job is like. I wouldn't do it if the president of the United States wasn't at risk. You understand what the stakes are here."

"Of course I understand," she snapped. "I just don't know if what you're asking will help."

Tems lowered his voice. "I'm going to do it either way. But I'll have a better shot if you're with me." For the first time since they arrived, he looked grim. "And we both know we make a good team, sweetheart."

Sydney tightened her lips. He was right—to a certain extent. She'd admired his diligence during training, even the numerous rogue ideas he'd come up with to pass certain assignments. They had traded banter during their graduation ceremony, then gotten along easily in Stockholm, could speak to each other in the clipped kind of language that secret agents shared which no one else could understand.

Sauda would kill them. But the orders were to bring Tems back alive, regardless of what it might do to his mission.

They didn't say what to do if Tems refused to return, because none of them had expected it to be an issue. Who would have assumed that he might not want to escape at all? What was she supposed to do—drug him and drag him unconscious onto a plane?

The thought was vaguely satisfying. But if she stayed and helped him, then she and Winter could fulfill their own duty. Tems would be back on a plane with them right after the gala, as originally proposed, and the president would be safe.

"And you?" Tems shifted his attention to Winter and pretended not to notice his mood. "I suppose I should ask your opinion, out of common courtesy. Are you in?"

Sydney looked at Winter. He would do it, she knew. But putting him at the center of the plot at the gala was different from merely using him to just get into the venue. Panacea had nearly gotten him killed in London. What if something happened to him here?

"This isn't what you signed up for," she said to Winter.

His eyes went to Tems, and the two held each other's gaze, neither backing down.

"I signed up to be your partner," Winter replied. "That's not changing, as far as I can tell."

Tems glanced at him with a look of vague dismissal. "Good," he said, a condescending lilt to his voice. "Because it looks like your golden ticket might come in handy again."

Winter narrowed his eyes. "What do you mean?"

"You've got your own box reserved for your people at the Warcross concert, right?"

"Always."

Tems nodded. "Then extend invitations to the entire Singaporean cabinet. It should go over well—I heard that the CEO has already invited the prime minister and the president. I'm sure Emika Chen would approve the cabinet. Tell her it's a sign of your gratitude to the government for your visit. Can you do that in time for tomorrow night?"

Winter was quiet before he nodded.

Tems looked back at Sydney. "Will you be in that box during the concert?"

Sydney sighed and rubbed her temples. This mission had gone wildly off the rails within their first hour of arrival. "Yes," she replied. "Other security will be scattered down with the crowd." She glanced at Winter. "But the box will have the best views of the scene from above. If I'm stationed there as your personal bodyguard, I can keep a better eye on you."

"What if we come out empty-handed?" Winter said.

"Then we've failed," Tems said simply, "and the president dies. But no pressure."

Winter looked at Sydney, and she wanted to bury her face in her hands. This was going to be even worse than London.

Tems's grave expression wavered at their silence, and a wicked smile spread across his face. "Is that you both agreeing?"

Sydney glared at him. "This would be so much easier if it wasn't you," she replied.

"As in, you're more personally invested because of me?" Tems asked.

"As in, I dislike you enough that I'm considering sacrificing the security of the entire world just to drag you home, instead of going through with your absurd plan."

"Well," he said, taking another sip of his drink. "The world's stability hangs on it, so take your time."

Some people never changed. Sydney glared at him, knowing full well what her answer would be. He knew it, too, and the satisfaction on his face was almost more than she could bear.

We both know we make a good team, sweetheart.

"Fine," she said through gritted teeth.

"Fine," Winter echoed, his voice just as tight.

"Fine," Tems said with a smile. He straightened in his seat and clapped his hands together, as if they'd just had the most congenial conversation. "Our fun begins tomorrow."

Haunted Pasts

Even at night, humidity hung in the air.

Winter didn't mind it much—in the darkness, the moisture felt good on his skin, and warm breezes combed through his hair as he leaned against his balcony to admire the city beyond the ink-black bay, a seemingly endless expanse of glittering skyscrapers and curving freeways.

It was long past midnight, and Gavi was already asleep in her bed, but Winter's jet lag still hadn't worn off, and Tems's bargain with them hadn't helped stop his mind from whirling. So he found himself out here instead, on a video call with his mother.

This time, at least, she was back in her apartment, and she'd picked up after the first two rings. Winter tapped an option on his screen that broadcast her as a three-dimensional figure from his phone, then set the phone down on the balcony's wide ledge. The image of his mother hovered beside him, as if she were really there.

"I caught up on the news about your book," she said to him. "I'm sorry, baby bear."

She looked healthy today, he thought with relief—her hair was tidily braided over one of her shoulders, and her eyes looked alert, not lost in grief or desperate for distraction.

Winter shrugged and looked out at the city lights. "It's not my book," he said. "But thank you."

"Xiàn zài zai na? Back in LA?"

He gave her a polite smile and shook his head. "Singapore."

"Singapore? That's lovely."

He'd told her about his upcoming trip on their last call, but she hadn't remembered. "What about you, Mom?" he said instead. "Are you staying home for a bit?"

She shook her head. "Heading to Portugal tomorrow, actually."

That was another thing about his mother. She never stayed put in one place for long—instead always off to some other corner of the globe, whether it be a friend's house in upstate New York or a beach in Thailand, as if running away from the haunting of old memories. It was something she'd done even when he was young.

But he just said, "Have fun. Do you have new cash for the trip?"

"I've got it." She tapped her side where he couldn't see, as if to reassure him.

He nodded. She couldn't bring herself to touch bills with wrinkles in them, something that had once stranded her in Paris until he could fly to her to help out. "What about your medications?"

"I've got everything. You don't need to worry."

"Okay."

"You're there alone?"

He glanced to his side, to the adjacent balcony that led into Sydney's room. "Not exactly."

"I thought I saw someone in the room behind you. Are they nice?"

He looked over his shoulder, realizing that his mother could see the sleeping figure of Gavi in the rumpled bed. He turned the phone a bit. "It's just Gavi. And she's got her own bed. We're not back together."

"Well, you have a nice time there," his mother said, in the way she had of answering him without quite listening to him at all. "Don't worry too much about the book. And be safe."

He smiled a little. "You too."

They hung up without another word. Winter usually tried to say "I love you," although he didn't often hear it back, and tonight, he felt too weary to even try. So instead, he just let his mother hang up first, which she always did. Her virtual figure disappeared, and he was alone again on the balcony.

His gaze went to the glass domes at the bottom of the hotel, the all-indoors botanical gardens called the Gardens by the Bay. By day, he could see the lush field of green beneath the dome, the hundreds of thousands of plants that lived in the futuristic, air-conditioned space. At night, tree-like sculptures nearby were lit up, giving him the impression of underwater, bioluminescent creatures.

I'm not really going far, his mother used to say when he was still a kid. She would disappear on her trips and leave him on his own for days. *I'll be back in no time.*

Then she would be gone, and he would go to school alone, walk home alone, forage for frozen dinners in the fridge and eat alone. Sometimes, he'd sleep over at a friend's house. Other times, he'd bring his blanket and pillow and sleep on the old couch in their backyard, where he would pretend he was camping. Still other times, he would dial his older brother's former phone number, daring to let it ring a couple of times before anyone picked up, then end the call and tell himself that Artie was still alive, still would have answered had he stayed on the line longer.

If Artie hadn't died, would his mother be more attentive to Winter now? Would she be more curious about how he was doing, call him more often, congratulate him instead of needing him to remind her about what was happening in his life?

Maybe not. Artie had always been their mother's favorite, her beloved firstborn, the boy she'd had with a man she'd loved. Then she'd lost that husband and gotten pregnant with a man she'd ended up hating, had married him anyway, and had tumbled into the depression of a new baby and a horrible second husband. That wouldn't have changed, had Artie lived.

But then Artie had died, had been killed overseas, and his mother had lost herself—as well as the shreds of devotion she'd given to Winter.

Winter shook his head and grimaced. It didn't matter, anyway. He knew he loved her all the same, and that she loved him, in her own way. Still, he let himself feel her absence. He let himself feel the absence of his brother. And he let himself feel that familiar suffocation, the feeling of wanting to talk to someone else, to let out some of the emotions bottling up in his chest.

His phone buzzed. He was too scared to look at the screen, for fear it might be Claire warning him about some other bombshell that had been leaked from the tell-all book. Instead, he let it buzz until it went silent again.

A movement in his peripheral vision made him turn his head.

It was Sydney, leaning against her balcony in a T-shirt and baggy shorts.

They looked at each other at the same time, then blinked in unison, surprised. The sight of her cut through Winter's brooding feelings, and he felt himself smile a little.

"Jet lag?" she said.

He shrugged. "You?"

"Checking out the view," she answered, nodding down at the city.

He nodded. "It is nice."

They fell into silence for a beat.

"Gavi's asleep?" Sydney asked.

"She's always been a good sleeper." Winter let out a laugh. "Wish I had that kind of peace of mind."

Sydney smiled. "Niall says sound sleepers make for poor agents. So I suppose it's for the best that you don't."

Winter chuckled, then studied her face. "You don't like that he's retiring."

Something about his words made her shrink inward, as if there were walls going up around her heart. She shrugged. "Just makes my life harder, is all," she said. "I won't know whoever it is that'll replace him, and the thought of getting to know a new analyst makes me feel tired."

"Is that it?"

Sydney said nothing, and for a while, they stood on their separate balconies and just stared out at the nightscape.

"Winter," Sydney said after a while, and he turned to look at her. "Do you remember that night, in London, when you couldn't sleep?"

"You'll have to be more specific. I remember several sleepless nights."

She snorted. "The one where you went downstairs and danced in the living room."

He struggled to remember, and then recalled a night when he'd woken up in the middle of the night and gone downstairs to walk off his insomnia.

"I didn't know you heard me that night," he admitted. "I thought you were still asleep."

She shook her head. "I go, you go. What kind of bodyguard would I be otherwise?"

"Why are you asking about it?"

She hesitated, then looked back at him. "Was that the night when you wrote those song lyrics about me?"

Immediately, he knew what she was talking about. The little leather notebook that always traveled with him had been open on his nightstand that night when he'd returned to his bedroom. And when he'd started writing down lyrics, they had been about Sydney.

The words returned to him, as solidly as if they'd been seared into his mind.

Do you ever feel guilty for everyone's mistakes?
Ever wish you could take someone else's place?
Do you ever feel like dying?
Do you ever want to live forever?
And this hurricane goes on and on
Every time I look at you
You are my meditation
Am I ever yours, too?

He cleared his throat, his cheeks reddening at the realization that Sydney had remembered those lyrics.

"It was," he said slowly. "Why?"

"How did you know that?"

He blinked. "Know what?"

She took a moment to answer. "There was that line . . . about feeling guilty for others' mistakes. Well, I do."

"Really?"

"When I was a little girl, I thought I was the reason why my mother got sick. She took care of me too much, and it exhausted her, so she went to the hospital. My father used to tell me that she went because of the way me and my brother ran her ragged. I thought I was the reason why my father drank, because I was so much trouble." She paused. "I feel like I'm the reason why Niall was unable to be a part of his own daughter's childhood, because he was too busy training recruits like me, because his job—me—took him away from his real family."

In a flash, Winter understood. "You think Niall leaving Panacea is a punishment that you deserve."

She looked at him, and in her eyes, he thought he saw surprise. It faded away quickly, and she tightened her lips before turning back to the cityscape. "My fault for thinking it," she said. "He's my boss, not my parent."

"There you go, feeling guilty again," he said, and she let out a humorless laugh. Then he added, "It's not you, you know."

"I know," she said. "Still. I can't help thinking it."

"I think my mother is the way she is," he said, "because of me. I think, sometimes, if she could have broken it off with my father before I was born, then she could have healed from him, could have moved on more easily with her life. But here I am." He held his hands out.

Sydney nodded, although she didn't respond. And somehow, Winter was grateful she didn't, that she didn't try to say something reassuring, that she didn't try to sugarcoat his words.

"I didn't know that about you," he explained carefully. "I just knew that about me. And I guess I felt like knowing you made me face those thoughts. You are my meditation, you know?" He smiled a little, apologetically. "You weren't supposed to see those lyrics. They don't mean anything, I promise. They're just for me."

Sydney didn't respond, but in the darkness, he thought he saw a subtle nod of her head. They sank back into silence, the air between them somehow lighter now that they had both gotten something off their chest.

"I've never told anyone that before," Sydney finally said, her eyes turned out to the city.

"Same," Winter replied, his attention also on the nightscape.

And even though they stood on separate balconies, it felt a little like they were side by side, like he could feel the warmth of her nearness. It made him want to stay out there a little longer, want to rack his brain for something else to keep their conversation going, anything to keep her with him a little longer.

"Winter?"

Then he heard Gavi's voice behind him, and when he turned around, he saw her silk-robed figure emerge onto the balcony, her hair in disarray and her eyes sleepy. She glanced over at the adjacent balcony at the same time he did.

But Sydney was already gone, like a ghost, and her balcony looked as if no one had ever been there.

Gavi looked at him with a skeptical smile. "Talking to yourself out here? It's two in the morning."

"Can't sleep," Winter answered, forcing himself not to look back toward Sydney's balcony.

Gavi turned around and put her hands in the pockets of her robe. "Well, you'd better get some rest before tomorrow, unless you want more rumors spreading about what we might be up to at night."

Winter forced himself not to look back toward Sydney's balcony. He hadn't even heard her leave, she was so quiet—even Gavi probably hadn't seen her, even though she must have guessed that Sydney was there. So he followed Gavi inside, his own lyrics haunting his mind.

You are my meditation
Am I ever yours, too?

12

Spiraling

t didn't matter how many years Sydney had spent as a Panacea agent—she still felt like a new recruit whenever she was with Niall.

"Tems still isn't answering," she explained the next morning, as they sat across from each other at a table in a bustling hawker market. All around them, people wandered from stall to stall under the massive, open-air building, balancing trays of steaming hot food and glasses of ice-cold sugar cane drinks. "Have you heard from him since you landed?"

"No," Niall replied. With his sunglasses and tropical shirt and cheeks flushed from the heat, the analyst looked less like an agent and more like a grumpy tourist. He picked up his chopsticks and took another bite of chicken. "Although his phone's tracker still pings in the city. Did you call him?"

She nodded through a bite of stir-fried rice noodles. "No answer for the last twenty-four hours, although my tracker also places him in the city."

"Where, exactly?"

"A lamp post at the corner of Dalvey and Evans Road," Sydney answered, nodding at a row of similar posts near the market, all mobile network towers in disguise. "He must have been passing through. Maybe on his way to the botanic gardens for a nice stroll."

Niall chuckled humorlessly. "And when did you get that location?"

Niall's questions were always designed to poke holes in a poor lie, even if he was speaking to his own team. Sydney kept her voice smooth. "Just an hour ago," she said. "What do you want us to do?"

There was a brief silence from Niall, and for an instant, Sydney imagined the conversation that could happen next.

Where is he? Niall would say. *I know you're lying.*

And Sydney would break down and tell him everything. A part of her ached to confess—to just let Niall know about Tems's plans, about the danger the president was in.

But instead, Niall said, "Stand by and keep trying. Nothing changes. If we connect, I'll confirm with you. Otherwise, plan to be at the gala."

"Yes, sir," she said.

Niall chewed thoughtfully, studying her from under his bushy eyebrows, before he returned to his chicken. Sydney watched him, gauging his mood.

"You're unhappy," she said after a while, taking a sip of her sugar cane drink.

He grunted. "Surely you're used to that by now."

"No—I mean, you're really unhappy."

He finished his bite before he leaned forward against the table and lowered his voice. "I haven't been able to ID your attacker," he muttered.

Sydney felt her chest tighten. "I figured."

"And there haven't been any other incidents since?"

"No."

He nodded. "Good."

Sydney put her drink down and forced a smile. "Stop worrying. I'll be fine."

"You've never been on your own like this before," Niall said.

"I'm not alone. Winter's with me. And I've been through years of training."

"You know what I mean. You've always had someone back at head-quarters wholly dedicated to following your whereabouts."

"You think I'm silly enough to get myself into trouble like Tems has?"

"I'm not saying anything of the sort. Tems has always been more . . . emotional than you, more reactionary. But I'm saying that anything can happen. Anytime."

Sydney folded her arms against the table. "Niall, have you ever aborted a mission because things didn't go as planned?"

He shook his head.

"My point exactly." She quieted. Her words to Winter last night came back to her now. *I feel like I'm the reason why Niall was unable to be a part of his own daughter's childhood.* "You deserve to take a break . . . from all this."

"Sure. But for now, I'm still on your mission." He pointed his chop-sticks at her. "And I expect you to remain careful. Don't go off chasing wild leads or doing something stupid, not without running it by me first."

Sydney felt another pang as she looked at the man. How long had Niall been in Panacea? More than twenty years? And yet here he was, dragging his feet toward freedom. "Were you always like this with Quinn, too?"

The mention of his daughter made him pause, and for a moment, Niall just ate in silence. "Back at headquarters, I tracked her whereabouts all the time."

"You had surveillance on her?"

"I'm not proud of it. I know I'm not supposed to." He shook his head.

"Mr. O'Sullivan," Sydney scolded the man teasingly. "Talk about a helicopter parent."

"It did once involve a literal helicopter. Don't tell Sauda. But I couldn't help it." He sighed. "I always wanted her to be safe, but I couldn't do the one thing that would have kept her safest—staying her father, staying near her."

"You're keeping the world safe."

"And she was the sacrifice."

"Do you regret having her?"

He looked at Sydney. "Never," he said.

"Then you did what you had to do."

"It's okay, Syd," he said quietly. "It is my fault, and I've owned that."

"You've always kept me safe. You're here, even now."

"I'm not your father."

"I know. But sometimes I feel like you are." She smiled. "For better or worse."

"More better than worse, I hope," he replied. And Sydney saw him look hopefully at her. Her heart bled a little. What kind of life was this, to have a family you could never see, then to love a woman you could never be with? She thought of Winter, leaning against his balcony and letting the wind comb through his hair.

What kind of life was that? Could she bear it?

She looked back at Niall, at the closest thing she had to a father. She was going to miss him—but she didn't have to quite yet. "You're not a bad option, as far as dads go," she said.

He snorted. "We'll see what Quinn ends up saying about that."

"You did the best you could."

He hesitated, taking a few more bites of food, then looking around as if he didn't know what else to do. "I wrote her a long letter," he finally said in a low, gravelly voice. "Months ago."

"Did she read it?"

He shook his head. "It's still sitting in my desk drawer. I haven't had the courage to send it yet."

"What's in it?" she decided to ask.

He prodded his plate with his chopsticks. "An apology," he rumbled, grief clouding his words. "Of sorts. I told her everything I could, at least."

Sydney swallowed, fighting back a tide of jealousy and bitterness, wondering what it would be like to get an apology from her own father. "You don't want her to see it?" she said.

"I want her to see it more than anything." He fell silent, then muttered, "Maybe I'm just a coward."

Sydney forced down her own resentment. It wasn't fair to Niall, her feeling this way. But she felt it, all the same. "You're not a coward," she said gently.

"I just . . ." He trailed off. "I'll hand it to her in person. If she'll see me."

"I think she will."

Niall looked afraid, and the sight made Sydney's heart bleed. "And if she won't?"

"Then give me the letter, for chrissakes, and I'll hand it to her myself."

Niall laughed, and Sydney stored the sound away in her memory, wishing she had a recorder on. "Deal," he said.

"To being competent." Sydney raised her drink to him.

"To being competent," Niall answered, clinking glasses, and nodded at her. "Make me proud, kid."

By the time they arrived at the stadium, the lines and clusters of fans on the streets had turned into a tidal wave, and as their car passed by, the wave seemed to crash against the concrete barricades lining the road, the thousands of people shrieking in delight at the sight of them. Some wore the augmented reality glasses that were required for watching the Warcross Opening Ceremony; still others likely had the contact lens version, as Sydney watched them gesture or wave at things she couldn't see. Their driver honked irritably as people at one walkway jumped over the barricade to get in the middle of the street, prompting officers to force them back.

"The games are even more popular than I remember," Gavi mused from her passenger seat. "Wasn't there a scandal a few years back?"

Today she looked even more resplendent than usual, her dress an ocean of lemon-yellow silks complemented by delicate gold jewelry. Sydney never cared about her clothing when she was undercover, but she couldn't help feeling a little self-conscious this time in her black suit.

"They restructured after their previous CEO was arrested—a data breach of some sort," Sydney answered. "Doesn't mean people stop liking something, though. Haven't you played before?"

"No. I don't do games—at least, not online ones."

"Well, think of it as virtual soccer, with dragons. It's even bigger in Asia than it is overseas."

"I'll say," Gavi replied as she stared out the window.

As they made it through the jam and sped up, Winter rolled down the window just enough to stick one hand out and wave. The gesture sent the crowd into a frenzy.

They drove through a private gate leading into the stadium, where the crowds finally were forced back, and stopped before a small entrance. Here, a guard opened the door for them, and Sydney stepped out to wait for Winter. As he emerged with Gavi on his arm, she fell into step behind him and headed into the building, yellow silks floating behind her.

"This way, miss," one of the guards told her as they walked along the stadium's interior hall. "Mr. Young, you're headed to the stage."

Winter approached her and held out an earpiece, along with a sound clip. "Here," he said.

Sydney took them. "Test?"

He nodded, then waited as she plugged the piece into her ear and clipped the sound device to the back of her trousers. As she did, Winter put in an identical earpiece, then walked around her to touch the device clipped to her. His fingers briefly brushed against the edge of her pants; she felt the slight pressure of them and shivered in spite of herself.

"Testing, testing," he said in a low voice. "Hear that?"

The sound came in crisp and clear from Sydney's earpiece, a near-perfect echo of Winter's voice. She nodded. "Testing, testing in return," she replied.

He turned the knob a little on her clip, then went to his own, adjusting it until he finally nodded. She couldn't help studying his serious expression for a minute, the way his hair fell over his eyes as he tilted his head down in concentration.

Behind him, Sydney saw Gavi watching them impatiently with her arms crossed.

"If I see anything suspicious from the box," Sydney told him, "you'll hear it in your earpiece. Do the same if you spot something in the crowd that makes you uncomfortable."

"Yes, ma'am," he murmured with a slight smile. "Hope we don't hear from each other until the concert's done."

"That's the plan," Sydney replied, answering his smile with her own polite one. Somehow, the eyes of their security team felt like more than she could stand. She took a step away and nodded toward the stadium, where fans were leading each other in rounds of chants and cheers. "Good luck out there," she said.

"You too," he replied. He gave her a polite hug, but as he pulled away, he murmured in her ear, "Stay safe."

Her stomach fluttered again at the warmth of him near her, of his concerned words. She nodded, unable to find the right reply.

Then the rest of Winter's security staff gathered around him. He cast a final glance over his shoulder at Sydney before he turned away and headed down the hall toward the practice rooms.

Sydney walked slightly behind Gavi as they were ushered in the opposite direction. She'd been in stadiums before, but never one like this.

The walls looked alive, their surfaces curved screens that responded to their presence as if aware of them—images of flowers bloomed as they walked by, along with music notes and specialized ads for luxury perfumes and couture outfits. Even the floor reacted to them, glowing pale blue under their every step.

At last, they headed down a flight of stairs and emerged through a lush entrance draped with real plants. Sydney found herself standing in a spacious box with a balcony that overlooked the stage, with a spectacular view of the rest of the stadium.

Already, most of the seats were filled, while on the stage below, she could see workers testing an enormous prop of Winter's logo, a rabbit with ears shaped like two halves of a broken heart.

Gavi left Sydney's side without a second glance, her attention focused on the many important people in the room. Sydney watched her go, noting the way the girl's chin tilted higher, her poise sharpening as she entered her element—charming her way through a circle of strangers. Already, she could see one of the gentlemen turning in Gavi's direction, chuckling as she grabbed a drink, pointed down toward the stage, and said something with an affecting grin.

She couldn't help feeling a little respect for the girl's fearlessness. Sauda would like her.

Sydney moved automatically to the edge of the room, where she could see other security staff standing by, staying out of the way of the guests while keeping an eye on everyone. Her gaze wandered from person to person before hitching on the one they were here for.

Mr. Seah stood near the edge of the balcony, speaking in an animated voice to a woman she recognized as Emika Chen, the CEO of Henka Games, who sported a rainbow-dyed bob and a sleek red jumpsuit, as well as Hideo Tanaka, the company's director and her fiancé.

Seah looked relaxed and friendly—if he was indeed in on the assassination job, he certainly gave none of it away.

As if he'd heard her thinking about him, Tems's voice came on unexpectedly in her earpiece. "Get closer when you can," he said.

She fought to keep the scowl off her face. This was the other reason why she had this earpiece—to everyone else, Sydney was using it to communicate with her client, but to her, it was a line that Tems also had access to.

He was watching her through the box's security cams, she knew. She didn't look toward them, but she did purposely turn so that the cam could see her clearly.

"I'm not an amateur," she snapped quietly.

"Just a friendly reminder," Tems said. "See if you can focus on his jacket. I want to know if any of the medals on his decorated uniform give away a clue."

"Working on it," she muttered, and moved away from the wall, heading carefully through the throngs until she reached the edge of the balcony where the cabinet member was standing. Sydney kept her eyes on the stage down below, as if scanning the crowds and waiting for Winter to appear. Idly, she listened in on pieces of the man's conversation.

"—to see such a large audience for the ceremony," he was saying now to Emika Chen.

The woman nodded politely with her arms crossed as she stood close to her fiancé. "Yes, it helps to get a great opening act," she replied.

"I hear he's attending the prime minister's gala?" asked Hideo.

"Yes," Mr. Seah replied with a smile. "It'll be quite the party with Mr. Young in attendance. Will you both . . ."

As the conversation went on, Gavi reappeared nearby, her dress gliding gently against the floor.

"Shrimp wonton?" Sydney heard one of the servers ask Gavi politely.

"Yes, please," she said, then took a bite of her food and came to stand by the balcony, her gold earrings clinking.

"You like him," she said without looking at Sydney.

Her words were enough to make Sydney turn from the stadium to face her. "Ma'am?" she asked.

"I know you were out on your balcony last night, having a nice night-time chat with Winter," Gavi said, popping the rest of the wonton in her mouth.

"We were discussing security for today," Sydney answered.

"I've seen a million people fall for Winter. You think you're immune?"

Careful, Sydney told herself. "I think you might be projecting your own feelings for Mr. Young onto others, ma'am," she said.

Something about those words seemed to get under Gavi's skin, and for an instant, the girl's eyes flashed. She smiled at Sydney. "I think you might be doing the same."

"Ma'am," Sydney said in her most condescendingly professional tone, "it's my job to take interest in everything about my clients, in order to keep them safe."

Gavi smiled and looked back down at the stage. "I'm sure that's what you tell yourself," she replied. "You don't need to give me the excuses— I've lived it. I know how you feel." She leaned closer to Sydney. "Listen to me. Winter doesn't do relationships—not the kind that you might want, at least. If you're lucky, he'll make you a part of his work. But you'll always be second place to that work. So if you're going to go after him, just have the fun. That's all he is. Trust me."

Sydney let her expression stay cool and unbothered as Gavi turned away. But the girl's words buzzed in her head, stubborn and unrelenting, burrowing deep into her thoughts.

"Always dangerous to fall for your partner, isn't it?" Tems said, his voice teasing.

Damn this earpiece, she thought. Gavi was still too close for Sydney to reply, but her hands closed so tightly against the railing of the box that the skin over her knuckles turned white.

At her silence, Tems went on. "I didn't think superstars were your type, to be honest."

Gavi finally moved far enough away, her attention now turned to Emika Chen. "He's not," Sydney whispered into her earpiece. "And I don't think you know much about my type, Bourton."

"Don't I? I think I know a little, Cossette."

"You think you're my type?"

"I think if we had the chance to do it all over again, then yes."

She rolled her eyes. "Optimistic of you."

"You're still angry about the passport. I didn't think I had to explain it to you, of all people."

"I didn't ask for an explanation."

"I know. Because we're a good pair, Syd. You and I."

There was an inflection in his tone that made Syd's heart twist a little, reminded her of why she'd kissed him on that snowy day in the hotel, why she'd let him take her to bed. "We were never a pair, Tems."

The stadium darkened, and down on the stage, the rabbit logo illuminated, sending the mass of fans into an explosion of cheers that shook the floor.

Above the noise, Sydney heard Tems utter a low laugh. "Give me a call when you're done with your new boy, Syd."

Sydney's temper flared, and she was about to retort, but the static in her earpiece cut off abruptly, signaling his departure.

Down on the stage, the first deep beats of Winter's intro music came on. Sydney recognized it immediately as the opening single from his new album. She listened as everyone else around her cheered and clapped, murmuring in admiration as the staged shifted and changed with the music, as if it were made up of massive tectonic plates.

Then Winter appeared on the stage. The entire stadium came alive with wild cheering—even the ministers around her in the box all turned to clap, their attention riveted on nothing but the boy in a silken black suit studded with diamonds.

Winter didn't look up in their direction. He kept his focus on the broader stadium, his face bright with energy, his voice filling the air as his dancers spread out to fill the rest of the stage. As he went, her gaze followed the ripples of motion in the audience standing nearest him. They moved like water, their hands reaching up for him whenever he passed by. And even though Sydney was here to track suspicious activity among the crowd, she couldn't help going back to Winter over and over again. The diamonds on his suit caught the sweeping spotlights and turned him blindingly bright.

And his voice. His voice was effortlessly clear and powerful, filling the entire space, reverberating in her chest, making tears well unexpectedly in her eyes.

Her jaw clenched. No, Gavi couldn't have caught on to any attraction she had for Winter, because they were done. She could still her heart around Winter. She could treat him exactly the way she was supposed to treat him: as a professional partner. Nothing more, nothing less.

She thought of Niall's words over breakfast, the tragic, faraway look in his eyes when he spoke of family, of love and mistakes.

Winter blew through two more of his biggest hits before the upbeat tempo calmed into something deep and melancholy. The lights on the stage changed, and Winter's backup dancers filed away, leaving Winter seated on a lone stool, a guitar propped on his leg. The audience cheered, then stilled in anticipation.

It wasn't until he began singing that Sydney recognized, with a start, the song he was performing.

And this hurricane goes on and on
Every time I look at you
You are my meditation
Am I ever yours, too?

It was the one he'd never released, the song he had been writing in London when they were on their first mission together, the song they'd opened up about last night.

It was the song he'd written about her.

It was one thing to read the lyrics scrawled on paper, one thing to listen as he admitted that it'd been about her—and quite another to hear it here, in a performance watched by millions, the words brought to life by an acoustic guitar and his velvet voice, which had transformed from its earlier power into something vulnerable and exquisite.

No. Goddamn it, Winter. Terror seized her—she looked quickly away from him, but not before it brought back a surge of everything that had happened during their previous mission. The fear she'd felt for him when she'd arrived back at their empty London apartment. The lump in her throat when he'd told her that this song was about her. The feeling of him lifting her into his arms and carrying her into the pool, of his lips on hers and her arms around his neck and legs straddling him in the water, the searing heat of his skin.

She thought of the words they'd exchanged before they parted ways, of how he'd leaned his head against hers and closed his eyes.

A little like the sun and the moon, aren't we? Never in the sky at the same time.

But sometimes the sun and the moon were visible together. Sometimes *they* were. And sometimes she couldn't hold her breath any longer around him, couldn't deny that she felt pulled to him in every way, that here, she felt like everything around her was spiraling out of her control.

As he sang, he looked steadily around the stadium, pausing now and then to focus on the crowd. His gaze made its way up until it reached the reserved box where Sydney stood. And there, he let his eyes fixate briefly on her, locking on her so surely that Sydney could almost feel it click into place.

Then he moved on to the rest of the crowd. But the embers of their brief stare still seemed to drift in the air, and heat flared on her cheeks as surely as if she'd been burned.

She wanted to scream at him for pointing his attention at her, for bringing this song to life before an entire audience. She couldn't bear the emotion that the song was surfacing in her chest, whole tendrils of her heart exposed to the open air. She needed to replace it with something else, with anything else.

He shouldn't have done this. It was a good song, too good, the kind where people would hunt down information on who inspired it, where they would dissect every lyric, where everyone in the world would soon be singing it. And if they started digging deeply enough, would they find out who he was singing about? Would they somehow connect it to her? Sure, he had looked around the entire stadium—but to her, the moment when he'd settled on her felt like the only thing people might notice.

You are my meditation.

The light on Winter went out with the final note of the song. The stadium burst into thunderous cheers. Sydney let out her breath, her skin still hot, her throat thick from holding back tears.

Then, in the midst of the noise, as she fought to collect herself—she saw Mr. Seah bow his head at his guests.

"Excuse me," she heard him say. Then he stepped away from the cluster of people watching at the balcony and headed for the door.

Sydney forced herself to calm her breathing, to focus. Then she moved like a shadow out of the distracted crowd. No one watched her leave. Like a phantom, she headed toward the door, her eyes trained on where Seah stepped through the sliding glass door and out into the hall.

As she went, she tried to push the memory of Winter's performance from her mind. But it stayed there, refusing to leave, along with the ghost of Gavi's words and Tems's bold bet. Her heart hammered frantically. They couldn't do this, this little dance around each other. Every time they drew close, the world around them drew closer, suffocating them, threatening to crush them. They had every reason to not work and no reason to be together.

Besides. They were dangerous together. Too dangerous. What would happen if others really caught on? What would happen if Gavi started spreading public rumors about them, or Dameon started connecting the dots? Compromising their cover, revealing such a weakness, could kill them.

No time, no time. She simply had no time to think about what it meant that Winter performed that song. She gritted her teeth, shoved him out of her mind again, cleared her throat, and filled her heart with anger. *That*, she knew how to do. She let herself be angry about the unfairness of it all, that she should have to think about nonsense like this while on a life-threatening mission. And as the anger built in her chest, it began scalding away her confusion. She let it burn and burn, until she could focus again, until she saw not Winter in her head, but the corridor before her.

She was here for a job. And she'd be damned if she'd screw it up over a boy.

There weren't many people outside. Security guards patrolled up and down the corridor, their eyes flickering to the occasional person hurrying along the hall. Sydney blended in with the guards, her black suit matching theirs, and as she went, a few of them seemed to acknowledge her with a terse nod, as if she were one of them, tasked with maintaining order at this concert.

A new song had started inside the stadium. The screams from the crowd were so loud now that Sydney could feel the floor vibrating. She walked near the wall as Seah headed down the corridor, his figure disappearing through the sparse crowd. For a moment, she thought perhaps she'd been mistaken, and that all he was doing was heading to the restrooms.

But then she saw him reach the curve at the end of the hall and glance momentarily over his shoulder. Sydney stayed where she was, silent and still.

When Seah finally disappeared, she moved, walking as quietly as she could.

Abruptly, the hall widened into an open-air section of the corridor, the wall turning into a long railing that overlooked the parking structure and then the tangle of thick trees beyond.

Sydney froze and pressed herself against the wall, blending into the shadows of a doorway.

The silhouette of Seah appeared again—this time while standing over part of the railing, with his back turned to Sydney. His head was tilted slightly to one side, and his hand was pressed against his ear, as if he were trying to hear someone on the phone.

Right away, she could tell that Seah was speaking in Mandarin. But one Western name stuck out, the sound startling and clear.

Rosen.

Walking on a Blade

Y ou promised me he would be at the table."

Sydney could barely make out his syllables, but it was enough for her to understand the Mandarin.

"No, I *did* pass it on."

She missed the next few lines. Then his words came back into focus.

"But I expect him to be there. If you want me to pull through, you'll have to—"

Him? Sydney wondered.

His words seemed to turn into a hiss here, as he momentarily lost his composure and stabbed the air with a finger. As he turned his head slightly, Sydney lost the trail of his words, only to see glimpses of his moving lips as he paced a little against the railing, ignoring the occasional fan or security guard passing by.

Her heart pulled tight as she continued to piece together his conversation. There was no direct mention of the president's name again, not that she could discern, but she saw pieces of other words.

Gala.

Others.

Table.

Intermixed within these was a word she couldn't quite decipher.

Kǔ.

She frowned, trying to understand the context. Her Mandarin was good for a foreigner, but one of her weaker languages. She thought through the basic characters that matched. *Kǔ* could mean "bitter" or "hardship" in one intonation, or "to cry" in another. Neither quite worked in the context of Seah's conversation, though. In this moment, she wished desperately that Winter was at her side, that maybe he knew better.

As if he'd heard her, Winter shifted seamlessly into a new song inside the stadium, and the audience responded with a fresh burst of cheers. By the railing, Seah stopped talking to glare in annoyance toward the building's interior. At the same time, Tems's voice returned on her earpiece.

"Whoever Seah's talking to," he murmured to Sydney, "the person's also here at the stadium."

Sydney stiffened, her gaze searching the general area. Tems must be able to see her location on his tracker. "Near where we are?" she whispered.

"I'm tracking the signal on his call. It's not a phone. It's on a local area network. The other person's right outside the stadium's perimeters."

As Sydney looked on, Seah hunched lower to continue speaking, his lips obscured by the phone.

Over time, Sydney had learned to recognize the subtle differences between a suspicious conversation and a simply nervous one. Seah seemed like a somewhat awkward man, perhaps prone to anxiety, but there was something about the stiffness of his stance, the way he kept looking at his watch as if he needed to be somewhere.

Back at the reserved box, she thought. He knew he couldn't be absent for too long.

After a while, he straightened his jacket and started walking back in the direction of the box.

Sydney sank deeper into the shadows as he left, then followed him with her gaze. "He's heading back now," she whispered into her earpiece. "ID on the other person?"

"Still outside," Tems replied. "Hasn't moved. You should follow Seah."

"On it," she murmured. She hoped that she'd managed to capture some of the video and audio of the cabinet member's conversation. Then she materialized from the shadows of the plants, turned in the direction of the reserved box, and straightened her sleeves.

That was when she saw it. A red dot of light flickering against the fabric of her suit, inches above her stomach.

A laser sight from a gun.

She didn't think; she just moved.

In an instant, she had darted behind one of the pillars of the balcony where Seah was standing just minutes earlier, her body hidden completely behind the stone. When she looked down again, the red dot was no longer there.

The other person's right outside the stadium's perimeters.

She could hear blood roaring in her ears. Someone had a target on her right now—someone located out in the trees beyond the stadium—and she had just narrowly avoided getting shot in the chest. She looked around, her eyes skipping from the few passersby in the hall—a trio of young attendees searching for their seats, a couple heading for the nearest bathrooms, a pair of security officers. None of them paid her any attention.

Whoever it was out there must either have been watching her or Seah, must have been scouting out this place—scouting *her*—for a while. Was it the same person who'd been at the airport?

She switched the frequency of her earpiece from Winter to Tems. "Tems," she whispered, covering her mouth with a subtle hand to prevent anyone watching from reading her lips. "There's a target on me."

He answered immediately. "Where?"

"Open hall between entrances three and four." She could feel her hands trembling at the encounter as she looked down the hall. "Seah was just here."

"That's near the other person's location."

"I'm calling Niall," she whispered. "See if he can get someone to intercept our mysterious interloper."

"Can you get back on your own?"

His voice was low, quiet, and urgent. It calmed her somewhat, a reminder that there was another seasoned Panacea agent here paying attention to her—and with that thought, she looked down the hall and gauged her options.

"Don't come," she whispered. "Note my location and make sure I'm still moving."

"I've got you," he answered.

She let his words still her, then turned her focus back on the hall. There were other scattered security guards here, patrolling the corridor, as well as the occasional cluster of concert attendees hurrying along, giggling and laughing, oblivious to what might have happened here, to a laser point fixed on her.

Would they try shooting her in public like this, with witnesses scattered all over the place? Surely they wouldn't want to cause a scene.

Sydney took a deep breath, silently counted for ten seconds—and then stepped out from the safety of the pillar, moving as precisely as if she were walking on a blade.

She immediately passed a pair of guards heading in the opposite direction, then kept pace with a group of laughing friends, all giggling about the new merchandise they'd just purchased from the stadium's front stands. Her pace stayed steady, even as she braced for the feeling of a bullet ripping into her body.

It didn't. Not yet, at least.

The hall's population thinned again. Now she was nearly alone, and a long, open corridor stretched between her and the location of the box.

So the sniper—whoever they were—didn't want to gun her down in front of a crowd, or else they would have pulled the trigger minutes ago. It'd given her a little leeway, but she needed to get back immediately, needed to warn the others.

Then, as she saw two security officers round the bend, she stepped out into the open and began walking back to the box.

From her periphery, she caught a glimpse of the red dot glimmering again on her sleeve. She forced herself to continue walking calmly, although everything in her screamed to bolt. One of the security officers gave her a disinterested nod as she approached him.

"Excuse me," she said, trying to sound sheepish. "I'm supposed to be in the reserved box as a bodyguard for Winter Young, but they won't let me back inside. Could you come with me to speak with them? I have all my identification."

The officer shook his head. "I'm sorry, ma'am," he said. "We're expected at the entrance on the other side of the stadium in a few minutes. What's your name?"

"Ashley Miller, sir."

"I'll radio them," he said, already starting to turn away. "They'll know you're coming."

She cursed inwardly as she started walking again, too, her head still turned toward them—but on the surface she gave them both a pleasant smile and a nod. "That would be so great," she replied. "Thank you."

He nodded back at her before he and his partner turned around and continued down the path. The protection of their proximity waned—and as Sydney turned back around to face the empty hall, she braced herself for gunfire. Her eyes darted around, looking for any more cover she could use.

"Ashley?"

Then the familiar voice came around the turn of the corridor—and Sydney found herself bumping right into Gavi.

"Oh!" Gavi let out a startled yelp before she rolled her eyes and gave Sydney a wry smile that looked more like a grimace. "They said you were lost out here. I stepped out to grab you."

Relief washed over Sydney. It took all of her willpower not to grab Gavi and hug her senseless. Instead, she chuckled dryly and looked down, as if embarrassed. "I appreciate the help, miss," she said as Gavi began leading them back the way she had come.

Gavi shrugged before folding her arms together and leaning closer to her. "In all honesty," she muttered, "I was trying to get a break from a minister in there who keeps loitering near me. You're a good excuse. Now, stay close so I don't have to keep talking to the guy."

Sydney felt a twinge of guilt at using Gavi as a shield from her attacker. Still, the girl was completely unaware, and the shot never came. By the time they rounded the corner and the glass doors of the box came into view, the laser sight hadn't reappeared. The moment her assailant had wanted to take advantage of was gone now.

So was Gavi's sense of camaraderie. The instant they returned to the space, she made a beeline for a woman standing near the food trays, sipping on a cup of tea. Sydney recognized her as the prime minister's assistant. So much for sticking near Gavi—but Sydney did nevertheless, feeling both weak with relief after her encounter and uneasy with the idea of an assassin lying in wait outside for her.

Down below, Winter's performance continued. He had taken off his glittering suit jacket, revealing a silver shirt made out of a gleaming, rippling fabric that moved like water when he did. His smile now was genuine, full of mischief as he belted out a high note and then winked at the audience, making the stadium burst into delighted screams.

She was glad that he hadn't been with her out in the hall. It ruled out her hypothesis that her airport assailant had been there for Winter instead of her. Perhaps he had a stalker of his own, but this—this was a deliberate targeting of Sydney.

She imagined the way his eyes would constrict in fear if she told him what had happened, and the uneasiness churned in her stomach again. It was the same look he'd had on his face during their most dangerous moments in London, when it seemed for a while that they might not make it out alive.

It was the act of him worrying that bothered her, the fact that her well-being could affect his emotions so visibly. She was too used to walking alone through life. Sure, Sauda and Niall cared about her safety—but *this*, this attention from Winter, this sudden tethering of another person's emotions . . . was different. This scared her.

Tethers like this cost lives.

"All's well?" Tems murmured through her earpiece as she came to stand near Gavi.

"All's well," she murmured in return. "For now."

"I'm doing surveillance of the surroundings for your attacker," Tems asked. Unlike Winter's concern, Tems took the danger she'd been in and reacted in the way an agent should. With cool, even cold, professionalism. It felt familiar to her, safer. "They must be stationed in the parking structure."

"Did you send it to Niall yet?"

"Not yet. Are you reaching out to him?"

"On it."

Sydney sent her coordinates to Niall, along with a quick note about the laser target. She waited until another of Winter's songs had started and the people around her turned their attention toward the stage.

Niall buzzed her earpiece almost immediately. "Target was unmistakably on you?" he said, without a greeting.

"Yes," Sydney replied.

"Get yourself inside immediately."

"Heading in now." She made sure her back was facing a wall and tapped her phone. When it did, she synced it to her earpiece and played the recording for the analyst. "Here's what I overheard."

"Send it."

She could hear the tension in his voice, knew that he was worried for her, and it made her stomach tighten. "Does the term *kǔ* mean anything to you? I can't parse the meaning in the conversation, even though I heard it several times."

For a moment, there was silence on the other end. Down on center stage, Winter's harnesses launched him high into the air, and the audience let out a chorus of screams that shook the stadium. As everyone around her burst into cheers, Niall's voice came back on again.

"Found something on the term *kǔ*. I've traced it to a new drug on the black market in the East. Apparently it was entered into our Eastern databases earlier in the year. Kǔ. It's a neurotoxin."

Down below, Winter did a somersault high in midair and landed on a floating platform. The audience screamed. Sydney felt a warning buzz in her head.

Seah was going to poison the president.

Traitors Always Stay Close

By the time Winter arrived with Gavi and Sydney at their hotel's after-party, the dancing was in full swing. From the rooftop, past the lush foliage spilling over from the ledge, Winter could see the entire expanse of Singapore, a glittering sheet of skyscrapers lit up by advertisements and blinking lights.

Gavi clung tightly to his arm and smiled at the bevy of reporters and cameramen that swarmed around them as they entered the space. As she struck a pose for one news agency, Winter glanced to his side and glimpsed Sydney standing a short distance from them, her eyes searching the deck for suspicious activity, an uneasy scowl on her face.

Sydney hadn't said a single word since she met him backstage after his show. No smiles, either. Her eyes had looked as cold and brooding as ever as she'd fallen into step right behind him and followed him out of the venue without a word. The only giveaway that something was wrong was the tension in her shoulders, a stiffness he recognized immediately as her indication that she was on high alert.

Something had happened during his concert, though he didn't know what it was.

The instant they arrived, two bodyguards showed up to usher them to a private booth. As they walked, Gavi leaned up to Winter's ear.

"Those ministers over there?" she murmured, nodding toward a group of people wearing Singapore flag pins on their lapels. "They were in the box with me and couldn't seem to care less about you—and look at them now, coming to the after-party in the hopes of bumping into you."

"Maybe they're here for *you*," Winter replied, giving the group a nod and smile as they passed by.

Gavi flipped her hair over her shoulder and giggled, her nose brushing against Winter's cheek. "Too bad for them," she said. "I charge a fee for photos."

Winter glanced over his shoulder again at Sydney. Her eyes were turned toward the ministers, too, so intently that he could have sworn she was purposely avoiding his gaze.

They reached the private booth on the other side of a long firepit set in a stone table. Dameon was already here, seated across from them with a few others that Winter recognized as some of the local crew that had worked on their set. Winter slid into the seat opposite them with a sigh, while Gavi settled in beside him.

Sydney remained standing at the end of the booth, still inspecting the crowds around her. He tried to meet her gaze, but again, she seemed to avoid him. Winter could feel her presence at his back every time he looked away, and the weight of it made him uncomfortable. He shifted a few times before he finally glanced up at her.

"Hey," he called up. She looked down at him as he gestured at the booth. "Do you want to sit down?"

"I'm guarding you," she said stiffly. She seemed pale.

"You can rest your legs at the same time," he said.

She just shook her head and went back to surveying the space. "Later," she replied quietly.

It was all she needed to say to tell him that something had gone wrong tonight. He looked around, trying to guess what she knew that he didn't. Tems was nowhere to be seen on the dance floor—in fact, it didn't look like he'd made an appearance here at all.

Dameon's voice made him turn away from Sydney and look across the firepit to his friends. "Wasn't I right?" he said with a serene smile. "Making you include 'Eyes on the Prize' in our set list tonight? Did you hear the crowd?"

"You're always right," Winter replied as he leaned forward, his elbows resting on his knees.

Dameon took an egg roll off of a tray that a waiter offered to them. "'Meditation' was a surprise, though." He looked archly at Winter. "Did you have that in your catalog? I don't remember it."

"I found it several days ago," he said. "Thought it made a good interlude."

"It was nice," Dameon agreed.

Beside him, Gavi leaned against Winter's shoulder and tapped her glass against his. "To a good concert," she said.

Winter toasted her back and took a sip of his drink. "Glad you enjoyed it."

"I always enjoy your concerts. You just don't invite me to enough of them."

"Well, it gets a little awkward when we haven't spoken in over a year."

"Does that mean things have changed now?" She smiled curiously. "Or are we going back to silence when we return to the States?"

Winter shook his head and looked at the fire. In his head, "You Are My Meditation" was still playing, and he could still feel Sydney's quiet presence nearby. "I don't know," he admitted. "I don't think it's a good idea."

"Fine." She shrugged. "Then I'll have to catch the rest of your concerts on the screen, like everyone else."

"They're all going to be the same, anyway. Besides," he added, looking at her, "you hate repeating a concert."

"It's true." Gavi laughed idly and brought her drink back up to her lips. "As much as you hate cigar smoke."

Winter glanced at her with a blank look. "Cigar smoke?" he said.

Gavi looked at him, then gave him a quick smile. "What?"

But Winter had known her long enough by now to recognize the hesitation in her voice, the first hints of a secret hidden in her words. She had let something slip by accident. "How do you know that?" he asked.

"It was always pretty obvious, Winter."

He angled his body toward her. "No, it couldn't have been, because we've never been anywhere together with cigar smoke. I know I've never mentioned it before. So how do you know I hate cigar smoke?"

"I can just tell, all right?" She tossed her hair. "Don't get so worked up about it."

A memory was already resurfacing in his mind, though—the cloud of cigar smoke that would surround his father when he sat in the kitchen, the way Winter would avoid coming to dinner whenever he smelled it downstairs, the way the smoke clung to his father's coat.

He looked at Gavi's face. She was lying to him. But he had caught her by surprise this time—perhaps she'd misremembered where she'd learned it. Perhaps she thought Winter had been the one who'd told her.

"Did my mother tell you?" he asked.

Gavi looked at him, and he could see the answer in her eyes. *No.* His heart twisted with dread. There was only one other person who could have told her.

"Did you find out from my father?" he asked.

Another beat of silence. She sighed. "Oh, Winter."

"What aren't you telling me, Gavi?" he said quietly.

She hesitated at the look on his face. "It was just for the week, all right?" she murmured, keeping her voice low. "And I didn't give him anything."

Him. Something in her tone brought on a lurch of nausea. "Give who?" he asked. "My father?"

One look at the expression that flashed across her face told him everything he needed to know. He started shaking his head. "My dad reached out to you? When? How? When he heard that I'd invited you along to this?" he said.

Gavi's stare went to the rest of the party, then back to him. Across the fire, Dameon glanced over at them, his smile wavering at the stricken look on Winter's face.

"No," she whispered. Another pause. "In Honolulu."

So that was the real reason why Gavi had showed up at his hotel that night. Why she had left her date at the movie premiere. Hadn't Dameon warned him about this? After all this time, he should have known that Gavi always had a good reason for her actions—a selfish reason—and yet, each time, he still found himself in this position. Caught off guard.

"This is for the book, isn't it?" he asked tightly.

Gavi's eyes were downcast now. Even she, it seemed, could feel shame. "He just asked me to pass along anything interesting that happened," she said, "that he could insert into the book. He also wanted me to soften you up to the idea of the publication, maybe pull back your lawyers a bit."

The nausea was making him light-headed. Winter looked around, the party's sounds suddenly dull and menacing, the fire crackling nearby suddenly too overwhelmingly hot.

Gavi put a hand on his arm. He barely felt it. "I didn't tell him anything too bad," she said.

"What *did* you tell him?"

She swallowed. "Just where you were staying, what your schedule was."

"That's not all, is it? What else?"

She hesitated. "Okay, a couple of stories from when we were together. I told him about the time you were stabbed. How you kept it a secret."

The time when he'd been stabbed outside a party, how he'd fallen across Claire's lap, bleeding, and how he'd insisted they not go to a hospital because of the stories that would follow. Gavi had figured it out on her own because he'd had to cancel a date with her that week, and because she'd found the scar when he'd slept over at her place a month later. And now she'd told his father, and his father had put it in his book. No wonder it'd been one of the headlines on the tabloids when they'd left for Singapore.

"What else?" he pressed quietly.

"I told him you like your bodyguard."

Sydney.

"You're feeding him straight rumors, then," Winter snapped, fear rising in his throat.

Her eyes flashed. "I just tell him what I see. It's not my responsibility to confirm or deny things."

He threw his hands up. "No. It's just common decency. Why, Gavi? Why would you do this? How much did he pay you? Did he promise you a piece of the book's profits?"

She didn't say anything, confirming his guess. He winced and looked at the fire. Even a small fraction of those profits could be worth millions.

"So that's it, then?" he snapped. "Just sold me out for the money?"

"Your father scares me, Winter," she whispered. Her eyes were wide, her brows furrowed. "He told me that if I helped him, he'd make sure not to put anything scandalous in the book about me."

He narrowed his eyes. "I thought you didn't care what others thought of you as long as you got the attention."

She scowled back at him, and in that, he saw at last that she did care. That maybe she really was afraid of what his father might have published about her.

Winter stood up, the nausea even more powerful standing. Sydney looked at him, eyes searching his, but he just shook his head. "I'm going to head back early," he said, nodding to Dameon across the firepit.

Dameon turned away from his date to give Winter—then Gavi—a questioning look. "Already?" he said.

"Headache," Winter said. "I'll catch up with you guys at breakfast tomorrow."

"Winter, wait," Gavi called after him.

But she didn't make a move to follow him, as if she knew her words were futile, and he didn't make an effort to say anything in return. He just stepped away from the booth and, without bothering to see if Sydney was following him, turned from the rest of the festivities and back toward the elevators.

The Reason You Strive

Their hotel floor was quiet and empty, a stark contrast from the booming celebration upstairs. Winter's ears were still ringing as he stopped before his door, swiping it unlocked with his key and stepping into the hallway of his suite. Everything around him seemed to be rippling, as if submerged—the side table in the hallway was made of moving lines, the view from the windows shimmered and trembled. He blinked and steadied himself against the wall.

Nothing felt real anymore. Not the reason why he was here, not the mission he was on, not the people around him. He hadn't seen his father in at least five years, hadn't even heard his mother mention him. How could his father be back now, barreling into his life like a nightmare?

He closed his eyes. His room disappeared, and in the darkness, he saw himself standing once again in his childhood bedroom, his head hanging as he stood before his father. The man had just found a drawer full of lyrics that Winter had scrawled on notebook paper. He held them up, then tossed them unceremoniously in the trash.

What a waste of time, he'd said. *Who'd want to listen to you?*

His father had hated his love for music, had taunted and scolded and ridiculed him for it his entire life. It seemed impossible that he was the author behind the tell-all book, that the same man who had thrown away his music could now stand to make millions off of it.

On a whim, he took out his phone. His father's number was no longer on it, but he could remember it all the same, and now he dialed with a shaking hand, wondering if it would still reach him.

It rang for so long that Winter was ready to pocket the phone again—but the ringing stopped at the last second, and his reflection disappeared to make way for an older man.

They both stared at each other.

Winter looked exactly like him. It was the quality that had both vaulted him into global fame and destroyed his relationship with his mother—Winter had inherited the same lush hair and dark, thick-lashed eyes, the same subtle grace in his walk, the same smile that could shift between shy and mischievous. His mother couldn't even look at Winter without remembering the traumatic relationship she'd had with the man, couldn't be in the same room with Winter without wanting to leave, couldn't tell Winter she loved him without feeling like she was validating a marriage that she regretted with her entire soul.

His father recovered first, the surprise on his face fading into a sneer, the cold glint in his eyes something that Winter, thankfully, hadn't inherited.

"Well," the man said. "What a surprise."

"You're releasing the tell-all?" Winter replied, the words tumbling from his lips in a hoarse, angry rush. "You're the author?"

His father turned away, as if busy with some task in his house, then looked back up at Winter, unconcerned. "Did your girlfriend confess everything to you?"

Everything in Winter's chest felt like it was bubbling up now, years of suppressed rage and grief and loneliness. "Leave her out of this," he said. "I figured it out myself. Pull the book."

His father lifted an eyebrow. "We don't speak for five years, and this is the first thing you say when you decide to call?"

There was always something manipulative in his father's voice, a disappointment that made Winter feel like he was a child again, that he was at fault no matter what they were talking about.

He gritted his teeth. "I wasn't the one who chose to leave."

His father sighed. "It's a shame that the first conclusion you jump to about the book is so negative. The book isn't a hit piece on you."

"Then what is it?"

"I want to set the record straight about me, given your status as a public figure. I deserve to tell my side of the story."

"I've never talked about you in interviews."

"I hear there are rumors about me based on music you've written."

"People can assume whatever they want. I've never written a song about you."

"How about this." His father's voice turned compromising, even consoling. "Let me send you a copy of the manuscript. I've been meaning to do so. We can sit down together, catch up properly instead of abruptly on a call like this. We can decide what you like and what you don't. Maybe you can fill in a few details?"

"No, how about this. You pull the book and return the money you were paid in advance."

At Winter's hard tone, the man narrowed his eyes. "I'm your father."

"That wasn't a choice I could make."

He sneered. "You think I didn't pay your mother to keep you fed after I left? Things may not have worked out between us, but the food on your table was bought by *my* hard-earned money."

Again, a familiar sinking feeling settled in Winter's stomach at his father's disappointment in him.

"You were *supposed* to take care of us," Winter said. "Spending money to feed me isn't a loan I need to repay."

He made a disgusted sigh. "Your mother never taught you to be grateful."

Winter recognized the mind-games part of his father's personality. "At least she was there."

"I think you're giving her more credit than she deserves." He tilted his head mockingly at Winter, challenging him in the way that used to make him feel so small. "I remember calling the house and getting no one but you on the line. Her being gone for days while you were home alone. Is that what you call *being there*?"

Winter could feel his temper boiling over. "And where were you? Mom was buried in those pills and struggling, and no one helped her. The government didn't; we had no relatives; we were alone." His voice hardened into steel. "Mom needed help. So *where. Were. You?*"

His father's eyes remained cold, sly, cruel. "Why didn't *you* help her?" he said mildly. "Surely you have the resources now?"

Winter swallowed hard, trying to contain his fury. He knew his father wanted to see him explode now, was using that manipulation again. "Pull the book," he said.

"I see you've learned to raise your voice."

Winter's lip curled into a snarl. "*Pull the book*," he snapped.

"Or you'll do what?" His father regarded him coolly. "Send your lawyers?"

"Every last one of them."

At that, his father's lips tightened. "Do you think you deserve this life, Winter?" he asked.

It was a simple question, said in a simple tone. But his father had always known how to push a needle into his heart, and Winter felt the stab now, felt himself wince at the hit.

When he didn't answer right away, his father smiled, knowing he'd struck true. The man leaned against his table and regarded Winter closely. "Why do you strive?" he asked.

"What?"

"Ambition tends to be fueled by something lacking in you. So what's yours? What's lacking?"

Winter didn't answer. He could feel his father's probing questions surrounding him, suffocating him with their accusations.

"Do you strive because you have something to prove? Because you're trying to cover up for your inadequacies? Do you strive because you feel like the world owes you something, like you somehow deserve better? Do you strive because you think so highly of yourself that you want everyone to acknowledge it?"

"You don't know anything about me," Winter snapped.

"Is it because of me?" His smile turned cruel. "Am I the reason you strive?"

Winter refused to give him that satisfaction. "I never think about you."

"That so?" His father leaned closer to the camera. "Let me enlighten you. You're nothing but a lucky boy. You don't work any harder than anyone else. You certainly aren't more talented. You don't deserve to be here any more than the rest of us. You're only famous because you got my face and your mother's voice, and you didn't work for any of that. So why do you get to have millions, when everyone else who works just as hard as you doesn't? What's so great about you?" He raised an eyebrow at him. "Am I right?"

Yes. Winter could feel the insecurities that haunted him being dragged to the surface, his father pulling just the right strings to haul them up.

"Call me if you have something to add to the book," the man said as he straightened. "Otherwise, put your feet back on the ground, kid. You're just smoke and mirrors. You're nothing."

Winter opened his mouth to reply, but his father had already hung up. He found himself staring at his own face again, pale and stunned in the darkness of the room.

He threw the phone at the couch and squeezed his eyes shut, raking his hands through his hair. Sickness roiled in his stomach. The world around him felt like it was spinning. What the hell was he doing, cold-calling his father like that? Did he think it would have done any good, that making demands of him would somehow make his father change his mind?

You're just smoke and mirrors. You're nothing.

All the late nights he'd stay up rehearsing or writing lyrics, humming new melodies, putting together new songs, working, working, working. His father had so successfully reduced it to nothingness, made him feel like it was trash. And wasn't that the real reason he pushed himself? Wasn't his father right all along? Because he desperately needed to prove the man wrong, that he deserved to be heard? To be loved? Wasn't that why he kept going back to Gavi, even when she hurt him over and over?

Winter paced the entryway, then slammed both fists against the wall.

As if on cue, a knock rapped on his door.

Still in a maelstrom of fury and frustration, Winter lunged at the door and swung it angrily open.

"What?" he snapped.

And found himself staring at Sydney.

An Ocean Between Two Hearts

She hurried past him without a word. When the door clicked shut behind her, she turned to face him with her arms crossed. Her expression cut momentarily through the whirlwind in his head. Something had gone very wrong.

"I got a recording of Minister Seah in the middle of your concert," she said. Her voice was stretched tight. "Tems thinks it's solid enough evidence for what we need. He's passing it along to the CIA now."

Winter's heart was still pounding from the call with his father, and Sydney's words seemed to come to him through an underwater filter. He ran a hand through his hair, swallowed hard, and forced himself to concentrate. "Okay," he managed to say. "Let me hear it."

Sydney played the recording from her phone. As it finished, she pocketed her phone. "Tems is searching for the identity of the caller on the other line."

"The guy keeps mentioning something called kǔ," Winter said.

She nodded. "I was going to ask if you happened to know what it meant. Niall says it's the name of a new neurotoxin making its way through the East's underground scene."

"Makes sense," Winter said, clearing his throat and forcing himself to think. "Kǔ was an ancient Chinese ritual of putting poisonous creatures in a jar and seeing which emerged alive and victorious. The poison from that victorious creature would then be used on a target. I researched it once for a song."

"'Magic Poison'?" Sydney asked.

Winter looked at her in surprise. "So you *have* listened to the album."

She scowled even deeper and looked toward the window. "Niall thinks Seah may attempt to use the neurotoxin on President Rosen at the gala."

Everything was falling apart. "What's the plan, then?" Winter asked quietly.

"Tems gathered intel during the ceremony that Seah's car will be parked along the palace's side entrance during the gala, along with the other ministers' rides. Our assumption is that he's going to make an early exit after he does his job, so that by the time Rosen reacts to the poison, Seah's already gone."

"So we cut him off from his escape route," Winter said.

"We cut him off," Sydney agreed.

Winter studied her face. There was a paleness about her that seemed not quite right, as if there was more to her words than she was letting on. "What else?" he pressed.

"Is that not reason enough to be worried?" she said with a scowl. The edge in her voice returned, a thin film holding back a tide of . . . fear? Anger? He couldn't tell. "We have a potential assassination on our hands. Seah's going to be seated next to Rosen at the gala, and we have twenty-four hours to stop him."

He looked carefully at her. "Something happened to you," he said.

She folded her arms and tightened her lips. Her weight shifted from one foot to the other, as if she ached to move. But when she spoke again, she said, "What happened to me is that, as I figured out the severity of the mission we're on, you decided to sing that song onstage."

Her answer startled him. "What?" he said.

"The song," she repeated. There was an urgency in her voice and a speed to her words that nearly bordered on panic. "You pull it out now, of all times, in front of the entire world? When we chatted on the balcony that other night, you told me that you never meant for me to see those lyrics. You made it sound like it was a private track just for you, that maybe it should be something we keep a secret."

He shook his head. "Are you afraid because you think it could have compromised us?" he asked incredulously.

"Who knows? That's always the risk, isn't it?" Sydney turned away from him, walked a few paces, and came back. "Do you understand that we are undercover right now?" she murmured, narrowing her eyes at him. "Do you understand that any unnecessary attention puts us in danger?"

His heart tightened. The world had started to spin again. "No one knows it's about you. I've told no one—not even my producers. Not even Claire. There's nothing in those lyrics to identify you in any way, something I did very intentionally. It could be about anyone."

"That song's not on your official album. You never released it."

"I perform surprise songs all the time. No one will find that strange."

"But they *will* analyze it. They do all the time."

"The lyrics don't say, '*Sydney Cossette is a secret agent.*'"

Sydney threw her hands up. "You draw attention to those closest to you when you hint at your love life like that, especially with the way you turned in my direction at specific parts in the song."

He frowned at her. "You're that afraid of the song?"

"Of you blowing the damn lid off our cover, yes."

"I don't think that's why you're scared."

"Well, it is." She tore her eyes away. "Your ex-girlfriend is here with you as your date. We're about to risk our lives tomorrow. Why are you releasing this song *now*? Why add to all this?" She turned back to him and pressed a finger into his chest. "Were you planning to put that song in your original set list before we arrived?"

"No," he said.

"You added it after our conversation, didn't you?"

"I'm sorry, all right?" he snapped. "It's a spontaneous interlude. I have one in every concert. I didn't think it'd bother you. After our talk . . . I thought, well, never mind. If it concerns you that much, I won't perform it anymore. It'll never see the light of day again."

"Why does it matter so much to you, anyway?" Everything seemed to hurtle out of her. "It's just a song."

She seemed to regret her words the instant they came out, but it was too late. Winter winced and took a step away from her. Her statement stirred the whispers that haunted him all his life, echoing the conversation he'd just had with his father.

You're just smoke and mirrors. You're nothing.

"It's not just a song," he said quietly.

She paused, taking a deep breath, and lowered her voice. "Look, Winter," she said. "It's not even the song. But we're on a mission together—have you forgotten that?"

He closed his eyes. Everything in his chest felt ready to boil over.

"That's our purpose, nothing more," she went on. There were tears shining in her eyes now. "So why did you do it?"

"Because I've thought about you every single day since London!" he blurted out.

Sydney flinched as if she'd been struck. "What? No, you haven't."

But Winter couldn't stop anymore. Too much had happened—Gavi's betrayal, his father's cruel words, this. A dam had broken in him, and he had no desire to fix it. He was tired of bottling it all up. He was tired of holding himself together. "I tried my best, you know," he said in a low, urgent voice. "Every day, I wished you would show up unannounced on my doorstep or in my practice room or anywhere I happened to be, and whisk me back into your world. Every day, I missed you. And you know what? I was okay with that. I'm not a fool. I know we aren't meant to be, and I was ready to move on. Then you appeared out of nowhere and pulled me right back in, and now we're here and I have no idea what to do. I tried my best, but now I think I'm losing my mind. So I sang the damn song, okay?"

"Stop," she whispered.

He held up his hands. "I know what I'm saying. I know how it sounds. I get that this, whatever this is between us, is a dead end. I know I don't deserve you. I don't deserve any of this. But I'm telling you right now that I've had a hell of a time getting you out of my head. And when you came back, everything I'd done to wall myself away from you came crashing down. That song is all I have of you, some private illusion that I might ever get a chance with you." His voice faded to a murmur. "That's all it is. I need you to understand that."

He felt foolish the instant he stopped talking. Dameon had always told him he was good at keeping his secrets close—why couldn't he keep this one? But it was too late to take any of it back now.

Sydney just stared at him, her eyes the color of a storm, her lips pressed tight. He couldn't tell what she thought of him now, whether or not she could make out the hurt that he knew must be on his face. He swallowed hard. Suddenly, he couldn't bear looking at her. His eyes turned down. He took in the pattern on the rug of his suite, forcing himself to follow the fabric's lines, as if it might lead him out of this torturous place.

After another agonizing silence, Sydney took a deep breath. Winter looked back up to see her turn away. "I can't do this," she whispered.

He barely caught her words. As she headed to the door, everything in him wanted to tell her to stop, to wait, that he didn't mean any of that, that he didn't know what he was thinking.

But he stayed frozen where he was.

I can't do this.

As always, she seemed impenetrable, the walls around her heart a fortress. It had taken a vial of poison for her to drop them last time—perhaps that would be the only time he ever saw a glimpse of the softness in her.

So all he could do was watch as she slipped out into the hall, the lock clicking shut behind her. For a while, he just stood there, trying to will it to open again.

It didn't.

A Halfway Love

Somewhere here on the rooftop deck, the party was still going. But Sydney didn't head in its direction, nor did she want to be anywhere in the adjoining suite near Winter. She needed to be far from the others, where she could calm down.

What a strange concept. Never in her career had Sydney ever struggled to keep a cool head during a mission, especially not over a partner. But she could still see Winter's stricken expression as he poured his heart out, then as she reacted by leaving. She felt sick to her stomach, like someone had kicked her. Like she had kicked someone.

Why did it matter so much to her how he felt? She couldn't understand it, this feeling of terror and disgust twisting in her stomach. She certainly wasn't in love with him. Was she? Perhaps it was a confluence of being here, having her life threatened at every turn, having a sniper's target on her body just hours earlier, having to work with Tems to keep the world order. But she had been in predicaments before. She had been able to manage things.

Winter. Winter was the reason. Winter was the difference. She stopped in a quiet corner of the rooftop beside a cluster of trees and breathed deeply, trying to settle her stomach. She hated that Winter was right. Why was she getting so worked up about the song? There was no way anyone could trace it to her, not logically, not beyond it being some vague rumor to join the thousands of vague rumors swirling around Winter every day. But she was afraid all the same, terrified that something between them had broken down, that some barrier had been shattered. She felt a soft spot exposed in her heart, ready to be wounded.

And this wasn't a line of business where she could afford to be wounded by a personal bond.

An incoming call made her look at her phone. It was Niall.

She inhaled deeply, composed herself, and picked up. "Je suis toute seule," she said. *I'm alone.*

"Good," Niall said. "So where's Tems?"

She blinked. The beat of hesitation gave her away. Niall had figured out their secret.

"Next time I see you," he grumbled, "you can try explaining to me why you lied to my face."

"I don't know where he is, Niall," she said in a low voice. "Not right now, at least. He's not staying at our hotel."

"But you've both made contact with him. You've seen him in person."

She bit her lip. "Yes."

Niall let out a long sigh. "Okay," he said. "Why?"

She could keep her promise to Tems and not let Niall in on everything. But the argument she'd just had with Winter had left her raw and bleeding. "Tems uncovered our lead on Seah first," she said. "That's why I trailed him at the stadium."

"Tems roped you into a rogue mission?"

"We made the choice ourselves. He was afraid that you'd force him back before he could get to the bottom of the ploy."

Niall made some sort of swearing sound on the other end, although Sydney couldn't quite make out what he said. "He never changes, that boy," the man muttered.

"Are you going to pull us off the mission?" she asked tightly.

Niall hesitated, and for a moment, all Sydney could hear was the whistling of the wind and distant laughter from the party. "The plan was to set you all up properly at the gala tomorrow," he finally said. "It's too late to pull Winter back without ruffling feathers and drawing attention."

A ribbon of hope cut through Sydney's roiling emotions. "You'll still be there, then?"

"The CIA has me stationed at the side entrance," he said. "You'll still see my car waiting there."

"And our flight out?" she asked.

"Will still be at the airfield for you and Tems. But I'm warning you, Cossette. No more antics."

"You don't want to see Rosen harmed any more than we do," she replied.

"Something I'm sure you were banking on." He sighed. "I had a feeling Tems would be a bad influence on you."

"I'm a bad enough influence all on my own."

Niall snorted, and Sydney imagined him smiling on the other side, in spite of himself. It was a small comfort, at least, to hear him in this moment. "Listen carefully. We still can't track the identity of your attacker. And although the guest list at the gala is tightly vetted, with no firearms allowed in, I can't promise that you won't be in danger at the venue."

"I've been targeted before," Sydney said. "I'll be in my suit. I've got all my toys, too."

"Just keep your eyes open. It's likely that Seah has others working with him there."

"I'll be careful," she said gently. "I promise."

There was another pause, but Niall seemed satisfied enough. "Don't let Tems lead you and Winter too astray."

"You know he absolutely will."

"Yeah, I know." Niall made another annoyed sound in his throat. "Sometimes, I swear, it's not worth the effort to save him."

Sydney let herself smile a little at that. "We're all lucky to have you, sir."

Niall grunted. "Get some rest tonight. You'll need it."

She didn't mention the fight between her and Winter. Far be it from her to add more stress to Niall's mission. "You too," she replied.

Niall hung up first. Sydney put her phone down and stared out at the nightscape, her thoughts a blur, letting the weight of the mission push against her.

Will still be at the airfield for you and Tems.

If all went according to plan, she had twelve hours left with Winter before they separated again. Most likely, it'd be a separation even more abrupt than their first mission—no proper goodbyes, no farewell embrace. And with the way their conversation had unraveled tonight, maybe not even the feeling of a dignified ending. They'd simply turn their backs on each other, hurting and full of grief, and walk away.

And wasn't that fine? Did it even matter, if they'd never see each other again?

A movement in the shadows near her made her startle. She whirled, her body already tensing into a defensive attack posture—only to see Tems emerge from the darkness with his hands in his pockets.

"Syd," he said in greeting, coming over to stand next to her.

She lowered her arms. "Hey," she said.

He stared out at the cityscape with her. "That was Niall, wasn't it?" he said.

She glanced at him. "Didn't think anyone was close enough to hear."

"I didn't. I just figured, since you look stressed."

"I think you're mistaking your feelings about Niall for mine."

He laughed a little. "Fair enough." He was silent for a moment. "He knows, doesn't he?"

"He knows," she replied with a nod.

"Is he going to let us proceed?"

"Yes."

Tems lowered his shoulders and seemed to relax a little at that. "Confirmation of our plane at the airfield tomorrow evening?"

"Yes. Niall confirmed. Nineteen hundred hours."

"Good," he said. "We won't have time afterward to delay. It'll need to be ready by the time we are."

"It'll be ready." She turned from the scene to face him. "Does the CIA have the footage? Do I need to contact them?"

"They've got everything," Tems said. "No need to make contact. I'll check that they're in place for us."

"Ordering them around now, are you?" she said with a raised eyebrow.

He gave her a sidelong smile. "I've built a nice enough rapport with them."

"What about Seah?"

"Force him to get up out of his seat, however you can, as soon as you can. Before he can settle down to do anything. We'll need to move fast and immediately."

Sydney nodded. "This will be a better job for Winter."

"Fine." An edge appeared in Tems's voice. "Whatever works. Have Winter get Seah to the hallway leading to the main entrance, past the coat check. I'll be waiting there with the CIA to arrest him. We need him *away* from the president, understood? I have a suspicion he has a backup plan in case things go wrong, and we can't afford for him to be near Rosen when he realizes we're onto him."

"And then we head out for the waiting plane," she finished. "Winter returns to his team."

"And we're done," he said.

And we're done.

"Done," Sydney confirmed, keeping her answer crisp and cool. But the storm in her chest twisted painfully.

In the silence that followed, Tems glanced down at his feet. "Syd, do you remember the day we graduated from Panacea?"

It had been an unseasonably warm afternoon in May, the sky overcast. Sydney had sat at a table in the Claremont's restaurant with Tems and several other graduates, had listened to a series of speeches, had received the hotel's business card and tucked it into her wallet.

"Of course," she said.

"Do you remember what we said to each other that day?"

She'd only exchanged a line or two with Tems, who had been seated at the opposite end of the table. "I told you, 'Congrats on marrying our work.'"

He smiled at her. "And I told you, 'Thanks for coming to my wedding.'"

They both had to chuckle at the memory, and Sydney found herself missing that more innocent version of themselves. They were so young and so eager to get out in the field, so excited to dedicate their entire lives to this profession, so clueless over what that sacrifice really meant.

"I shouldn't have left you behind in Stockholm," he said after a pause.

She glanced at him. "Why did you leave so suddenly, anyway?"

"A friend of mine had been killed that night." He stared out at the city. "I had to act quickly, before his attacker got away."

Killed in action. So that was the reason. "I'm sorry," she said.

"It's all part of marrying this job, isn't it?"

"You never told me."

He gave her a sidelong look. "You know I couldn't have."

And he was right, of course. They had grown closer during that unexpected tryst, their paths intersecting longer than they should have. Tems was never meant to share the details of that mission with her.

"I know," she replied.

"It's hard to have casual conversations," he went on, "when you don't know whether or not you'll live or die the next day."

She imagined what might happen tomorrow, how a million things could go wrong. How they might not make it out at the end. She remembered the stricken look in Winter's eyes, the fear that had shot through his expression after the first attempt on her life. This was familiar ground, at least, this not knowing. Tonight might be the last time she exchanged words with any of them.

"It's all part of marrying this job," she said, echoing his earlier words.

Tems nodded. "If it weren't," he said, "I'd ask you if you'd like to go on a date sometime. I'd ask you what your favorite restaurant was, what you like to eat." He gave her a crooked smile in the night. "I'd ask you if you wanted to stay over, or if you wanted to take it slow."

Sydney didn't know what to say to that. Was there anything? She found herself thinking of Winter, of the impossibility of being together. Sometimes, she had a fantasy of what it would be like if they just stepped away from their lives right now. Him from the spotlight, her from the secret world. What it would be like if they could just disappear together into the crowded street outside of their hotel, safe in the anonymity of a mass of humanity.

In another life, that could be the easiest decision in the world.

But it wasn't—they were in this life, and in this life, the scenario was impossible. So what was the point of thinking it? She and Winter had less than twelve hours left together on this mission, and after that stretched another unknown period of time, where she might not see him again for months, maybe years.

Or maybe ever again.

But Tems, at least, walked in the shadows like she did. He understood the nature of her work, knew what could happen and what couldn't. He didn't hang on to wild dreams in the way Winter did. He didn't have that optimism and poetry in his heart. Tems could have a fling and move on without a word. He saw the world the way it was. They could meet on and off for their entire career, if Sydney let them, if they decided to do it.

Maybe Sydney couldn't imagine a love life, but she could imagine a halfway love with Tems, in the way Sauda and Niall managed—nothing exclusive, nothing permanent, just the occasional meetup whenever their missions intersected. A lifetime of unspoken, knowing glances and speaking in secrets.

The thought did not excite her. But she could see herself doing it. She could find small moments of joy in that.

"Are you trying to ask me something, Tems?" she said quietly.

He smiled wryly at her. "An agent never asks directly," he replied. "They only know what makes sense."

What makes sense. And, in a way, they did. She let them stay where they were, standing apart, not speaking. Maybe this was the better, more sensible way.

"If we survive," she said.

"If we survive," he echoed. "So let's try to make it through."

She thought of Winter again, felt the knife twisting in her heart. Then she rebuilt the steel walls around herself, until the fire that consumed her every time she was with him chilled against the metal, trapped and contained. She let the fire wither until it was nothing but ash and deadwood littering the floor of her chest.

Maybe it was for the best that she'd left Winter behind. Best to turn around early on a dead-end street before you walked the entire length of it.

When the wind blew again, Sydney straightened. "Let's just make it through," she agreed.

Showdown

The Istana, the official home of Singapore's president, had been draped for the gala that evening in long red and white banners, the country's national colors, and soldiers in matching uniforms stood in two lines leading from the golden gates to the marble steps leading up to the building's grand entrance. The colors contrasted boldly with the lush green foliage that framed the palace at every corner. Lining the top of the steps were members of the national guard, rifles hoisted against their shoulders.

Gavi walked in silence next to Winter. The fight they'd had the night before was fresh in Winter's mind, but the mission was still on, and that meant he still had a part to play with her at his side. He didn't look at her, though, and she didn't look at him. They walked without touching hands, pretending to admire the decorations in the palace.

Winter's custom suit stood out against the bursts of color. It only made him feel more exposed, as if he might see a target on the fabric at any moment. Behind him, Sydney kept a reasonable distance, looking more severe today in her bodyguard's suit, her hair pulled tightly back with a long pin tucked through it. Her gaze was trained on a corner or a hall or a cluster of people, never on him. But he couldn't help lingering on her, and now, as she passed between a red, flowering vine and was momentarily shrouded in crimson, he imagined it as a scarlet dress trailing behind her. It didn't matter what she was wearing, really. There were hundreds of guests here draped in luxury, but none of them stood out to him like she did.

He turned away and took a deep breath. Maybe it was for the best that their mission would end today. He could go home, Gavi could go her separate way, and he and Sydney wouldn't have to deal with the messiness they had unearthed between them.

The thought still left a pang in his heart.

Servers in flowing robes bustled in and out of the reception hall, offering the entering guests platters of ice-cold fruits and champagne. Winter took glasses of champagne for him and Gavi, then handed one to her as politely as he could muster.

"Thanks," she muttered.

He didn't reply. Instead, his eyes darted beyond the reception hall to the long entryway past the main doorway, where security gathered thick.

They were everywhere he looked—police in suits and sunglasses, talking quietly to each other on their earpieces, their eyes jumping to each guest in suspicion before they bowed politely and looked away. He wondered if any of them were the CIA agents in disguise that Tems had mentioned. He wondered if Niall was on the grounds, if he had already parked his car in preparation for helping them get to the airfield and waiting plane.

It seemed hard to believe that any assassination could be attempted in a place like this. But as they headed into the main hall, Tems came into view, his face an unwelcome reminder of all the things that had to go right in order for them to call this mission a success.

He was dressed tonight like the US president's entourage, his black suit blending him in with the rest of the bodyguards and assistants. As they approached, Tems smiled.

"Mr. Young!" he said with a smile. "Everyone in my family is a fan of yours. What a pleasure to see you tonight."

The sight of him made Winter's stomach lurch in anticipation of their plan. He chanced a glance at Sydney. Tems had ignored her completely, of course, and she'd done the same. Her lips were tight, her calm expression veiling tension in her step. Her eyes flickered to him, and at his gaze, her lips pressed tighter.

She looked away as they glided past Tems. As Sydney passed him, though, Winter saw him slide something small into the pocket of her suit. She didn't pause at all, but her hand went into her pocket to check that she had received it.

Of course Winter knew what Tems was doing—handing her a ticket that they would need when Winter made his move. But the jealousy rose hot and swift in his chest all the same. The memory of Sydney's vulnerable gaze from the night before flooded his thoughts, and Winter swallowed hard, forcing himself to keep the smile on his face and follow the stream of guests farther into the palace.

"Hey," Gavi said in a low voice as they reached the end of the hall, stopping in front of the coat check desk. "I don't want us to spend the entire night lingering on this whole mess about your father. I'm sorry. I really, truly am. I never should have agreed to it."

He sighed, his eyes fixed on the main atrium that they now entered. "Let's just walk together and pretend like we're cordial, all right?"

Gavi straightened and frowned. "So all the headlines tomorrow are gossiping about how miserable we looked?"

"It'd be nice if there were no headlines at all, because no one cares."

Gavi sighed. When he looked at her, she seemed sober, her face unusually serious. "Look, Winter," she said quietly. "I don't know how to apologize for last night."

"For starters," he said coldly, "you could stop working with my dad."

"I've stopped. I promise."

"I don't believe you."

"Winter, please." She struggled for words for a moment. "I know I owe you a favor after all that. Maybe a lot of favors. I'm sorry. Can't we talk about it?"

He sighed. "You know, it's always a game with you."

Her expression darkened. "I'm not playing right now."

He turned away from her. "I just want this day to end," he said. "So we can go our separate ways. Let's leave it at that."

Gavi fell into a sullen silence as they headed into the banquet hall.

Round tables dotted the space, around which milled an assortment of guests, some of whom Winter recognized. There were presidents and foreign dignitaries, ambassadors wearing sashes in their nation's colors and celebrities sporting pins of their country's flags.

Winter searched for Rosen. The US president hadn't arrived yet.

"Laugh with me," he murmured to Gavi as they went.

Gavi, to her credit, transformed from her irritated, sullen state into a smiling girl with sparkling eyes. She giggled at him, one of her gloved hands coming up to cover her mouth.

Winter sensed Sydney turning to look at them—but when he glanced at her, she was focused on the banquet tables again.

They made their way amicably through the crowd before they finally reached one of the tables in the center of the room. There, they sat together at their place settings. As Gavi turned away to talk to one of their tablemates, an editor from a prominent French magazine, Winter looked around the room, searching for the people they were here to see. His heart pounded steadily against his ribs, and he could hear a roar in his ears, as if his body were bracing itself for impact.

A soft nudge from Sydney's boot under the table made him turn his head toward her. She turned her head slightly to her right as she sipped her water.

There. He could see Minister Seah standing a few feet from his banquet table, laughing at something that the ambassador from Argentina was saying. A short distance away, flanked by two bodyguards, President Rosen chatted casually with several other heads of state.

A tingle of anticipation ran down his spine. The president had shown up, and Winter needed to make his move soon.

Sydney leaned toward Winter, as if they were deep in conversation. As she did, she pulled out what Tems had given her. It was a small red ticket, and on it was written a number.

4262

The ticket was printed twice, as if the attendant had failed to rip it in two. Sydney made a show of frowning visibly, then leaned toward his ear. If anyone was watching them, they'd just think it was an error on a ticket. "The valet code for Seah's hat and umbrella," she replied.

Winter nodded, a knot forming in his throat. It was his cue; he would use the code to approach Seah and get him to follow Winter to where Tems had CIA agents lying in wait to arrest him.

Sydney met his eyes. The awkwardness between them faded, and for a moment, they looked at each other meaningfully. "Ready?" she said.

Winter didn't answer, but he gave a nearly imperceptible nod, then touched her hand briefly before sitting straight and glancing around the chamber. At his side, Gavi paused in her conversation with the editor to look up at him.

"Don't stare, keep moving," Sydney murmured to Winter, her eyes downcast as she took one more sip of her water. "Now that Seah's here, the clock's ticking."

He did as Sydney said, his eyes skimming right past where the president now stopped to smile and shake hands with the Singaporean prime minister. He was about to take his seat. Beside him, Seah had already settled into his own chair.

Just like a performance, Winter recited to himself. Then they rose from their table in unison, Sydney falling into step right behind him as his bodyguard, and headed down the hall.

As they arrived back at the coat check, the clerk saw Winter, and the light of recognition went off in her eyes. Winter saw her lips quiver slightly as she smiled, then offered him a polite nod.

"Back again, Mr. Young?" she said.

He smiled at her, his nerves now hidden behind a veil of charisma. Beside him, Sydney put her hands together and waited quietly. "I'm heading out onto the deck for the sunset," he told the clerk conspiratorially, rubbing one of his sleeves for emphasis. "Thought I'd get my hat back."

She nodded in hurried agreement. "Code, sir?"

"Forty-two sixty-two," he said, handing her the ticket from Sydney.

She took it, then hurried off to the back room. A moment later, she returned with the deep blue top hat that belonged to Seah.

Winter's heart hammered in his chest, but on the surface, he gave her a thoughtful frown. "Ah," he said. "I don't think that's mine."

Her eager face transformed into one of mortification. She looked at the hat again, as if willing it to change. "Oh! I'm terribly sorry about the mix-up. The correct ticket must have been handed to another patron."

"It's okay," Winter said, holding his hand out for the hat. "I recognize it—it belongs to Mr. Seah. He probably has my ticket."

"I'm so sorry," the clerk said again, her cheeks flushed. She handed the hat to Winter, and Winter flipped it around his hand with a flourish before grabbing it.

"No worries," he said, winking at her. "I saw him in the dining hall."

Then he turned and went back the way he came. Sydney walked beside him, her position tight now against him. Her sleeve brushed against his purposefully, as if she were offering him encouragement.

So far, so good, he thought.

As he headed back into the dining hall, he saw that the president was now seated at his table. Odd. The president should have moved out of the dining hall by now. From the corner of his eye, he could see Sydney's slight frown too as she noticed the same thing.

Winter let his eyes rove around the room, as if he weren't sure where Seah was, until settling on where the man was ordering a drink at the bar.

"Mr. Seah?" Winter said as he approached him.

The man turned calmly to him, but something stiff about his movements and the brief widening of his eyes told Winter that he'd probably been startled by the approach. He quickly masked it with a smile, his eyes darting from Winter to Sydney. "Mr. Young!" he exclaimed, holding a hand out in greeting. "I thought I saw you coming in. What a wonderful concert you put on yesterday."

Will I survive you? Winter thought grimly, but he flashed an easy smile and shook his hand warmly. As he did, he saw Seah's eyes jump to the hat in his hand.

"Always glad to have impressed a fan," Winter replied with a wink. Then he gestured at the hat and gave Seah an apologetic look. "I'm so sorry to bother you right before the dinner starts, but I think the attendant may have mixed up our tickets. Is this yours?"

He nodded and took the hat. "That's the one."

"I thought I recognized it from when you headed inside," Winter said. "Would you mind if we . . . ?" He nodded back toward the coat check hall.

Seah glanced once at the bartender, who held up his finished drink to let him know he'd save it for him. There was the slightest hint of hesitation, and Winter noticed the man's eyes dart briefly to his table, where the president sat. "No worries," he finally said. Then he headed for the corridor with Winter at his side.

"I didn't know the sun set so early here," Winter remarked, trying to keep Seah distracted with small talk as they went.

Winter noticed how the man's eyes skipped around the hall, searching. "Everyone thinks that," Seah answered. "As if the heat means sunshine around the clock, eh?"

Now every muscle in his body seemed tense. Winter's own gaze hopped to the end of the corridor, where Tems should be readying the agents to pounce.

"One can hope," Winter said with a light shrug, and Seah laughed.

But as they reached the coat check, Seah seemed to hesitate. He nodded at the clerk and brushed a nervous hand across his forehead. "It seems like we've switched tickets," he said, fumbling around in his pocket for a ticket. "And I don't know where mine's gone. I got this one."

The clerk took his hat and went to the back room to retrieve Winter's. As she did, Seah gave Winter an uncomfortable smile, one that Winter returned.

The plot was closing now. Winter could see the time ticking away on the man's face, could see that with every passing second, his nerves tightened a little more, knowing that Winter was cutting into his plan's time.

Hurry up, Tems, Winter thought.

The clerk didn't re-emerge. Seah shuffled from foot to foot, let out a frustrated laugh, and nodded at Winter. "Their valet service leaves something to be desired, doesn't it?" he muttered.

Winter chuckled in agreement. But he knew that it must mean that Tems had successfully made contact with the clerk. The Americans would be out in the hall soon.

Suddenly, at the last minute, Seah began walking abruptly down the corridor, away from the dining hall.

Beside him, Sydney tensed. *Go,* her body language seemed to say.

"Mr. Seah?" Winter said, and fell quickly into step behind him. The man was trying to make a getaway.

Seah didn't answer. Instead, he broke into a run. He had sniffed out the trap.

Now, Tems! Winter wanted to scream. *What are you waiting for?*

"Mr. Seah, wait!" he called out.

The man ignored him and rounded a corner. For an instant, Winter thought the trap would fail—he was about to escape. Thoughts flashed through his mind. What if he tackled Seah? Would that blow their cover?

Just when he was about to lunge—

They turned the corner and stuttered to a halt.

Half a dozen CIA agents—some dressed in black, others in gala clothes as attendees—were blocking the hall right before the main entrance, guns drawn and pointed straight at Seah.

"Hands up!" one of them snapped.

Seah turned around, eyes wild, and bolted back down the corridor, straight at Winter.

Sydney moved on instinct, blocking the man's sprint. With a snarl, he lunged at her in a desperate attempt to get her out of the way. Sydney's defense lessons flashed through Winter's mind—in an instant, he was at her side, his arms going up to defend her.

But the agents were on the man before he could make his attack. Seah had only a second to look Winter in the eye, bewildered, before he went down, shoved to the marble floor by two agents. The man let out a choked sob as one of the agents pressed his knee harshly into his back.

Winter could feel the rush of adrenaline surging in his limbs, leaving him shaking. He looked up to see Tems standing nearby now—where had he come from? His eyes turned to meet Winter's.

Winter felt a torrent of relief flood his veins and an overwhelming desire to collapse. It was over.

As the agents hauled Seah to his feet and clipped handcuffs on his wrists and ankles, Tems flashed Winter a smile. It was there and gone in a second, so as not to tie Winter to them—but in it was all the ease that Winter had suddenly felt.

Ethan Seah was under arrest. The president was safe back in the dining hall.

But when Winter looked over at Sydney, she seemed bothered, something clouding her face instead of the relief that he expected to see.

"What is it?" he said.

"Something's not right," she replied.

He had no idea what she meant. But they had no time to stop and think now. As the agents surrounded Seah, Tems hurried over to them both. "We need to get out of here," he whispered to Sydney. "Got a flight to catch."

But Sydney had already turned her back and was rushing toward the dining hall.

Winter exchanged a confused look with Tems, but neither of them hesitated in following in her wake.

She knows something, Winter thought, *and she has no time to tell us.*

They passed the hall they were supposed to use to exit the building. Where the hell was Sydney taking them? They had exactly thirty minutes to reach the airfield and get back on the plane.

Right as they turned into the dining hall, Winter felt Sydney touch his sleeve. "No," she gasped out.

He glanced wildly around, looking for the source of her reaction.

His eyes went to where President Rosen was still seated. That was when the feeling of triumph vanished from Winter's chest.

As he looked, he saw the president suddenly freeze, as if he'd seen something.

Beside Winter, Tems jerked forward, as if to make a move.

But it was too late. At that moment, there was a sharp, unmistakable *pop*.

The president flinched. Winter saw crimson stain the man's jacket. Screams went up near him.

Then President Rosen collapsed, red blossoming on his chest.

19

Enemies on All Sides

Sydney knew something wasn't right the instant the CIA agents tackled Seah to the floor. She could feel the hairs prickling on the back of her neck.

He was supposed to have taken the hall to the right, she thought. The intel they'd been given was that Seah's escape route was the building's side entrance, where his car was waiting.

But right before the agents tackled him, he had turned abruptly to escape out the main entrance. There were no cars out the main entrance—the only people allowed there were security guards. He would have run headfirst into an onslaught of police.

Why would he do that?

Sydney had stared at the man on the floor as handcuffs went on him, a frown on her face. *Unless he wasn't operating alone,* she thought. Someone else was here.

"What is it?" Winter had asked her.

"Something's not right," she'd replied.

But she couldn't articulate it in the moment. She was just trying to figure out why Seah had changed his route, why when he lay on the floor, his eyes had turned wildly to the main entrance, as if expecting someone out there to intervene and help him.

The sixth sense in Sydney's mind had tingled so violently that she'd turned back in the direction of the dining hall. Had rushed there with Winter on her heels.

And then—had seen the president go down, had seen him collapse as the people around him jumped to their feet, screaming. Over by their own table, Gavi had darted upright and cupped her hands around her mouth in horror.

Had he been killed? Sydney had caught a glimpse of the president's hand over his chest, blood streaking his skin, seen his eyes roll up as security swarmed over him. It was enough of a glance to sink her heart.

Enough for her to see that the shot was fatal. That the man was dead.

Sydney faced Winter and Tems. "Go," she said harshly, then nodded at Winter. "You need to get Gavi out of here."

Winter was already moving. She caught the slightest hint of him nodding at her over his shoulder before he rushed off to Gavi, pulling her arm as she stood frozen by the sight and guiding her along with the stream of panicking guests toward the front entrance.

Tems was already turning back, his expression stricken. Within the minute, the entire building would be locked down—and they would be trapped. Security guards were already rushing past them as they flooded into the dining hall, while others at the front entrance had scattered across the front courtyard to search for anyone who might be connected.

Sydney's mind whirled as they ran. There was no question that the man was supposed to be behind it, that he was meant to be the one to carry out the assassination. They had thwarted that attempt. But Seah had clearly been working with others, and someone else at the party had fired a shot at Rosen.

But there was no time for Sydney to untangle it any further, nothing they could do for the president now. They had to get out and find Niall.

Tems reached the end of the hall first before he halted and started doubling back.

"Try the east wing," he said breathlessly. "They've already locked this one down."

They turned without hesitation and followed him. All around them were startled guests, many trying to find a way to escape the mystery shooter—but security at every exit blocked their steps. As they rushed past, Sydney could hear snatches of other languages as the guards apologized to various heads of state and politicians, telling them no one could enter or leave the property right now. Those guests, in turn, shouted heatedly at the guards, some pushing against their raised rifles.

The situation was quickly devolving.

The static in her earpiece abruptly came to life.

"We're coming," she said breathlessly.

"Hurry it up, Jackal," Niall answered. His voice sounded tight, with the kind of efficient calm he always seemed to display when things went terribly wrong.

"Two minutes!" she called back.

Suddenly, Tems halted before reaching the hall they were supposed to take. He swore.

"Soldiers at the end," he said.

Sydney glanced down the corridor to see the first few guards arriving at the far side of the hall, their guns drawn as one of them shouted orders. "Change of plans," she muttered, then veered sideways, heading now toward the back exit.

"What's happening?"

Gavi's breathless, panicked voice suddenly came into range, and Sydney turned to see Winter rushing up with her beside him. Her eyes were wide, pupils dilated in terror, and for the first time since Sydney had met her, she didn't look composed and ready for whatever situation she might find herself in. Her arms shook visibly.

"Was that the president?" she went on, her voice pinched with fright. She glanced at Winter before looking back at Sydney. "Was that a gunshot? I saw blood—"

"Take our car," Winter interrupted as he threw his jacket around her shoulders and guided her toward the main entrance. "Go now, before the situation deteriorates."

She turned wild eyes on him. "Just me?" she exclaimed. "What about you?"

He shook his head. "Too many prying eyes. I'll find my own ride. *Go now.* I'll call you."

He flashed Sydney a look, and the two of them exchanged a knowing glance. Winter couldn't go back yet with Gavi, not when there might be a sniper out in the bushes looking for him and Sydney. Sydney nodded at him, and he led Gavi to the parking attendant waiting at the main entrance, who ushered her down the stairway.

She looked back again at Winter, bewildered and terrified, before she disappeared from view.

Winter waited until she'd gotten into her car, then rushed back to Sydney and Tems. "What now?" he said in a low voice.

"Winter Young!" someone exclaimed.

Sydney glanced up to see one of the prime minister's aides running toward her.

"Convenient," Tems snapped, shooting Winter a hostile glare.

Winter returned the glare before he gave the aide a polite nod. "What's going on?" he asked, as if he were unaware.

The aide looked pale as a sheet, beads of sweat clinging to his forehead. He pointed back into the dining hall. "There's been a shooting," he said breathlessly. "I suggest you get to somewhere safe, sir. Follow me."

Winter stopped him before he could start dragging all of them back down the wrong hall. "I need a quiet place to get hold of my manager," he said. "Can you tell me how I can get to the nearest bathroom?"

The aide blinked at him, his eyes still wild with panic, then nodded and pointed in the direction of the back entrance. "Then I suggest you get to the front, sir," he said. "The guards are stopping everyone, but tell them it's urgent."

"Thank you," Winter nodded. Then the aide sprinted away, his encounter with Winter forgotten.

Sydney let out a breath. "Bathroom?" she said.

"When I went in there, they had small windows above the sink," he replied.

She nodded at Winter. Then they were off again. Sydney could hear Tems's grumbling even as they ran.

"The soldiers will be onto us before we can get out," he said.

"Name a better escape route, and we'll take it," she shot back.

The corridor to the bathrooms was quieter than those for the exits. As they turned and saw the two narrow bathroom doors, Sydney heard orders being barked out from a soldier in the dining hall. No one was going to leave this building for hours, at least—already, news about the US president's death must be filtering out to the rest of the world. They had little time to reach Niall, even less time for him to take them to the airfield.

Sydney reached the bathroom door first and shoved it open. Sure enough, a small, narrow window was situated above the sink, partially obscured by the green canopy of a fat-leaved tree.

She shot Winter a look as they ran to the sink. He looked like he was hanging back, as if he might not come.

"You can't stay here," she breathed. "Not by yourself."

"Claire will be calling immediately when she hears about what happened," he replied. "She'll panic if she can't get ahold of me."

"And she'll panic even more if you get yourself killed here. Have you forgotten who you are?" She nodded at him. "Come with us. For now. Please. I can't keep you safe if you're on your own. And Gavi already took your car."

He hesitated, and in that hesitation, Sydney realized that he was afraid to jeopardize her life, that he thought his presence might compromise them. Then the image of him being sniped from a tree flashed through her mind, of him being here without so much as a bodyguard to protect him while there were assassins on the loose.

"Come with me," she said again, her voice low and pleading.

Winter paused a second longer. Then he followed in her wake.

With little effort, Sydney jumped onto the sink's porcelain rim and grab the bottom ledge of the window. Her fingers ran along the bottom of the glass, then curled into a fist.

"Cover your eyes," she called to the boys below.

Then she stripped off her suit jacket and bundled it thickly around her hand.

She punched the window as hard as she could.

The glass shuddered and cracked. She punched it again, and this time, she felt the glass give away against her hand, raining down in pieces. She knocked a few more of the shards off before she removed the bundled jacket from her fist and flattened the clothing against the jagged bottom edge of the window.

When she glanced down to check on the others, Winter nodded for her to go first.

The side garden that they managed to crawl out into was still empty, but Sydney could hear the soldiers shouting at each other at the front and back gates. *Shit,* she swore to herself as she eyed the gate. They'd need to scale this fence to get to the other side, where she could jury-rig a car for their escape.

"I'll boost you," Tems muttered as he emerged behind her through the window. Winter followed shortly after, grabbing Sydney's jacket as they went.

Sydney shook the glass shards from her jacket with one efficient flap and pulled it back on. Tems hurried to the gate and knelt there, hands ready. Sydney ran toward him. Her shoe landed in Tems's hands, and she felt his boost lift her as she reached for the top of the gate. She grabbed it with one hand.

The exertion sent a ripple of pain through her lungs, but she ignored it and hauled herself over the edge.

Immediately, her gaze settled on a parked car across the street, with an official license plate. A Singaporean government car. Inside, she saw the giant, unmistakable silhouette of Niall waiting for them.

Somehow, the familiar sight of him sent a rush of adrenaline through Sydney. At least he'd made it here—all they had to do was reach him. Maybe he would have an update from the CIA about what had gone wrong, something she knew they'd be in heated discussions over once they were in the air. No doubt he and Tems would have a shouting match about the mission—not that it would matter now.

Not now that the president was dead.

But she didn't have time to dwell on it. Niall must have spotted them at the same time, because the car lit up and reversed in their direction. All of her focus now zeroed in on the car, and she broke into a sprint at the same time as the rest. Maybe she couldn't solve this mission alone, or even with Winter and Tems—but with Panacea, they'd get to the bottom of this. They would find a way to solve the chaos that was about to engulf the world.

Then—

—from the corner of the palace, right out of sight—

—a second car came speeding straight at Niall's.

Sydney only had time to skid to a halt before the second car smashed, full-speed, into him with a deafening crash.

The force was so great that Niall's car flipped into the air, landing on its roof with a crunch of breaking glass and metal.

A scream tore out of Sydney's throat. "Niall!"

At the same time, Winter started bolting for the car. "Get him out!" he shouted.

Inside the car, Sydney caught a glimpse of Niall's clean-shaven face, dazed and dripping with blood, his body hanging upside down in his seat, held in place only by his seat belt. His head turned slightly in their direction, and his eyes found Sydney.

Sydney's horrified gaze met his grim one. Somehow, in this split second of a moment, she suddenly felt herself turn back into the person she was at fifteen, arriving at Panacea for the first time with Niall at her side, him vouching for her during the orientation, then her graduating from her program, Sauda saying her name, Niall handing her a folder and shaking her hand.

You're going to cause some good trouble, kid, he'd told her with a smile.

"Stop! *Stop!*"

It was Tems. He had caught up to Winter and yanked him backward, forcing him off balance so that he stumbled to the ground. Tems flung his other arm out sideways at Sydney. "*Get down!*" he screamed. His eyes locked in helpless desperation on his former mentor—

—and then on the second car, devoid of a driver.

Sydney halted, right as the car exploded.

Nowhere to Run

20

Whenever things devolved into chaos, Sydney's brain went on autopilot, and she saw time happen in snatches. In stills.

She experienced it now, this jolty, surreal, stilted moment. Chunks of metal and glass burning on the grass. Her view from the ground as she looked up at the flaming remains of the wreckage that contained Niall's body. Winter staring, stunned into silence, at the scene. Tems rushing toward the two cars, only to throw his hands up in defense as another explosion sent more fire and smoke in every direction.

Get up! Move!

She could hear Niall's voice in her thoughts, as if he were shouting at her, saving her even now. Sydney forced herself to her feet. Her ears rang. She reached out to Winter and seized his hand, yelled at him to come with her. She heard herself calling to Tems, who had already turned around and was running back toward them. Had he not shouted at them to stop, they would have all been caught in the firestorm.

Sydney's mind struggled to process it.

That was no accidental crash. She recognized the ferocity of the eruption as surely as if she were back in training, watching controlled experiments of various explosives in Panacea's underground facility. Niall had been killed by a professional device planted on the second car that had engulfed him in the blast.

Someone had murdered him.

All this time, she had been thinking of her own safety—Niall had been worried for her—when she should have been afraid for him.

Through hazy vision blurred with tears, she heard Tems's voice.

"We have to get out of here!" he shouted.

Their escape. Sydney's body kicked into high gear. The three of them sprinted across the lawn away from the explosion.

There. She saw another parked car along the street, with an official license plate. Winter must have seen the car at the same time, because they moved in sync toward it.

As soon as Sydney reached it, she snatched the long pin out of her hair and began working on the door handle.

"Two o'clock," Tems said as he caught up to them, and Sydney looked up. A guard had noticed them and pointed in their direction in the midst of the chaos. "Hurry up, Syd."

"Hurrying," she snapped, her voice hoarse.

As she went, her mind whirled. It was obvious someone else at the event was working with Seah—but Niall? Why did they want him dead?

The same mysterious reason they'd wanted Sydney dead. Why Tems had gone into hiding. Someone was targeting Panacea in order to silence them.

At last, Sydney heard the car door open with a gratifying pop. She immediately hopped into the driver's seat. Winter slid into the passenger side at the same time, while Tems went to the back.

"Who's the best driver in here?" Winter muttered.

"Me," Sydney and Tems said in unison. She glared at him through the rearview mirror.

"I've been in this city for three months. I know it like the back of my hand," Tems said. "Switch with me after it starts."

"Fine." Sydney pried open the car's ignition panel and stared at the tangle of wires.

The faint sound of sirens from the front of the estate now reached their ears. More police and emergency vehicles had been called in. If they didn't move within the next thirty seconds, they ran the real risk of being blockaded in on this side street.

"Come on," Sydney whispered to the car as she worked.

Seconds later—it felt like a lifetime—the car rewarded her with a satisfyingly smooth roar of ignition. Winter hopped out from the passenger side to the back seat, she slid nimbly to where he'd been, and Tems jumped forward into the driver's position.

"Go," Sydney snapped at Tems.

"We're already late," Tems replied. He stepped on the gas—they all jerked back against their seats as the car shot forward down the road.

"Easy, Tems," Sydney said through gritted teeth. "We're trying not to attract attention, remember?"

Tems eased the car into a legal speed limit, then glanced at her with a wry grimace. "I think we might be past stealth, sweetheart."

Then they reached a roundabout, and Sydney's retort died on her tongue as a police car turned at the opposite end of the traffic circle.

For a moment, the police car seemed to pause, as if watching them make their way around the turn. Through the rearview mirror, Sydney saw Winter's head turn slightly to keep the car in view.

"Don't look," she reminded him, her face turned resolutely in the direction of the road.

Winter followed her advice in an instant. As he did, she held her breath, waiting for the police car to turn with them and follow.

But at the other side of the roundabout, it went on in the direction of the gala building. Securing the estate must overrule anything else right now, she guessed.

Adrenaline was still surging through her veins, making her tremble all over. Now that their immediate flight was over, now that they were inside a car—Sydney could feel it overwhelming her, making her dizzy. She reached up over and over to wipe tears from her face. When she looked at Winter, she saw his face stunned into blankness, pale from shock. He was looking down at his phone.

"Claire?" she asked.

He nodded wordlessly. "No signal," he answered.

Tems shook his head, his face pale and stricken. "Who'd set up Niall like that?" he murmured.

Silence hung heavy in the car at his question.

Winter swallowed and said, "Maybe the same person who set up Seah."

"The bigger question is *why*," Sydney said.

"What do you mean?" Winter asked.

"Why bother creating two plans?" she went on, her voice still shaking. "It succeeded in leading us astray—but it also meant putting your enemies on high alert that something would happen to the president on this evening. It meant the gala had been crawling with soldiers and security, which would have made the entire operation trickier to execute. Better to have just a single plan and launch it as a shock." Her eyes met Winter's. "So why the trouble? Why not make it easier for themselves?"

"Unless this *was* easier," Winter replied.

Sydney turned back around in her seat. "It's not easier," she murmured. But Winter's answer echoed in her head until she realized that maybe he wasn't wrong.

Unless this was *easier.*

"They must want everyone to suspect a different person," Tems said as he pulled onto a freeway. "They wanted everyone to know, first of all, that Seah—who we were guided to target—was *not* the assassin. Then they wanted everyone to know that someone else *was*."

"What's the point of that?" Winter said.

"To set someone up," Tems replied. "Now the entire country is on a manhunt for who the president's real killer is, and who else might be behind the operation. When they find their culprit, they'll get the consequences they were aiming for."

"Don't look back," Winter suddenly said.

Sydney didn't. But she froze in her seat at his words. "Why?" she asked.

"The police car from that roundabout," Winter said calmly, his face forward in the rearview mirror. "It's behind us."

Sydney glanced up—and sure enough, there was the car, with the same license plate as the police vehicle that had been at the roundabout.

"*Shit*," Tems swore.

Sydney glanced at Tems. "Are we going as fast as possible?"

"As fast as possible?" Tems's face darkened. "Do you not remember how fast we were going during a motorcycle course in training? Of course I can go faster than this." Then he floored the gas pedal, and they shot forward.

Sydney clung to the sides of her seat with all her strength as they rocketed up to the taillight of the car in front of them, then swerved out of the way at the last second.

Behind them, the police car disappeared over the bend of the road.

Tems tapped on his phone, then tossed it aside in frustration. "Can't reach the CIA."

"Can you reach Sauda?" Winter asked Sydney.

"Trying," Sydney answered, looking down at her phone. She couldn't bear to think about Sauda's voice on the phone, about having to break the news to her. But the connectivity had already been low at the event. It was nonexistent now—and as they drove on, she saw the bars drop to nothing. An error message popped up on her screen.

Please still be at the airfield, she thought.

Tems glanced over at her. "If our attackers are targeting Panacea, then they might know about the airfield." He stared gloomily out at the road. "What time is it?"

"Eighteen twenty-two," Sydney said.

He nodded. "We're within the time limit that Sauda gave us—and at this pace, we'll arrive within the half hour."

Sydney found herself nodding along. He was right, of course. They'd be in the air long before any authorities could stop them. But no thought of escape could bring any of them relief. All this time and effort. All the sacrifice, arguments, fights—just for it to end horrifically. The president was dead. The diplomatic fallout from this would be catastrophic.

But Sydney couldn't even think about that right now. She could only think of Niall.

Niall was gone. Had died right before her eyes. She couldn't stop seeing the explosion over and over, couldn't stop remembering the dazed look in his eyes as he turned his gaze to Sydney, blood trickling down his face.

And that moment, right before the explosion, he'd looked like he knew he was going to die.

"There will be war," Winter said, his voice so quiet that Sydney could barely hear him. "Won't there?"

Tems gave him a subtle nod in the mirror. "If we're lucky, it will happen from a distance."

Sydney looked out the window at the airfield that now came into view and wondered, as her adrenaline surge began to level out, what *distance* really meant. What was the point, if everyone else would be swept up in it? If they hadn't accomplished what they came here to do?

As they pulled off the freeway, the tension in her gut surged again. Her eyes searched the airfield for the plane that Niall had described. *A Cessna Citation Longitude,* she told herself, looking for the airframe. He had said it would be parked here, at the east end of the private field, waiting for their arrival.

But all she saw was an empty field.

Other planes were in their hangars. The only aircraft in sight were two commercial liners waiting at their gates. But no other planes were here.

The tension in her gut churned into white-hot dread.

"It's not here," she whispered as they slowed to a stop at the end of the airfield.

Tems stared at the runway, his face pale. "It has to be here," he argued, searching for a plane that didn't exist.

Winter said nothing. He looked not at the field, but at Sydney, and as their eyes met in the rearview mirror, they seemed to telegraph the same sinking realization.

Panacea's plane had been forced to leave them behind.

21

On Your Own

The international airport has been locked down," Tems said as he scrolled through the news on his phone. "I'm seeing confirmation online. No planes allowed to take off, and no cars allowed through any of the airport's exit points."

They were barred from the airport while the government executed a manhunt for the president's killer—and while Niall's killers were likely still targeting them.

"What do we do?" Winter asked. His head had turned back in the direction they'd come.

Sydney realized right away that he was looking for the police car to reappear. It was this gesture that snapped her mind back into focus. She touched Tems once on his shoulder. "We need a place to hide," she said, "and make contact with Sauda."

"Thought Panacea phones had an encrypted booster?" Tems said.

"They do." She waved the phone once impatiently. "This isn't a standard blackout."

Tems nodded as he glanced over his shoulder. "Hold tight," he muttered.

Sydney braced herself right as Tems slammed his foot down on the pedal. The car screamed in reverse out of the airfield's narrow entrance road, spinning in a tight circle before jerking forward down the street.

"Where can we go?" Winter asked.

"We stay in the car for now," Sydney said as she tried once again to dial out on her phone. "Come *on*!"

At last, an incoming message popped up on her screen from an unknown source.

Name? it said.

Jackal, Sydney typed back.

The message disappeared, and a second later, a hologram appeared of Sauda. The woman looked like she was deep in conversation with someone out of frame—until the call connected, and her eyes snapped over to Sydney as if the woman were sitting in the car between her and Tems.

With a sinking feeling, Sydney realized that Sauda hadn't heard about Niall yet.

The first thing Sauda did was swivel her gaze to Tems. "Oh, good," she said coolly, annoyed. "I'm glad you got ahold of the Arsonist, so that we can scold him properly once we get you all back to the States. We can't land your plane. Working on an alternative. Is Niall driving? Put him on."

Tems had no retort. They all answered with silence—and in that silence, Sauda's expression changed, sobered. She looked at Sydney. "What's happened?" she said.

"It's Niall," Sydney said. The rest of her sentence halted as her voice choked off, and she had to swallow hard to get past the tears rising in her eyes. "It's Niall, ma'am," she could only manage.

She didn't need to say the details. She didn't need to tell Sauda exactly what had happened. Sauda knew immediately what she meant.

For a moment, her expression froze. Her eyes flickered from Sydney to Tems, as if searching for confirmation, or perhaps some hint that Niall was alive, that she had misunderstood.

But they said nothing.

"How?" Sauda finally said, her voice low and still.

"Car explosion," Tems replied as Sydney struggled for more words. "As we were trying to escape."

Their answers sounded so disjointed, so messy. "Another car smashed into Niall's as he tried to pick us up," Sydney finally managed to say. "We couldn't get him out."

Sauda nodded, more to herself than to them. Her lips had straightened into a thin line. Sydney could see a gloss against her eyes, although the woman didn't cry. "Okay," she murmured. "Okay."

"I'm sorry, Sauda," Sydney whispered. "I'm so sorry."

Sauda glanced around the car again, her eyes settling on Winter. She nodded, acknowledging that all three of them were together, before turning back to Sydney with a sober expression.

"Asset's down," Sydney added. She knew Sauda would understand her real meaning. *President Rosen was dead.*

Sauda nodded. "We can't land the plane," she repeated. "We reached Singapore's airspace right as the assassination happened. They're scrambling phone towers. We'd actually gone into descent before we were forced back into the skies. All passports are currently suspended. No timeline on when airports will reopen."

"What about in the US?" Winter asked.

"News just went public about the president's assassination," Sauda replied. The woman seemed to be speaking in a daze, as if she hadn't quite processed Niall's death. Maybe none of them had. "We'll work on making sure the American government doesn't have you on their hit list—but we can't help you in Singapore, not yet. Singapore will suspect any US intelligence agent right now, given the political nature of this attack."

"They won't grant us clearance," Sydney said. "We'll need another way."

And right as she said it, she saw Winter nod in the rearview mirror and point at himself. "The other way," he said.

Sauda's eyes skipped to him. "Can you get them out?"

Winter thought for a second, then nodded. "I once had to get out of France after a volcanic eruption in Iceland grounded most flights. France granted me an exemption."

Sauda nodded. "Singapore will have less reason to suspect a superstar. They might let you through."

"Let's say they do," Sydney said. "Then what?"

"There's a private airfield about fifty kilometers northwest of where you currently are," Sauda said. Her hologram disappeared briefly to make way for a map. "In Kampung Ladang, Malaysia. As it's across country borders, it is still operational, last we checked." The map disappeared, and Sauda came back. She looked at Winter. "Tell Claire to send your private plane there."

"How do we get across the border?" Winter asked.

"They'll be on alert, too," Sauda said. "But you're the superstar. See what you can do."

"Are you serious?" Tems muttered.

"Do you want to leave the country or not?" Winter snapped.

"Enough," Sauda interjected. "Get there as soon as you can."

"What about Niall's killer?" Sydney said. They had avoided bringing him up, as if not mentioning him could somehow make his death a fiction. The thought was unbearable to her. "What about what happened?"

"Get yourselves to safety first," Sauda said brusquely, and Sydney stopped short. Sauda rarely lost her temper. In her words, she could hear an unspeakable grief. "Let's not add to the body count."

The transmission cut off before Sydney could say a proper goodbye. She put down her phone and glanced in the rearview mirror again. There were a few more vehicles on the road now.

Then one of the cars caught her eye. She went cold.

"I hate to burst everyone's bubble," she said quietly. "But that white car's following us."

Immediately after she said it, the white car suddenly accelerated toward them. At the speed it was going, it would collide with their bumper.

Tems didn't hesitate. He stepped hard on the gas pedal, then swerved wildly across the lanes, wedging them in front of a series of trucks. "If someone's after us," he said over the screeching of tires, "they're going to guess where we're going. We can't go to the airfield right now. Winter's plane isn't even ready. We need to lose them first."

"Can we do it?" Sydney asked him.

"Let me find a shortcut," he said.

As an exit ramp appeared, he careened down it, hugging the curve tightly until he reached an intersection. He didn't even hesitate at the stoplight—instead, he blew through it, leaving two cars spinning out of control. One nearly collided with them, but Tems swung the car sideways, drifting it through a narrow gap between the two cars, before steadying it again and hurtling down the road.

It looked like an industrial park, with a side road blocked off with road closure signs.

"Not closed anymore," he said. Then he rammed right into the signs.

They flew apart, and the car went skidding through a construction site. Workers shouted at each other to jump out of the way as they zoomed through.

Sydney glanced behind them. The white car pursuing them had fallen out of view, but a second car was tailing them now—the same police car that they'd seen at the roundabout near the gala building.

"Tems," she said, nodding behind her.

"I know, I know," he answered.

They made a sharp turn at the end of the construction site. The car's wheels lurched as they drove right inside a concrete pipe, the sound of their engine suddenly echoing against the stone walls. When they emerged from the other side, they were speeding toward a flimsy wire fence secured with a padlock.

Tems smashed right into it, sending the gates flying as he went.

They crashed through a section of dirt before skipping back onto a road heading in the airfield's direction.

That was when Sydney saw the line ahead.

"Police barricade," she shouted.

And sure enough, even from this distance, they could see the faint line of flashing lights, unmistakably that of a police cavalry. Her heart sank— the military had caught up to them. It would be impossible to reach the airfield now.

Tems spat out a swear and threw them into reverse. The car screeched to a halt, vaulted backward, and then turned before he sped off in the opposite direction. "Where to?" he shouted.

"Into the city," Winter shouted back.

"Are you crazy?"

"I've done press here before," Winter said. "We're ten kilometers out of downtown. If you can get into the city, we can lose them in Little India."

Little India. Sydney suddenly realized it was Sunday. She had been through the area before—it was a colorful, vibrant, busy place, full of markets and temples. And on Sundays at this hour, it would be crowded with worshippers and tourists, all flooding the streets to chat and shop. It would mean giving up entirely on their flight out of the country for the night, but at least they would have a chance to hide.

Tems narrowed his eyes at Winter through the rearview mirror. "You're going to get us all killed."

"Would you rather be arrested at the barricade?" Winter shot back. "It's impossible to get through—we can all see that!"

"He's right," Sydney snapped. *"Go!"*

Tems's grip tightened against the steering wheel as he turned the car at an intersection. They zoomed down the road as the flashing lights behind them followed.

As they turned up a hill, the skyscrapers of Singapore came back into view. The car clipped down a narrow road before Tems finally screeched to a stop at a traffic light. Elaborate light decorations hung in rows down the street. All around them were delivery vans and bustling stalls—workers hanging thick garlands of fresh flowers on hooks, fruit vendor displays piled high with bananas and honey mangoes, cooks selling vadai, daal, and dosai with chutney.

Behind them, they could hear the sound of sirens.

"That alley," Winter said, pointing to a narrow corridor branching off to the right of their intersection. "No lights there."

"Hang on," Tems said. Then he spun the steering wheel all the way to the right and swerved into the alley.

It didn't look like their car could fit down a path this narrow—but somehow Tems made it work, the space so tight that their mirrors scraped against either side. They made their way down the alley until they reached a narrow crevice against one wall that gave them a little more room. It wasn't exactly a parking spot, but they didn't have time to consider that now. Tems stopped the car and cut the engine.

They sat in silence as the sirens gradually drew nearer—then zoomed by, one after another. Sydney held her breath as the sound's pitch lowered, drew more distant.

They waited a little longer. The sirens turned faint, then disappeared.

At last, she exchanged a glance with Tems and Winter, then emerged from the car.

Night had started to fall, thankfully, covering them in deeper shadows. But Sydney knew they couldn't stay out here until morning, not with the entire country on high alert. They traveled as far as they could from where they had left the car behind, taking a myriad of small streets until they emerged into another narrow street, where she saw a neon sign for a small, nondescript hotel.

"Think we can get in through the back?" she said.

"How the hell are we going to get a room at a hotel?" Tems said. "They'll want IDs. Pretty sure we're on a government blacklist right now."

Sydney nodded at Winter.

Winter frowned at her. "You want me to charm our way into a room?"

Sydney crossed her arms. "Think you can do it without drawing a crowd around this place?"

Winter stared at her for a second. He shrugged. "You underestimate me."

Hiding in Plain Sight

22

At least one thing was going their way today: only a lone recep-
tionist sat behind the tiny hotel's check-in counter, her feet
propped up on a chair and her nose buried in a magazine.

Good, Winter thought as he stepped inside the hotel's lobby by
himself, his hands in his pockets and his walk a graceful, carefully
practiced stroll that everyone always seemed to comment on whenever
he was photographed. His boots clicked sharply against the linoleum
floors.

Somewhere in the back hall of the hotel were Sydney and Tems, listening carefully for Winter's conversation and waiting for the right time
to sneak up the stairs.

The girl didn't bother looking up from her magazine as he approached
the counter. She just muttered, "Two hundred sing a night."

Winter cleared his throat politely and tried to sound lighthearted.
"That sounds perfect," he said, taking out his wallet. "I don't have change,
though. Can you break a one-thousand sing note?"

The girl let out a sigh, muttered something under her breath about
change and discontinued bills, and straightened from her chair, her head
still buried in her magazine. "How many nights?" she asked.

"Just one," he said.

At last, she glanced up reluctantly at him. "Your ID—" she started to say.

Her words died on her tongue as her eyes settled on his face.

She seemed confused for a second, blinking rapidly—and then her eyes widened into round discs. Her mouth opened in a wide O.

Winter held up his hands. "Please don't scream," he said in a hushed voice. "I'm trying not to draw a mob in here."

She bobbed her head, her face still in shock. Her hands came up nervously to smooth her hair down. "Yes, yes, I'm sorry!" she exclaimed. "It's—you're—are you really *Winter Young*?"

He gave her an apologetic smile. His eyes darted to her name tag. "Miss Goh, if you could keep my location quiet, I won't stir up any chaos in your hotel. There's been a lockdown at the airport—"

"Yes," she said in a breathless rush. "I just heard on the news."

"I'll take two rooms, then, for my team. We're trying to figure out our transport in the morning."

She jumped as if scalded by hot water. "Right! Of course!" She shook her head, embarrassed at herself, and began scrambling for keys. While she prepared them, Winter saw her gaze hop over his shoulder, momentarily distracted by a movement.

Winter casually shifted to see the shadow of Tems pass by the open door through the stairwell hall. He moved without a sound and disappeared in the blink of an eye.

Winter turned back to the girl, who seemed to have already shrugged off the coming and going of what she must have thought were other guests of the hotel. Her eyes were back on him, shining and bright, and he returned her smile, bringing forth all of the charm that he doled out whenever he did meets with his fans. She handed him two sets of keys.

"I can't tell you what a huge help this is. Thanks for our secret." He gave her a small smile, and to his satisfaction, she beamed in response.

A mutual secret between them—it might be enough to keep her from telling anyone they were here.

He headed toward the stairs. As he started climbing up, he saw the girl staring after him, still standing, looking around as if she wasn't sure how to process what had just happened.

Please keep our secret, Winter thought as he leapt up the stairs. As he went, he sent Sydney a quick message.

306. 335.

By the time he arrived at the third floor, Sydney and Tems were already there, waiting in front of the room's door. He swiped the key against the lock, and the three of them disappeared inside.

Winter gazed around. It was as simple a hotel room as there could be—he couldn't remember the last time he'd stayed in one like this. Maybe back when his mother had first divorced his father and they'd moved into an apartment that wasn't ready for a couple of weeks. Somehow, the stale smell of the carpet brought that memory back in full, and for a second, he felt like a child again, unmoored and lost.

As Sydney settled against the bed and Tems went to shut the blinds on the window, Winter tried calling Claire again. Again, his call failed to connect. Outside their window, they could hear the commotion of the street increasing as evening settled in thickly, the sounds of street hawkers their wares mixed with the putter of motorcycles.

It sounded as if everything was fine, like everyone was moving forward. As if their world wasn't crumbling around them.

"Still no word from the CIA," Tems muttered as he returned from the window. "Even they're blocked from making transmissions out."

Sydney shook her head. "Keep trying."

"Will do," Tems said. He nodded at the door. "I'll take 306. I'll keep an eye on the front street."

"We'll keep an eye on the back alley," Sydney replied.

They spoke as if on autopilot, unthinking. If Winter didn't dwell too hard on it, he could pretend this was a prep night before a big concert day, could fool himself into believing that they were just working on any other project. He could tell himself that he wasn't on the run with Sydney and her fellow agent, that not everything that could have gone wrong did.

Sydney rubbed her eyes. She looked more exhausted than Winter had ever seen her. "Whoever killed Niall is likely the same group that has been targeting you and me," she said to Tems.

"Seah was my key suspect," Tems replied darkly. "Apparently he was only part of the story."

Winter shuddered at the memory of Sydney's attacker at the airport. The walls around them felt like they were closing in. "Who else would want you all dead?"

"Whoever targeted the president," Sydney muttered, "must have known that Panacea was behind this effort to protect Rosen." She looked at Tems. "We should have gotten you out of the country when we first arrived."

At that, Tems narrowed his eyes at Sydney. "Are you saying this is my fault?"

"I'm saying Niall might be alive if we hadn't changed his plans."

"Niall would have come here," Tems snapped, "whether you changed your plans or not. Have you already forgotten that someone was targeting you the instant you and Winter landed in this country? You were all wrapped up in this."

"Niall was a seasoned agent," Sydney said. "To catch him off guard like that isn't normal. Nothing about this mission is normal."

"Give me an example of a normal mission," Tems said. "Or have all your missions been textbook? Because this isn't the first time mine have gone wrong."

"This is the first time I've lost someone," Sydney said.

"You're lucky, then," Tems snapped. "Because it's certainly not mine."

There was a hollowness in his eyes that struck Winter, a flash of fury that brought his brother back into his memory with startling clarity.

Suddenly, he saw his brother sitting here with his arms outstretched, his expression a cloud of frustration. Winter had only ever seen him like that once, two days after he'd returned from one of his trips: Winter had complained about something silly, asked his brother why he couldn't come along to an audition. Artie had exploded in return, had asked him why he couldn't do anything without Artie beside him, why he had to rely on him so much.

I'm sorry, Artie had said to him later that night. He'd said it with a shake of his head and a look in his eyes so sad that Winter had forgiven him without a second thought, just grateful to have his older brother back in the same house for a while.

At the time, Winter still thought Artie worked for the Peace Corps, not Panacea. Now he looked back and wondered what kind of mission Artie had really been on. Whether his brother had lost someone on that trip, too.

"Let it go," Winter said quietly.

Tems and Sydney looked at him in unison, eyes flashing, but Winter just stared grimly at them both.

"Grief takes the shortest path it can find," he said. "And the shortest path is at each other. Let it go. It won't help us now."

Tems glared at him, although he didn't answer with a retort. Instead, he straightened and headed toward the door. "Check in at zero three hundred," he called over his shoulder.

Winter watched him reach the door and swing it open. It clicked shut behind him, sealing them in silence.

He turned his eyes back to Sydney. She was looking out the window, her eyes far away. Perhaps she was lost in a memory of her own loved ones, people now forever out of her reach.

Again, he tried calling Claire. Again, no signal. He tried Dameon. No luck.

"Shit," he muttered.

He hesitated, staring down at the next number on his phone. Gavi.

She had gotten a local phone card. He might still be able to call through to her. They'd risk getting tracked—but their options were running out.

He dialed her. Sure enough, it went through. She picked up after the first ring.

"Winter," she said breathlessly. She sounded like she was in a chaotic crowd of voices. "Winter, thank god. Where are you?"

"I'm safe," he said.

"Where are"—her voice cut out for a second—"everyone's looking for you."

"You told me you owe me a favor," he said.

She seemed to suck in her breath, then quieted her voice. "I did."

"Go public with the news that I'm not there anymore. I'm not in the country."

"You—what? How did you get out?"

"I'm safe. I can't share where I am." He lowered his voice. "Tell everyone I'm not there anymore. And give the phone to Claire."

She hesitated, and he added, "Please, Gavi. Just this once, with no strings attached."

"All right." To her credit this time, she didn't fish for more details. "Here's Claire."

Her voice abruptly turned distant, and a second later, Claire's came on strong and clear. "*Winter?*" she said.

Relief flooded through him. "Claire," he muttered, looking at Sydney. "Don't kill me."

"Give me one good reason why I shouldn't," she snapped. "Where the hell are you? You're not in the country anymore?"

"Don't say a word out loud," Winter replied. "But I need you to send my plane to an airfield."

23

Love on a Dead-End Street

The clock on the nightstand, which read 10:30 P.M., was an old-fashioned one, which meant the ticking now sounded overwhelming in the silence of the room. Sydney spent the first hour pacing back and forth, peering through the window at the back alley of the hotel every few cycles.

"The gate's locked in the back," Winter said to her on one of the cycles.

"I know," she muttered.

But she kept checking anyway. She looked at her phone, waiting for a message from Tems, some warning for them to leave, some signal from Sauda. But there was nothing. Claire had gotten Winter's message, had kept it secret. Now all they could do was hope that the plane would be there for them tomorrow. All they could do was wait. As the night deepened, Sydney ran out of things to check, and her mind settled at last on what she was dreading.

She sat down on the edge of the bed. All she could hear in the silence was the crunch of metal as Niall's car flipped over, the scream that ripped from her throat as Niall looked at her with a dazed, bloody face, the explosion that threw her off her feet. Her ears still felt like they were ringing from the force of the blast. In the darkness, she felt like the world around her was still spinning, careening out of her control.

"Sydney."

She realized her eyes were closed, and opened them to see Winter sitting beside her, the weak light from the window painting stripes across him, his face pointed at her in concern.

"Hey," she said, rubbing her eyes.

"Hey," he replied.

He didn't ask if she was okay, and she leaned in his direction, grateful he understood.

He did the same lean, although she wasn't sure if he was aware of it. Still, neither of them touched shoulders. They were careful to stay apart, their bodies so used to keeping distance between them.

"After I lost my brother," he said slowly, "I realized that maybe I'd been anticipating losing him my entire life. That was why I felt so afraid every time he left on a trip."

Sydney studied his face. "Like he might never come back."

Winter looked at her. "Have you ever missed a person even while they're still next to you? Like you're waiting for their absence someday, so you try desperately to hang on to the moment, so much so that you can barely exist in the present with them?"

She knew exactly what he meant. "Yes," she answered.

He nodded absently, as if his mind were somewhere else. "That was how I felt whenever I was with my brother. Like he was gone already. Like I already knew what would happen to him."

His words hit true. It was how she'd felt when her mother was still alive, when they'd sit together by the river to watch the freight trains, or take walks together to the grocery store. *This will pass,* she remembered thinking at the time. *She will be gone someday.* And the thought would send a pang of missing through her. She'd felt that same fear whenever Niall trained her for a new mission, like that would be the last time they ever spoke. She'd felt it when Niall had announced his retirement, the inevitable realization that, someday, Niall wouldn't be there for her anymore. And she'd felt it when she and Winter had strolled through Kew Gardens at the end of their last mission together, knowing that their lives were going to take them in opposite directions.

She had spent her entire life missing people who were still beside her.

"I know we're not alone," she said softly. "But I feel like it."

"I know," Winter replied. Here, in the shadows and highlights of midnight, he looked like someone not entirely real, the glow from the neon signs outside the window painting his skin in a pattern of colors.

"There was nothing we could have done," he whispered in the silence.

She nodded wordlessly, even though she didn't quite believe him.

There was nothing she could do to let the world know of Niall's sacrifice, either. She thought of his biological daughter, who would now never know her father had loved her, whom he had wanted to see the instant he left the agency. Sauda could never tell anyone outside of Panacea that she had loved him, never share her grief over his death. And as for herself—she would have to move on and pretend outwardly that nothing had happened, that she had never known this man. As if he had never existed.

It's the loneliest job. Sauda's old words to her echoed in her mind.

It took her another moment to realize that she was finally crying. Tears were dripping down her chin, and her lungs hurt from the squeeze of each silent sob. She reached up to hurriedly wipe the tears away, but they kept coming, and she turned her face away from Winter, embarrassed to let him see her like this. She couldn't stop. All she could see was Niall's face during their last meeting, that small, grumpy smile. His freshly shaven face.

Make me proud, kid.

Winter said nothing. Sydney was glad that he knew instinctively to stay back and let her cry. He waited patiently, his face turned down to the carpet. Sydney concentrated on the pain in her lungs, let herself feel the ache of them and the wound in her heart and the weight on her chest. She wiped at her tears again and again. She could barely keep up with them.

"Here," Winter said gently.

She realized he'd gone to the bathroom and brought back a washcloth for her, still warm from being soaked in hot water. She put it on her face, let it calm her.

She didn't know how long it took before the tears finally slowed, before she could open her eyes and see clearly again. The stripes of light against Winter had changed. Idly, she realized that they should switch on a lamp.

Sydney turned her eyes back up to him. His hair was rumpled, as if he'd been raking his hands through it, and his gaze seemed tired and yearning. Yearning, always, for something out of reach.

Her heart tugged painfully. She knew that feeling all too well.

She took a deep breath and stared off into the darkness.

"I'm sorry," she said.

He frowned. "For what?"

She didn't answer right away, because she wasn't sure. Instead, she turned from him and toward the window, trying to understand why she'd said it.

When she'd been on a job with Tems, when they'd had their brief fling, had she felt this way?

No, she thought automatically. No, that had been different in every sense. They'd had a fling because they were snowed in to their hotel room, she was bored, and he was being charming. It had been fast and careless, something to pass the time. And that was before he'd stranded her overseas.

This . . . She wasn't sure what this was. But when she studied Winter's face, there was a warmth in her chest, an ache in her stomach. There was a lump in her throat when she remembered the words he had blurted out last night.

I have thought about you every single day since London.

"It's not just a song," she finally said.

He blinked, then laughed softly. "It's okay."

She shook her head. "I think what I mean is—when you agreed to join Panacea, I promised you that I was going to be your partner. Where you go, I go. But you were trying to tell me something, and I refused to listen to you."

Winter shifted, and for a moment, his expression seemed lost and young. "Look," he said, "forget everything I said. I shouldn't have put that on you."

Sydney hesitated. "There is something about you that scares me, Winter."

He looked back at her. "Why?" he asked.

She opened her mouth, then closed it again, searching for the right explanation. "My father and I always had a violent relationship," she began. "He's not a good man. He hit my mother, hit me and my brother. But one time, someone broke into our home and stole a box of cash that he'd been saving up. It had over twelve hundred dollars in it. I never knew what he was saving it up for, but I saw him stash a few dollars every time he staggered home from a late-night shift. He'd take it out sometimes and count it, and I swear it was the only time I ever saw him genuinely happy. Like that box held something that could change his life." She paused again. "When it was stolen, my dad went sprinting down the street, as if he might be able to catch the thief, who'd long gone. Then he went missing for several days and came home dead drunk."

The image reappeared in her mind of her father staggering away from the house, his figure illuminated by a streetlight against cracked pavement before he was swallowed by the darkness beyond.

Winter searched her gaze. "I'm sorry," he said.

She looked out the window. "Never in my life had I ever sympathized with my father. But I felt sorry for him that night. I'd saved up some money from my part-time jobs that summer, so I got it from my room and went to him and tried to give it to him. I told him he could have it, if it'd cheer him up."

Winter stayed quiet as she took a deep breath.

"He started yelling at me. Took the money from my hands and threw it back in my face. Accused me of trying to humiliate him, like he couldn't make his own money, asking me why I spied on him, why I knew the money was missing. Said someone stole it because I must have mentioned it in public somewhere. Said I was good for nothing." She paused, then lifted her shirt sleeve all the way up to her shoulder. There, where her joints met, was a round scar in the shape of a cigarette burn. "My eye was swollen shut for a week after that, and I told myself it was my fault. My fault, for opening my heart like that. And so after my mother died, after I left for Panacea, I closed it tight. It made me stronger, you know?"

"I know," he said softly.

Her eyes stayed on the cement wall outside their window, the faint sounds from the night market still echoing out in the dark. "Close your heart," she murmured, "and no one can tell you you're worthless."

He looked away, his gaze distant, lost in his own thoughts.

"You're not," he said to the window. "You must know that."

"I do," she answered. "But . . . sometimes, late at night, the voice in my head tells me otherwise." She swallowed again, focusing on the words struggling to come out. "Winter, I'm here because I'm trying to prove something to myself. What it is, I don't know. Maybe that I deserve to be here, that I can survive without being tethered to anyone else, no matter where I am or what trouble I'm in. That I don't need anyone. And then I met you."

She chanced a look at him and found him watching her patiently.

"I don't know why listening to you sing that song scared me so much," she said. "Like there's a rope attached to you that's tightening around my wrist. I'm afraid you're going to tug me into the water, and I'm not going to be able to come back."

"Why?" he asked.

"Because I can't swim," she answered quietly. "That's what I'm afraid of, Winter. I don't know how to follow you."

"Then don't," he replied.

She searched his gaze. "What?"

He moved closer to her, until she could feel the warmth radiating from him. His body brushed against hers. "I'll come to you."

She looked up into his face and saw the answer there, the realization that she was bound to him whether she wanted to be or not.

"Winter," she murmured hoarsely, swallowing, terrified. "Winter, I don't understand how you can live with an open heart. Everyone hurts you. Why don't you protect yourself better? Put up walls?"

"What if protecting yourself kills you in the end?" he said. "What if the thing your heart needs most is right on the other side of that wall? I know it's dangerous to expose yourself to everything the world wants to throw at it, to everyone who wants to take something for themselves. But I still leave it open, just in case something beautiful comes in."

She didn't believe his words, not entirely, but a lump rose in her throat nevertheless, lodging there, threatening to choke off her words.

"There are those who see your worth, Winter," she whispered back. "Not for gain. Not for money. Just for you."

He searched her gaze, and for a moment, she thought about looking away again, turning her back, and asking him to leave.

"Not everyone you love will leave you behind," he whispered.

She felt herself leaning toward him, felt him leaning down to her, felt her hand touch his sleeve as he wrapped his arm around her waist and pulled her closer. The tether between them pulled taut, and she felt the pain of it in her chest as surely as if her lungs had squeezed. But she couldn't break away now. She didn't want to.

And then he was kissing her.

He pressed his hands against the sides of her face and kissed her deeply. She didn't know what was happening, didn't understand it, was too afraid to disturb it. Her mind buzzed with something akin to panic.

She pulled at his shirt's buttons, impatiently undoing each one. He was doing the same, tugging off her suit jacket and loosening the collar of her shirt, pulling its tails out from her trousers. She let him slide the shirt off her shoulders and shrugged it away. His shirt was open now, too—she had pulled it down his arms to reveal his bare chest.

His kisses moved from her mouth to her jaw to her neck. One of his hands unhooked her bra and ran along the smooth skin of her back. She felt feverishly hot against his lips.

"What are we doing?" he murmured in her ear. "Syd—what are we doing?"

"I don't know," she whispered, her head tilted back, eyes closed, a small noise escaping her as his lips worked along her neck. "I don't care."

There was a warning buzzing somewhere far in her mind, telling her that this would be a mistake, that they would both regret it, that it could end their friendship, this fragile partnership. It felt like stolen time. Wrong, illicit, unbearable. But she didn't want to care about that right now. The door was closed; their room was silent; no one else was here. And right now, all she wanted was to forget about everything gone wrong in the world. All she wanted was to indulge this fear in her chest, give in to the thoughts that had been tugging at her heart for a year.

All she wanted was him.

So they tore frantically at each other, leaving a heap of clothes on the floor before he pushed her against the fabric of the bedframe, her arms wrapped around his neck, his hands gripping her bare hips. Her breaths came shallow and rapid against his ear. He smelled like hints of cologne and sweat and champagne.

She met his gaze. His eyes were hooded with desire, so searing that it sent a thrill of fear through her.

"What are we doing?" she whispered again, echoing his words from earlier.

"What do you want me to do?" he rasped back.

A wild recklessness surged in her chest. "Surprise me."

His eyes looked dark with want. He pressed his lips against her ear. "Stay still."

She did.

He kissed her jawline gently, then her collarbone, her shoulder, then trailed down her body, making her skin tingle with each contact. His lips studied her every softness, slowed down and lingered wherever she shivered with pleasure, worked reverently on her until she arched, shuddering, a small cry emerging from her throat. She could tell that he had been with plenty of others before, that he knew exactly what to do and how to do it, and it left her in a heady fog of both envy and ecstasy.

"Winter," she murmured, meeting his gaze with her hazy one.

"Tell me," he whispered. "Do you like that?"

She closed her eyes. "Yes."

"Do you like this?"

A shiver rippled through her body. "Yes," she gasped.

"This?"

She sucked in her breath sharply. "Winter," she whispered, her voice breaking. "Winter, I can't—"

"Then don't," he whispered back.

Now she was seeing stars, could barely tell the difference between the fuzzy contour of his body and the darkness of the night. What he was doing to her made it too difficult for her to gather her thoughts, so she gave up and gave in, let her body go.

Pull me into the water with you, she thought. *Just this once.*

She had no concept of how much time had passed, whether they had been like this for seconds or hours. Eventually, she realized she had wrapped her arms around his upper back and pulled him down to her, that she was kissing his lips hungrily, their bare skin sticking. She raked her hands through his damp hair, memorized the sound of their bodies together and his gasps and the whisper of her name on his lips. He was trembling just as much as she was, and in the dimness, she could make out the ache in his gaze, could see herself in his dark irises.

"Sydney," he whispered feverishly against her neck as he moved. "Sydney. Let me stay."

She couldn't tell exactly what he meant by that, and perhaps he didn't know, either. Perhaps he was too caught up in the moment, feeling as intoxicated as she had, saying things he didn't quite mean, feeling things he couldn't quite articulate. Maybe he wouldn't even remember by morning. But he whispered it again, nevertheless.

Let me stay.

She pressed her lips against his cheek and murmured something in response. She knew he'd heard her, knew that it must have pierced his heart as surely as it had pierced her own, but he didn't say anything. Maybe that was for the best.

Keep me in your songs.

Afterward, Sydney lay awake, studying the patterns of faint light against the walls. Her gaze went to the boy beside her, his mess of black hair fanning across the pillow. His eyes were closed, his breathing slow and even, but he wasn't asleep, because his hand was still running idly along the curve of her side, sending pleasant tingles through her body. He looked serene and delicate, vulnerable in a way that she found heartbreaking. She let herself take him in without thinking, savoring these few, precious minutes, admiring his every exquisite detail.

It was strange, how she could both remember everything that they had just done—and yet recall it only through a frame of fog, as if she'd had the most vivid dream of her life.

She watched him for a while, then reached over and brushed his hair gently back with a finger.

He stirred at her motion, a quiet murmur in his throat, and his eyelids fluttered. A second later, she found herself looking into a pair of dark eyes.

They said nothing to each other. Perhaps they were both too afraid.

Instead, Winter put his hand next to where hers rested against the sheets. His fingers brushed hers, just slightly. She echoed his movement, putting her own hand so that their fingers just barely overlapped, and gave in to this warmth, the pull of him that she couldn't resist, the promise of something that could be magical, if only.

If only, if only. She felt his fingers move against hers, the gentlest of caresses, the kind of touch that passed between those who trusted each other the most—and wished with all her heart that she could just stay in this pocket of time.

Safe. Her mind buzzed, always alert for the danger in letting her guard down. She pulled her hand away, her breath shallow. It took everything in her to turn her face away from him.

He leaned away, too. The moment ended—his hand pulled away, and he straightened without a word in the bed, sitting on the edge with his arms propped up on either side. She stared at his smooth back, studied the contours of his muscles.

Then she rose, too, and began grabbing her clothes off the floor.

Neither uttered a word. There was simply nothing else to add.

We can't.

The decision hung in the air, keeping them from leaning in again, from reaching for each other's hands, from looking at each other.

They dressed in silence.

As Sydney passed him to head to the bathroom, she paused to look at him.

"Winter," she began, then faltered.

He took a step toward her, wrapped an arm around the small of her back, and rested his forehead gently against hers. His eyes were closed, his brow furrowed. He was so warm.

"I know," he murmured to her.

Then he stepped away without kissing her, and she continued on to the bathroom, and neither looked back at each other.

An hour before dawn, an alert came from Tems.

Minutes later, he was knocking on their door. When Sydney opened it, she saw him standing there, breathless, eyes narrowed. He rushed in past her.

"Three twenty," he muttered.

Winter gave Sydney a questioning look.

"Someone's on our tail," she whispered to him. She turned to Tems. "Who is it?"

"Come with me," he said. "Leave the keys. We're not coming back."

Sydney knew better than to question it. She and Winter followed Tems out into the hall, closing the door behind them with a soft click. Then they made their way down the corridor to a window that overlooked the front of the hotel.

They stayed in the hall's shadows. Tems nodded down at the street.

At first glance, it was just another passerby, hurrying off to some early morning work at the markets—an older lady dressed in a linen shirt and traditional pants.

"Her?" she whispered.

"I saw her pass by fifteen minutes earlier," he said grimly. "Could be state eyes, could be CIA. Could be a spy for Rosen's killers."

Sydney's blood ran cold. It was something she always checked for when she was out in the field—if a passerby was really just a common pedestrian, she would never see them again. If there was a reappearance of a pedestrian, though—well. She was being followed.

Sydney looked away from the window and headed toward the stairwell.

"We need to go. *Now.*"

24

Famous Enough to Hide

During the brief time of their training and partnership, Winter had learned this about Sydney—when she told him to do something without any explanation, he would do it without hesitation.

At least no one else was wandering around at this hour. Winter shivered at the cool air as they passed by the open windows and made their way down the back stairwell. The feeling of unease that prickled his neck felt familiar—like how people could locate him no matter where he was, whether at some secret café he told no one about, or on a walk at an obscure park, or at his friend's house in the middle of the night.

How had someone followed them here? His call with Gavi, perhaps. Or the girl who had checked him into the hotel. Had she sensed something wrong when she'd glimpsed Tems and Sydney heading up the stairwell behind him? Had she been so excited about seeing him that she'd told a friend?

It didn't matter in the moment, as they arrived at a metal door leading to the back alley.

"Locked," Sydney whispered as she reached it. Immediately, she pulled the pin from her hair and jammed the metal into the keyhole. It only took seconds for her to grimace. "Damn it all. This lock's broken." Winter bent down to watch her work as she went on. "I'm amazed they can lock it at all with a key—they must have to jiggle it every time. I can't hook the pin to the mechanism inside."

Winter glanced back the way they'd come. From the dim hall, he could see the lights on in the lobby and hear the faint sound of voices.

"It's going to take too long to pick it open," Tems whispered, barely containing his exasperation.

Sydney glared up at him. "Would you like to waltz through the front lobby?"

But Winter rose and took a step down the hall. Now he could make out the voices more distinctly—one was the girl from last night, high-pitched and friendly, if a little puzzled. The other was an older woman, someone who spoke with an accent too exaggerated to be native Mandarin.

He looked back over his shoulder to where Sydney continued working on the lock, her face tight with concentration.

Then he heard footsteps coming from the lobby.

"Forget the lock," he hissed at Sydney as he hurried back to them. They both looked up at him in unison. "They're coming."

Tems glanced toward the lobby, then at the only other door in the corridor. He went to it and pulled it open. A supply closet with no windows.

He nodded wordlessly to the others. Sydney straightened and rubbed her shirt hurriedly on the back-door handle, erasing her fingerprints. Then she stepped inside the closet with Winter and Tems.

They stood ramrod straight, silent and tense, as the footsteps grew closer. "But, ma'am, only half of our rooms are occupied tonight, lah," Winter could hear the attendant saying in Mandarin. "If you'd like, I can give you an hourly rate if you only need to stay for part of the day—"

"I'd like that room, then," the woman replied. Again, Winter heard the exaggeration in her accent. Their voices faded as they headed up the stairwell.

"There's a security camera in the front lobby," Sydney whispered in the darkness as silence settled around them again. "If we go that way, we're going to get on video."

"Not if we get rid of the camera first," came Tems's whisper from the blackness.

"They'll know we were here for sure, then. We'll leave an official mark for them to trace."

Winter craned his neck up as he heard the girl's distinct clicking heels walking down the hallway above them. There was no second set of footsteps—which meant the older lady must still be in the halls by herself. Maybe the girl had left her in the hotel room she'd asked for, not wanting to make an older woman go back down the stairs. It meant they had someone actively searching for them upstairs now. She would figure out in the next few minutes that their room was empty.

"We don't have time to hang around and mess with a broken lock," Winter muttered.

"I'll do it," Tems said. "The security cam. You two get to the alley and find us a ride."

No more time to argue. Winter stepped out first, swinging the utility door open as quietly as he could and slipping out through the crack. The lobby was still empty.

Sydney was moving so soundlessly behind him that he had to glance back once to make sure she was still there. They headed into the lobby's glaring brightness, careful to stick to the edge of the wall underneath the security cam.

Tems came up behind them like a shadow. With a hop, he made it onto a chair in the lobby and leaned up, his long arm stretching up to the security cam. He swiped one hand over the round lens, then nodded down at them.

Go.

Winter didn't hesitate. He stole across the room, Sydney at his back. Behind them, he heard the attendant girl's heels tapping against the wood of the stairs. She was going to arrive any moment now.

They slid into the shadows outside in the narrow street. Immediately, Winter headed to the alley by the hotel. There, he froze.

Police lights flashed blue against the wall at the end of the alley.

He glanced back at Sydney, whose eyes were fixed on the lights as well.

"They're already here," she whispered. She whirled and checked the other end of the street.

Sure enough, there were the faint, telltale flickers of light against the far walls at the end of the street. Sydney had been right—the woman must have backup here already, waiting for her signal to move in.

Sydney swore under her breath. "Don't tell me we have to steal a cop car," she muttered.

Winter stared at the blue glow strobing against the wall. If they stole a car now, they'd never be able to get past the border. They were too far; there would be barricades set up to stop them immediately. And it would be too obvious that Winter was in the car with Sydney—not only would he be added to the fugitives list, but his cover for Panacea would be blown.

Then it occurred to him.

Realization dawned on Sydney's face at the same time.

"Maybe we don't have to steal it," he whispered.

If Winter could have taken a photo of the police officer at the street corner, it would have been a shot frozen in time of a mouth dropping open in shock, of eyes widening in disbelief, at the sight of the world's most famous superstar walking down the middle of the street toward the barricade, hands in his pockets.

As he approached, he pulled his hands out and held them up

purposefully, letting them see that he had no weapons. He let out a sigh of relief, his eyes welling with intentional tears.

"Thank god," he said.

The man's gun was in his hand, but at the sight of Winter, it wavered and he lowered it. "Mr. Winter Young?" he said skeptically.

"Yes," Winter said with a nod. He looked from the first officer to a second one standing nearby. Everyone's eyes were on him now, all with the same shocked expression. "That's why you're all here, aren't you? I called my manager to ask if I could be taken to the border, where she has a plane arranged for me in Malaysia."

The first officer blinked skeptically at him before the other hurried up to them. He glanced at Winter in exhausted frustration. "Mr. Young, you're not supposed to be here."

Winter threw his hands up in exasperation. "Of course I'm not supposed to be here," he began. "I'm supposed to be in Melbourne, Australia, right now, getting ready for the next leg of my tour, but then the lockdown happened, and I don't have my team with me out here. I can't be in the streets—unless you'd like to deal with a riot." He stopped and blinked at the officers. "Why? Why are *you* here, if not to be my escorts? What did Claire say?"

"Who?" the first officer said.

The second officer sighed wearily at having to handle a celebrity. "Mr. Young's manager," he said. "I've seen her on TV."

"Then you understand." Winter stared pointedly at them. "She's arranged a team from Malaysia to meet me at the private airfield in Kampung Ladang. I have to leave immediately. And if someone doesn't escort me, I'm going to have to go on my own in broad daylight along this street. Not sure you want to deal with the chaos of that."

Winter looked expectantly at the men. His mind, however, was elsewhere—counting the seconds as Sydney quietly made her way toward the police barricade.

At last, the first officer shook his head and looked back at the second.

"I'll take him in the SUV," he said. "The rest of you stay here and wait for orders. I'll be back in an hour."

Then he looked at Winter and nodded. "Follow me, Mr. Young," he said.

"Thank you," Winter replied with a polite nod. He resisted looking over his shoulder toward the hotel and wondering if Tems had finished yet. *Come on,* he thought as they headed to a police SUV parked at the back of the barricade. *We're running out of time.*

As they neared the car, Winter felt the phone in his pocket buzz once. Sydney's signal. His heart tensed in anticipation. On the surface, he smiled and thanked the officer as the man opened the back door of the car for him.

"I'd recommend keeping your hat down, Mr. Young," the officer said before he shut the door. He handed him a standard black face mask. "Here, put one on. We'll be passing through a bit of downtown, and traffic is starting to build up. Lots of eyes."

"Believe me, sir, I know all about it," Winter said conspiratorially, and it earned him a little laugh from the officer.

As the door shut, Winter pulled out his phone and took a quick look at Sydney's message and location.

His heart leapt. She was already in the car, hiding in the SUV's trunk space.

He resisted the urge to turn around, as if he could see through the row of seats to where she must be curled up tight. How did she move so quickly? She must have done it in the instant he'd distracted the police, must have popped the back and crept in while everyone was gaping at him.

Then he processed the text that she'd sent.

Tems nh.

He'd gotten used to her quirky shorthand texts. *NH* stood for *Not Here.* Tems hadn't come when he was supposed to.

Winter's teeth clenched. Of course something had gone wrong—or perhaps Tems was just taking his time, being as insufferable as ever. But Winter could feel the drop in his stomach. Sydney had a better radar than he did for Tems's timing—she knew something had happened to him.

But it was too late to change gears now. The driver's door opened, and the officer climbed into the seat.

"Well," he said, glancing back once at Winter. "This will be a first for me, driving a celebrity. Can I trouble you for an autograph when we arrive?"

Winter gave him his practiced smile, full of all his charisma, and he saw the officer's face brighten. "You don't have to ask, sir," Winter said. "It's the least I can do."

"Ah! Thank you, then." The man laughed and began reversing the car out of the barricade. "My daughter is a big fan of yours. She has your posters all over her wall. She's going to faint from excitement when she hears about this."

Winter laughed along and chatted with him, but his mind was on the barricade, on the police that were closing in on Tems, who was now on his own. It was on Sydney, curled in the SUV's trunk space and rendered helpless for the ride. Every muscle in his body felt poised to jump, ready to run.

But there was nowhere to go. So Winter leaned back and went along as if nothing had happened.

A Well of Secrets

Winter slouched down in the car seat and pulled his hat lower. Through the narrow slit between the hat's rim and his mask, he could see glimpses of the city outside slowly awakening. Street vendors bustled around their stalls, setting up wares and firing up grills. Giant shallow skillets gave off clouds of smoke and steam as cooks turned fluffy meat buns on their surfaces. Clothes, bags, and jewelry hung from the sides of stalls, glittering in the strengthening dawn.

"You sure got unlucky with your tour stop's timing," the police officer said, his gruff voice breaking the silence in the car.

Winter snorted and looked at him gloomily. "I've gotten stuck before," he replied, "but this kind of lockdown is definitely a first."

The officer nodded. "I'm sorry about your president."

The reminder sent another ribbon of nausea through Winter. He shook his head grimly. "I don't know what this is going to mean," he said.

"Well, the rest of us know what it means when you poke the American bear." The officer let out a laugh that wasn't a laugh at all. "If tanks and soldiers from your military start showing up next week, I won't be surprised."

"Singapore didn't sanction this," Winter said with a shrug. "Even if the suspect is from their ranks."

"The Americans won't care," the officer replied. "Even if they do, they'll assume someone else forced our hand."

"China?"

The officer nodded. "I guarantee your government's huddled in a war room right now, discussing sanctions against China for paying a Singaporean official to assassinate your president. Wondering if they can handle a war."

It aligned with the briefing that he and Sydney had gotten. Tems had said the same. But hearing it from the officer made his heart constrict. *War.*

Winter held his hands up. "I hope it all gets sorted out soon," he said.

"You and me both," the officer said with a sigh. "Maybe then the CIA will leave us alone."

The CIA.

Something about the man's words hooked in Winter's mind. *The CIA.*

Tems and Niall had been working with the CIA for weeks now, but Tems had been unable to reach the CIA ever since the assassination. Yet it sounded like the CIA had no trouble staying in close contact with the police here. Why were they ghosting Tems?

"The CIA?" Winter asked curiously, careful to make his voice sound awed, and leaned forward. "You got to talk to a real CIA agent?"

The officer nodded, and Winter noticed him sit straighter in his seat, obviously pleased to have impressed him. "They're not as scary as they sound."

Winter nodded and murmured his admiration, but his mind was spinning. Multiple CIA agents meant that they had sent a task force, that there was another team working on the same case here without telling them. Why hadn't they reached out to Tems? Why hadn't they included Panacea on this? Unless they had gotten fed up with working with an outside agency.

Unless Tems had been cut unceremoniously from their communications. The thought sent a shiver down Winter's spine. He felt like he was trapped in a well of secrets, the water turning murkier the further he sank.

They traveled in silence for a while, until they neared the border. The car had started to feel claustrophobic, and Winter's feet bumped restlessly against each other, aching to get out. Up ahead, he could see concrete barriers on either side of the lanes, as well as a few guards standing at a station far at the end of the road.

As a soldier began walking toward their slowing vehicle, the officer asked, "How did you find yourself in Little India, anyway?"

The question was casual enough, asked with near indifference. But when he met the officer's gaze through the mirror, Winter could sense an ever-present suspicion behind the man's friendly nature.

"I got separated from my entourage after getting turned away from the airport," he replied. The man didn't react to his words.

Stay calm, Winter reminded himself. He thought of Sydney hiding in the back of the car, able to do nothing except hope that he would say the right thing.

He was about to explain further, when the soldier finally, mercifully, reached them. The police officer's attention turned from Winter, and he let himself relax slightly in gratitude.

The soldier greeted the officer in Mandarin with a shake of his head, and the officer responded with what sounded like a protest. Winter couldn't hear what they were saying—he could only watch as the soldier gestured back toward the station.

Border's closed, the soldier seemed to be explaining.

The officer made an annoyed sound in his throat and gestured behind him, as if telling the soldier to look at his passenger. Winter put on his polite smile as the soldier walked over to him and gave him a stern look.

"Nǐ hǎo," he greeted.

"Nǐ hǎo," the soldier responded, eyes narrowed.

Then he lit up. "Eh!" he exclaimed, exchanging a knowing glance with the officer. The officer gave him a smug smile.

"Mr. Winter Young?" the soldier said.

Winter nodded. "Just trying to pass through, sir," he replied in Mandarin, and the man beamed to hear him speaking it.

The soldier hesitated as the officer said something else to him. The two laughed for a second, and Winter felt himself relax more. For the first time since the assassination, a faint bloom of hope appeared in his chest. If they could get through, if they could just be in Malaysia, they could find a way to reach Panacea and fly out. Tems was hopefully still on his way, too. If they could just—

Then the officer turned around to look at him. "They'll let us through," he said. "But they'll need to inspect the vehicle. You'll need to step out. I'm sorry for the inconvenience, Mr. Young."

Winter's moment of hope vanished, turning into dread. A vehicle inspection. They would find Sydney for sure.

He swallowed, smiled, and unclipped his seat belt. "Of course," he replied.

As he started to rise, he hoped that Sydney had heard that conversation, that she understood the Mandarin well enough to be warned that they were about to check the car. But even if she did, where would she go?

Unless she had already moved, had managed to disappear into the foliage along the side of the road.

Winter stepped out into the humid air. As he did, he watched the soldier wave several others over. One of them opened the car's hood and peered at the engine. Another walked around to the far side of the car, tapping the tires.

Winter felt his muscles flood with adrenaline. What would they do if they found Sydney? He didn't know. He knew he couldn't leave her. He—

As one of the inspectors came around, his eyes focused on the ground below the vehicle, Winter saw a message from Sydney appear on his phone.

Move.

Move? Winter frowned. Then he looked over his shoulder—to see a distant dot heading rapidly toward them down the road.

Very rapidly.

It was a motorcycle, and it looked like it was going a hundred miles an hour.

Winter's eyes widened.

He whirled around and saw one of the soldiers heading to the back door of the SUV. His lips parted.

"*Get back!*" he shouted.

Every head whipped to the road in unison—just in time for the motorcycle to hurtle right into the car.

Do Me a Favor, Sweetheart

Sydney heard Tems coming before anyone else—she felt the vibration in the car and saw him through the SUV's rear window. Her head swam from being cramped in the back for half an hour, but she'd still managed to crane her neck enough to notice the advancing officer—and then, in the distance, the dot of the approaching motorcycle.

With a single glance, she recognized Tems's silhouette riding it—and knew that he was going much too fast, that he had no intention of stopping.

She brought her phone close to her lips and whispered a single word into it. "Move."

The text appeared on the screen. She sent it to Winter.

As she did, she saw the legs of one of the soldiers walking out into the road, then his shout in the direction of the motorcycle. "Checkpoint!" he yelled in Mandarin. "Border control!"

The motorcycle sped onward. The officer hesitated, then yelled again. "I said, *checkpoint!*"

Then she saw running feet. "Out of the way!" someone shouted.

And everyone around her suddenly burst into chaos.

Before she left the shelter of the SUV, she glanced wildly around for a glimpse of Winter. At last, she caught sight of his figure.

She gauged the jumble of running soldiers before she scrambled out from the back of the SUV. When she glanced over her shoulder, she saw Tems leap from the seat of the motorcycle right as it slammed into the police truck.

A screaming crunch of metal and glass. Everything seemed to explode behind her.

Sydney launched herself into the hedges lining the road. She didn't need to look to know that the truck had burst into flames—not from the impact, but from something that Tems must have thrown at the truck. She crouched in the hedges to survey the scene. The SUV was lying on its side, engulfed in fire. The motorcycle crashed into the side of the border station in a fiery ball.

Soldiers ran both toward and away from the wreckage, either to save themselves or investigate what had happened.

Then she saw Tems, his face half-covered with a mask, emerging from the smoke at a run. He sprinted through the border control entry, where the flaming motorcycle had crashed right through the bar.

Two soldiers gave chase. "Stop!" one shouted in English.

The other lifted his rifle and fired in Tems's direction. But he had already moved out of range, running to the side of the station where several police motorbikes were parked.

Sydney turned her attention to where Winter ran. He was still alongside the police officer who had taken him here, his expression stunned. Somehow, though, he seemed to know where she was—and when no one was looking at her, she caught his eye.

They exchanged a single, quick, meaningful glance.

Sydney left him to go his own way as the officer guided Winter into a waiting police vehicle on the other side of the border. She sprinted instead for Tems, who had tugged on a helmet hanging from the police vehicle and revved the engine. Her lungs stretched tight, aching.

He saw her coming, but didn't bother waiting for her. *Asshole until the end,* she thought wryly as she forced herself to sprint faster, her lungs heaving in a painful spasm.

She managed to grab his sleeve right as he took off, swinging herself onto the back of the motorcycle as they fled.

"Where's Winter headed?" he said over his shoulder.

Sydney heard the crack of two rifle shots behind them. Tems swerved into another lane, then back again, over and over.

"The private airfield," she called back.

Another rifle shot dinged the metal of one of the motorcycle's handlebars, and Tems's grip shook for a second. He steadied them again and took the first exit off the freeway, the signs written now in Malay. Behind them, Sydney could hear several motorcycles giving chase, the other soldiers finally on their trail.

"We're going to have to take the long route," Tems shouted. He blasted through a stoplight, then a second one, narrowly avoiding a collision between two cars.

"What delayed you back at the hotel?" Sydney asked.

"Police came to the lobby," he shouted. "Probably called there by the old lady. They were doing a search."

He sounded like he was saying more, but the roar of motorcycles behind them drowned him out. He made a sharp left turn, cutting off more traffic.

Then Sydney hissed. Up ahead, she could see more police. They were trying to fence them off.

Tems cursed, screeched to a stop, and reversed the motorbike. "Hold on tight," he shouted, and Sydney forced herself to wrap her arms tightly around his waist.

He sped back the way they'd come, blowing through another stoplight.

"Make a right!" she shouted at him. "Right!" She'd studied the map long enough before they came this way—if Tems didn't make a turn soon, he'd take them too far from the airfield. But he must not have heard her, because he kept going.

Then, suddenly, he braked hard.

Down the road from them came two more soldiers on motorbikes, rifles pointed in their direction.

Without warning, Tems swung down from the motorbike. He gave Sydney a hard look, then motioned for her to scoot forward on the bike. For her to go on.

"Go!" he shouted.

Sydney froze for a fraction of a second, watching in disbelief as Tems walked out to the middle of the road and held his hands up. He met her hesitation with another glare, one full of fire. Ahead of him, the two soldiers began to slow. As one of them swung off his bike, Tems broke his façade of surrender. He rushed at the soldier, knocking him off his feet with a well-placed blow to the neck. As the man fell, Tems grabbed his rifle.

"Do me a favor, sweetheart," he called over his shoulder. "And get the hell out of here!"

In a flash, she recalled when he'd told her what had happened in Stockholm.

A friend of mine on the mission was killed that night.

Was she going to lose someone else today?

Sydney couldn't afford to waste any more of the time that Tems was buying her. She scooted forward on the bike, then revved the engine hard and jerked forward. She had to get to Winter, make sure he was secure. Behind her, Tems raced for the second police motorbike.

Sydney veered the bike sharply around and, with the two soldiers distracted, zoomed down the road in the direction that they had come. She glanced over her shoulder one more time, expecting to see Tems on the bike behind her—

But he wasn't. Instead, his head was turned in the direction of two more soldiers blocking his path. He hadn't reached the motorbike, and now he was surrounded.

Sydney was about to turn the bike around for him when she saw him give her an angry shake of his head. A second later, one of the soldiers struck him in the chin with the butt of his rifle. She saw Tems go down.

Every ounce of her screamed to go back for him. But she gritted her teeth and turned to face the road again. They would take Tems in alive, for questioning. And it would do neither of them any good if she were to get arrested with him.

So she hardened her heart, and fled alone.

Those Who Know Us Best

B y the time Winter arrived at the airfield, the jet that Claire had commissioned to pick him up was already waiting and idling on the tarmac.

"Are you sure you can be here alone?" the officer asked as he rushed out of the car.

Winter nodded and pointed his head toward the plane. "Yes," he replied. "I'll do customs on board the plane. Thank you so much for the ride." He frowned in concern. "Will you be okay heading back? It was a firestorm back there."

"Part of our job," the officer said, but fear was written across his face. He looked at his car. "I don't know how you ended up in this mess, but get out of here as soon as you can."

Winter let out a long breath. "Yes, sir."

The officer seemed like he was already regretting leaving his team for so long. He looked at him a second longer. "Your manager meeting you here?" he asked.

"No. Claire's still in Singapore. She wants me out first. She's staying at the embassy for now."

"Right." Still, the officer wouldn't leave. Instead, he lingered.

Winter felt the tension building in his chest. He gave the man as polite a smile as he could. "I'll be all right," he reassured him. "Truly."

The officer shook his head. "I'm not about to be on the news for leaving you here on your own. Hurry up and get on board."

Winter silently cursed the man's sense of responsibility. He glanced quickly around the airfield, looking for any evidence of Sydney and Tems approaching. But he saw nothing.

Then, to his surprise, the plane's door swung open, and Dameon poked his head out. He caught sight of Winter and came hurrying down the steps.

"I didn't think you'd make it!" he said as he headed over to him. He nodded once respectfully at the officer, who gave him a hesitant nod in return. "Thank you, sir. We've been waiting for a while. The pilot kept asking where you were."

"There was trouble at the border," Winter said, giving the officer a meaningful look. "Can we really fly out from here?"

Dameon nodded. "If we leave soon. Did you call Claire? I can't reach her."

"Cell towers are all jammed in Singapore." He looked at his phone. "Might work here, though."

At the approach of Dameon, the officer had seemed to relax in his stance a little. He lingered a moment longer, awkwardly, then finally decided that it would be a good time for him to take his leave. He tipped his hat at Winter.

"All right," he said. "Stay safe, Mr. Winter."

Winter gave him a bow of his head. "You too," he said.

The officer looked at him one more time, then at the plane, then at the airfield. At last, he adjusted his hat and jogged back to his vehicle.

"You're safe," Dameon said, relief obvious in his voice. "I really thought we weren't going to find you in all the chaos."

Winter stepped toward him into a brief embrace. As he did, he watched the police car continue down the road, kicking up a cloud of dust until it finally turned the corner and disappeared from sight. Again, he found himself looking around for any signs of Sydney's arrival. No luck.

"If I'd gotten really desperate," Winter said with a single laugh against Dameon's shoulder, "I would've just stood in the middle of the street and called for help."

Dameon laughed at that, too. But when Winter stepped back from their hug, Dameon's eyes searched his, a new light of recognition in them.

"So we can follow the mob of fans?" he asked. "Or so that your other team could come get you?"

Winter stilled, brows furrowing in confusion. "What team?" he said.

Dameon put his hands in his pockets. "Winter, you know what I mean."

His heart began to hammer. "I honestly don't," he replied. But he could see the truth reflected in the boy's eyes, that uncanny ability to know everything about him, and in a flash, he knew that Dameon had figured him out.

Dameon gave him a sidelong look.

"Ashley Miller isn't really Ashley Miller, is she?" he said. "And she's not really here as your contracted bodyguard."

Winter shook his head again. This had been a lesson from Sydney, too, that when under suspicion, he needed to stick to his story at all costs. "No, she is," he said. "On both counts." He looked back around the field. "And I really need her to be here right now. She's supposed to arrive at the same time."

"Winter."

Dameon walked around until he faced him, so that Winter could look nowhere else but directly into his friend's eyes. "Winter, before we started on this trip, Claire told me to watch out for you and report back to her."

He blinked. "You've been tailing me?"

"Claire wanted me to stay close to you and make sure everything was okay . . . without telling you. She's been suspicious for a while now. Your moods during this trip have been . . . concerning." He shook his head. "I'm sorry for tailing you, but my gut also told me something was off." His voice quieted. "I know you're in danger, and I know it's not just because of this lockdown. So what can you tell me?"

Winter met his gaze and knew that Dameon could see the lie in his eyes, that he had known for a long time, that it was impossible to deny this secret that hung between them. Dameon seemed to notice the recognition in his gaze, because he gave Winter the smallest of nods.

Remember your training. The reminder rushed through Winter's mind and stabbed at his chest. When he spoke again, his voice was hoarse.

"There's nothing to tell," he said. "And I don't appreciate you and Claire keeping things from me."

Dameon studied him without a word. Then he nodded and said in a low voice, "Then let me tell you what I know," he said. "This afternoon, after you headed out, I overheard a conversation at the hotel about you, from two men dressed in business suits. I thought I misheard them at first, because they weren't talking about your concerts or why you were here. They were talking about your bodyguard. They called her Sydney." He narrowed his eyes. "And they weren't discussing her as your bodyguard, either."

Two men in business suits. Winter stilled. "What were they discussing?"

"They were talking about how to get rid of her, how they needed to report back to an agency."

Suddenly, the dread pooling in Winter's stomach vanished, burned away by fear. He stared in silence at Dameon, who met his gaze with a somber nod.

"Who were they?" Winter asked. "What did they look like?"

"White," Dameon replied. "They definitely weren't from Singapore."

"What accent did they have?"

And this time, when Dameon answered, Winter felt the ground beneath him shift.

"American."

Americans. Winter's stomach felt hollowed out. Why would Americans want Sydney dead? Why would Americans be after Panacea, after Niall? Dameon had said they were reporting to an agency. Who were they with?

His mind flashed to the moment when the police officer had told him about the CIA. How they had been cooperating with the Singaporean government, but not with Tems. How Tems couldn't reach them.

"Did you see where those men went?" Winter said.

Dameon crossed his arms. "They took a black car to the gala you attended. I tried calling you, but by then, the entire lockdown had happened, and I couldn't get through. No one could, except Gavi." He held up his hands as Winter opened his mouth. "So when I'm asking you what you know, it's because I can't help you without knowing. Whatever it is that you're involved in—your bodyguard, whoever she really is, is in danger, and so are you." He lowered his voice. "And that doesn't sit so well with me."

Winter closed his eyes. Looked back out at the airfield, to where he finally saw a cloud of smoke approaching from a distance. It was Sydney, and she was on a motorcycle. He took a deep breath.

"You want to know the truth?" he said, looking back at Dameon. "Well, you're about to find out."

New Enemies and Allies

The first thing Sydney felt as she approached the airfield was an overwhelming sense of relief. From the road, she could see the jet that Claire had commissioned for them, ready to take off whenever they were. But more importantly, she could see the unmistakable outline of Winter's figure waiting there, his face turned in her direction.

At least he had made it. At least he was safe.

The second thing she felt, though, was a prickling sensation that something monumental had shifted—because her gaze shot to the figure standing next to Winter. It was Dameon. And from his posture, he looked like he was expecting her.

When she slowed her motorbike to a stop in front of Winter, he walked up to her immediately, his eyes still searching.

"Are you hurt?" he said as she climbed off. Then, "Where's Tems?"

She shook her head to both questions and gave him a meaningful look before staring at Dameon.

"Glad you've made it," she said to him.

"Even more glad that you did," he replied, his arms still crossed as he surveyed her warily.

Sydney looked back at Winter. He gave her a pointed expression that told her everything she needed to know.

Her cover had been compromised.

"I don't know everything," Dameon said before she could speak again. "But I know enough. Your real name's Sydney Cossette. You're some kind of undercover agent, and you're here because you're working with Winter on something big, something that had to do with the president's assassination." He held his hands up. "I don't need more. And I'm not going to talk. But I'm here to tell you that your lives are in danger in more ways than you think."

She glared at Winter, who shook his head. "I didn't tell him," he said. "He learned your name on his own—because he overheard someone saying it in the lobby of our hotel."

She hadn't expected that. "What?"

"Americans," Winter added quietly.

He explained the rest. And as the story unfurled, as Winter told her about the CIA's early involvement, the men who had been speaking in the lobby, Sydney felt as if something cold and terrible had pooled in the pit of her stomach, a sheet of ice that turned everything upside down, that drowned everything she thought she had known about this mission.

"What if this is true?" Winter said in a low voice. "What if our own government is behind this assassination plot?"

Their own government, assassinating their own president. Americans, killing Niall. Americans, trying to kill her. If this was true, then this had just become a more ominous case than any of them had dared to fear.

Did it mean the CIA was behind it? Sydney couldn't begin to fathom that idea. Her mind spun frantically.

What if Panacea had been complicit, too?

The thought of being unable to trust Sauda and Niall was too improbable for her to bear.

"If our people are a part of this," she said slowly, "and if the CIA is involved, then Tems is in very real danger. He's been captured and arrested by the police. They're going to turn him in to the CIA."

Winter shook his head, still frowning. "None of this makes any sense. Why would the US want their president dead?"

"To start a war," she replied. The clarity hurt her heart.

"Why would the US want to start a war?"

"You think we don't start wars every other year?" She glanced at Dameon, who had turned ashen. "If we trigger a crisis and pin it on China, we get to wage war."

"It benefits no one."

"It would benefit someone. Military corporations. Weapons manufacturers."

Winter narrowed his eyes. "A rogue faction?"

Sydney nodded, her mind turning faster. A rogue faction in the CIA would make sense, and the thought terrified her to her core.

"Why do they want Panacea dead?" Winter asked quietly. "Niall? You? Tems?"

"Because we're in the way," she whispered back. She looked at Dameon. "Keep this to yourself, at all costs. All our lives depend on it. You are now officially a Panacea asset, and as such, you are both in our care and sworn to silence. Do it if you care for your own life." She nodded at Winter. "Or his."

She thought that Dameon might break down, that he might spiral into a panic attack. But the boy, as frightened as he looked, gave her a sober, resolute nod.

She looked at the jet. "Make sure this stays here for us. Tell Claire any lie that will keep her from asking too many questions." Then she looked at Winter. "Stay here."

"Like hell I will." He stepped forward.

She sighed. "What now?"

"You're off to rescue Tems, I'm guessing."

"He's our mission."

"And I'm your partner."

The way he said it made her catch her breath. There was a glint in his eyes that she recognized, a bright stubbornness that told her that forcing him to stay would cause her more trouble than it was worth. And again, she felt that panic rise in her chest, the feeling of being tethered to someone, the danger of that tether shredding her heart.

He took another step toward her. "I'm not leaving you behind," he said. "Not after everything. We're either getting out of here together, or not at all."

Dameon crossed his arms and frowned at Winter. "You know, I used to think Gavi was the most dangerous relationship you could be in," he muttered. "But this is definitely worse."

Sydney tightened her lips, hesitating. Then she turned away from Winter and walked toward the motorcycle. "Come on," she said.

She straddled the vehicle and felt him swing on behind her, his familiar, warm arms wrapping tightly around her waist. In spite of everything, she felt a rush of relief that he was with her, that she wasn't alone, that at least they could trust each other. And in this moment, she wished with all her heart that he could always be here.

"Where is he?" Winter asked.

"Being held at the border for now," she said. She revved the motorcycle's engine, and it let out a roar. "Not for long, though. I'm sure they've confiscated his tracker."

"If Tems complains about this rescue," Winter grumbled as Sydney gripped the handles, "I'm going to kill him."

And at that, Sydney found herself smiling.

29

Predator and Prey

The station reminded Sydney of one that she'd once broken into on the border of the Czech Republic—a simple affair, two stories of gray concrete inside a courtyard walled with stone and barbed wire.

They abandoned the motorcycle half a mile from the station and made their way toward the building until they finally stopped beside a trio of trees situated a hundred yards from the wall. One glance at the wall told Sydney that there were infrared cameras installed at each of the corners, the distinctive shape of their structure giving them away.

"What is it?" Winter whispered beside her.

She nodded subtly at the wall. "Infrared cameras. If we get any closer, they'll pick us up."

Winter reached for something in his pocket. Sydney looked over to see him produce the pen flare from his pocket that Niall had given him at Panacea's headquarters.

"How bright a distraction do we need to throw those cameras off, then?" he said.

Sydney smiled. "You still have that?"

"Saved it for an emergency," he replied with a sidelong wink.

Sydney took the flare from him. It would do. When it went off, it'd be bright enough to white out the footage from the cameras for several seconds—enough time for them to get close to the edge of the wall and make their way around to the back.

"What happens once we get in, though?" he whispered.

"When *I* get in," Sydney clarified. "You stay out here, make sure you're watching for trouble. We need our escape route to be foolproof." She cast him a skeptical glance. "You know how to ride the motorcycle?"

He shrugged. "I used one once for a stunt."

Sydney winced. "Good enough."

Up on the wall, she saw a faint, moving glow. A single guard was walking around inside the premises with a flashlight. She waited until the light had turned to the back of the building.

She and Winter exchanged a look. Then she clicked the pen, set up the flare, and tossed it near the entrance.

The shock of the flash was so bright that, even knowing to brace themselves, Sydney still flinched, the light washing out her closed lids so that even the darkness looked bright red. Instantly, she moved in the direction of the gate, her eyes still shut.

The light was there and gone in the span of three seconds. By the time she reached out and felt the stone cold and hard against her fingertips, the night had gone dark again.

Sydney opened her eyes. The flare had temporarily thrown off her night vision, leaving spots of color dotting her sight, and she fumbled against the wall for a second before feeling the edge of the gate. Her fingers found the lock. She pulled the pin from her hair, then went to work on it.

Inside the building, she heard a faint mutter of voices. English, although she couldn't make out what they were saying.

The lock finally made a satisfying click. Sydney shoved the pin back in her hair and slowly pulled the door open.

The lone guard making rounds in the complex was, as her timing had correctly estimated, still behind the building. Sydney slid inside and made her way through the shadows until she pressed herself against the building's wall. There, she paced herself, following the faint glow of the guard's flashlight until she had made her way to a window.

The light inside the window shone cold and fluorescent. Even before Sydney could edge her way to the side enough to peek in, she recognized the deep grate of Tems's voice.

"There's not enough time," he was saying.

"There's plenty," came a reply in an American accent.

She froze. Who was he talking to?

"They're going to come back, you know." That was Tems speaking again. "*I'm* her mission. She's not going to forfeit it, it's not in her nature."

Sydney felt her throat turn dry. She slowly edged forward just enough to catch a glimpse of the room.

It was a sparsely furnished space, just a single long table with four chairs, the fluorescent rectangle of light on the ceiling casting everything in a cold, harsh glow. Tems sat across from three others, his elbows resting on the tabletop, and together, they looked like they were deep in discussion.

Sydney stared at the scene as if it might be an illusion, racking her brain for understanding.

And right away, she recognized one of the other three officers sitting at the table. His face had been seared into her memory the moment he'd attacked her at the airport.

He was right here. It was unmistakable—the man who had lunged at her with the knife was now seated calmly across from Tems, his arms crossed.

A cold realization began seeping into Sydney's veins.

"Go back with her, then," one of the others, a woman, said.

"What about Panacea?" Tems asked. "I need to stay a little longer. There's a few loose threads."

"We'll take care of your loose threads," her attacker interrupted. "What is it, your luggage?"

Tems shook his head. He didn't look like a captive or the subject of an interrogation. There were no cuffs on his hands or feet, nothing binding him to the chair. His posture was relaxed, with no intention of bolting from the room. "My recorder in the hotel. I didn't have time to get it."

"We'll send someone."

"What are you going to tell the director?"

The man shrugged. "CIA needed some more time."

CIA. The man who had attacked her at the airport was a CIA agent. They were all agents, sent over by the government. Sydney felt her stomach twist sharply, the impossible questions bubbling up in her mind even as she answered them herself. Why was Tems sitting here, talking with them like they had all been working together? He had been unable to reach them after the assassination, had looked and sounded so frustrated. Why was he now talking about Sydney's mission as if it were an obstacle, like he had no intention of following through with their escape?

Unless he'd never intended to. Unless he had never really been here for Panacea.

His words came back to her from the night they'd talked at the hotel. When she'd asked him if she needed to contact the CIA.

No need to make contact, he'd said. *I'll check that they're in place for us.*

"You should have let Seah in on everything," Tems muttered now. "It would've made things less complicated for us."

"Seah couldn't know. He was a liability."

"You don't plan an assassination for six months just to risk it all on a loose asset."

"You should know. At least yours went smoothly."

Tems gave a single, cynical laugh and nodded. "At least mine did."

At least yours went smoothly.

Sydney had to lean against the wall for support. Her mind whirled, trying to make sense of what she'd just heard. It couldn't be true. But in her head, all she could see was Tems giving her a wry smile.

An agent never asks directly. They only know what makes sense.

And she knew, with a certainty that made her sick to her stomach.

Tems hadn't been here to work on his Panacea mission to stop the assassination. He had been here *for* an assassination. But not for Rosen. *Not for Rosen.* Sydney's breathing sped up until her lungs hurt.

At least yours went smoothly. At least yours went smoothly.

Tems had planned Niall's murder.

Walking a Tightrope

Sydney squeezed her eyes shut as she struggled to process it. How could it be true? Tems had been a Panacea agent for years. He had gone through training as part of her class—they had graduated at the same time—she had worked with him on a mission. Tems had taken the Panacea oath. There had been no signs of suspicion on him at all.

No. That wasn't true, though. There were warning signs. He had disobeyed orders on his first outing as a recruit, had set fire to an entire train line without permission from Panacea. He had stolen her passport in Stockholm and gone against protocol, had been sent to the Sapphire Cross for it. Niall had been constantly frustrated with him.

Sydney had gone rogue before, hadn't she? She had done things to defy authority, too. Many agents had, for the good of their missions.

But Tems was different. He hadn't defied Panacea in the past for the sake of a mission. He had always done it in reaction to something. Had always acted on emotional triggers. Hadn't Niall complained about that? Hadn't the analyst demoted him for it?

Now here he was, his words unmistakable.

Through the blur in Sydney's head came one of the questions that Tems had just asked the agents. *What are you going to tell the director?*

The director of the CIA.

Sydney's eyes opened again. That meant the director didn't know—that meant the rest of the CIA didn't know. That meant that this was a rogue cell operating within the CIA, a rogue cell that had been responsible for the assassination of the US president.

Tems had been working here with a CIA team targeting the president. They had gone through with the assassination, with his help.

And he had gotten Niall killed.

Had done it *on purpose*.

Sydney clutched her chest and gulped in lungfuls of air until it hurt.

Inside, Tems stood up. "I need to find my way back to them now," he muttered. "Otherwise they're going to be coming for me, and I'd rather we not make all of this even more complicated than it already is."

Sydney's thoughts spun as the trajectory of their mission changed in her head. Now it was less about Tems's safe exit out of the country as a fellow Panacea agent and more about getting him onto the plane in order to extradite him back to the States and have him—and indeed the rest of this rogue cell—arrested for treason.

That meant she needed to get out of here right now, before Tems discovered her snooping around. She needed to tell Winter what had happened, had to make sure they got back to the airfield and pretended they knew nothing of what had just occurred, and get Tems on the plane with them, playing along long enough until they landed and were in Panacea's cars.

Sydney pushed away from the wall and looked around. There were two guards circling now, perhaps as a result of the flash of light that had made the infrared cameras temporarily malfunction. She could see one of them making their way gradually in her direction, the glow from their flashlight trembling against the ground.

Her eyes darted up to the top of the station. Then she rose, placed her boot on the edge of the windowsill that no one could see, and pulled herself up right as the guard came around the corner.

She crouched in complete stillness against the outside of the balcony as the man drew near, his flashlight illuminating the gravel where she had just been. She held her breath, looking on as the man swiveled the light back and forth in a bored motion of habit. He shined the light toward the gate, finding nothing.

Then he pointed his flashlight again at the ground in front of the window where Sydney had just been. This time, he held the light still, studying the ground.

He must have noticed the sand that her boots had shifted.

Sydney cursed silently, listening as the guard called for his friend to come over.

"Hey," he said in Mandarin. Sydney crept quietly to the edge to see the man waving at the second guard.

The second guard, a woman, approached. "What is it?" she replied.

The man pointed his flashlight down at the ground. "Does this look like a different boot to you, or is it standard issue?"

The woman bent down to study the floor, pointing her own flashlight at the same spot. Then she shrugged. "It doesn't look like ours," she said. "Maybe it's the Americans."

"They didn't come to this window," the man said. He shined his flashlight on the windowsill. "There's some dirt here."

Sydney hated when guards were competent. She crept to the opposite side of the roof and glanced in the direction where she'd left Winter to wait. There was a drainpipe running along the side of the building here. If she could slide down quietly enough, she could make a run for the back gate before the two guards arrived on the scene—that is, if Winter could see her up here and unlock it for her.

She peered into the darkness, hoping he'd notice her, hoping she'd see him.

For an instant, she thought she had made a mistake, that they couldn't possibly connect in the darkness like this.

But then she saw a slight movement near the trees surrounding the outer rim of the wall. A second later, the flash of a hand signal she would recognize anywhere. His making a scissor movement.

Winter was watching. He had seen her.

Sydney pointed once at the back gate.

He didn't respond, but he didn't have to. She knew he had gotten the message, could tell that he was no longer near his position by the trees. A warmth pooled in her stomach, giving her a surge of comfort, reminding her that she still had a partner on her side.

Below her, she could still hear the guards talking. She swung one leg over the side of the roof and found her footing against the drainpipe. It was old and rusted, but it seemed like it would hold her weight. She didn't have time to debate it, anyway—a second later, she had swung onto it and slid down with a low hush of wind. Her boots hit the ground in a soft thud.

On the other side of the building, she could hear the people inside the room now talking to the guards through the window.

"I'm not sure that's a footprint," one said.

"Did you check the perimeter?" said another.

She didn't hear Tems's voice chiming in, and that was what made the hairs stand up on the back of her neck. Had he left the room? Sydney hurriedly smoothed the sand under her boot prints, but she didn't have time to erase her tracks the entire way. She made her way toward the back gate, hoping that Winter had already managed to get it unlocked. Toward the window, she heard the sound of feet as someone else joined the guards outside.

She reached the gate and put her hand on the handle. *Please open*, she thought. She pushed it gently.

It gave way. Her breath rushed out in a gasp of relief. Then she stepped out into the night, deep into the shadows.

And came face-to-face with Tems.

He furrowed his brows in concern at the sight of her. "Sydney!" he exclaimed, putting both hands on her shoulders. She shivered at his grip. "It's not safe here—you shouldn't have come."

She looked into his eyes, searching past his expression of worry to find the truth. Then she realized that she should have always known. Tems had always been a good liar. Too good at putting on a charismatic smile and then pulling the rug out from under her. Too good at pretending to be vulnerable, pretending to be friendly, pretending to be sorry. Maybe too good an agent.

Once, she had seen him as a comrade, someone she could rely on to understand her world, someone she could speak to as an equal, someone who could be her ally—and maybe more—whenever the time was right.

Now she only saw a killer.

Still, she feigned ignorance and let herself look at him in relief. "You're a goddamn pain in the ass," she whispered. "I have to get you out of here."

He hesitated, looking out into the darkness. She had purposely only said that she was here, but she knew he was still searching for Winter. Then he turned back to her. "Follow me," he whispered.

There was nothing she could do but go along with him. They made their way to the back of the complex, to where a jeep lay in wait.

"They won't notice for a few minutes yet—I managed to sneak out of the room while they were searching," he whispered as they went. His hand gripped hers tightly. "Is the plane ready for us?"

"Ready and waiting," Sydney confirmed, as if they were both still going along with their original plan.

He nodded, and she fought to keep her focus. But as they went, she let herself cast a glance out into the darkness, hoping that Winter could see her. Then she tapped the top of her left hand twice in a rapid motion.

Danger.

She turned back to Tems immediately, as if she'd done nothing out of the ordinary, as he reached the jeep. Sydney climbed into the passenger seat.

"They're going to hear you start this thing," she whispered to Tems. She turned toward the station, because she didn't want to look directly at him—lest he see the truth in her eyes.

"They won't catch up in time," he said. "It's their only vehicle here. Their motorbikes are all locked up in the back. We're going to need to drive with the lights off, though."

Sydney nodded, her heart still in her throat as she walked this tightrope of an act. *Just get him on the plane,* she reminded herself over and over. That was all she needed to do—make sure she trapped him in the air on the way back to the States. She could figure out a way to subdue him on board. But if she could just get him there—

Tems glanced at her as they clipped their seat belts in place. The jeep roared to life. "Did you hear what they were saying to me in there?" he asked.

Sydney shook her head. "Didn't catch it," she replied. "Did you get any clues?"

"I got one," Tems replied. Then his eyes darted to the windshield, as if he'd seen someone moving outside the jeep.

Sydney looked, too. A mistake.

And that was when she felt it—the sharp prick at her neck, then the feeling of Tems's cool hands gripping her throat.

When she looked back at him, all she saw was his expression, now stripped bare of any act, cold and disappointed and full of determination.

"Sorry, Syd," he muttered.

Then the world blurred around her, and Sydney felt herself go limp before the darkness closed in.

A Crack in the Heart

Sydney woke up to an argument and a searing light.

"This isn't a question, Mr. Bourton."

"I didn't answer it as a question," Tems snapped. Sydney could hear the clipped anger in his voice, a sound she recognized all too well. The loudness of the voices made her wince.

"Does Panacea know she's here?"

"You checked her for trackers yourself."

The light was fluorescent, that much Sydney could tell. She squinted as her eyes fluttered open, then shut again. She tried to lift a hand to block the light, but something weighed her wrists down. Vaguely, she realized that she was tied down in a chair, and her mouth felt like it'd been stuffed with cotton.

It made her want to gag. The nausea that made her stomach lurch shook her fully awake, and her eyes shot open again—to reveal the rest of the interrogation room at the police station.

The three men sitting at the far table stopped talking to look at her. Beside them stood Tems with his back turned to her, his hands in his pockets. He broke from his argument too at the sound of her stirring, then glanced at her over his shoulder. The scowl on his face shifted and softened as he turned to walk toward her.

"What do you remember?" he asked her first.

Sydney knew why he posed this question. He must have injected her with benzodiazepine, which—in addition to being a powerful tranquilizer—had the tendency to interfere with memory. She shook her head and regretted the motion immediately as her head exploded with agony, the migraine blooming from the back of her head to the front until it felt like her entire brain had been struck with a hammer.

"Oh my god," she whispered. Her lips cracked as she spoke.

Tems knelt down and looked up at her. "What do you remember?" he asked again firmly.

Sydney glared at him. "I remember you stabbing me with a goddamn needle. Didn't think you were a literal prick."

At that, Tems gave her a humorless smile. "Then I guess we all learned something today," he replied. "Glad you're okay. I was afraid I used too much."

Sydney didn't answer. Her eyes went to the other agents and committed every detail of their faces to memory. She didn't recognize two of them—but the third, she knew. Her attacker from the airport.

Now the agent met her stare and pulled out his gun with a sigh. Every muscle in Sydney tensed.

Tems shook his head without looking away from Sydney. "Put it away," he said coldly, addressing the agent with the gun. "I told you. You're not shooting her."

"What is Panacea going to do about it?" the man said without emotion.

"I'm going to shoot you back," Tems replied simply, pulling out his own weapon and resting his arm idly against his knee.

"She knows," another agent said.

"We can work something out," Tems said. He nodded at Sydney. "Won't we?"

Don't say a word, Sydney thought. There were no friends in this room with her—any word she uttered could be used against her, against Panacea, against Winter.

Against Winter.

She noticed that, so far, Tems hadn't mentioned him yet. Maybe the other agents didn't know she had a partner. Maybe Tems didn't think he was capable enough to come here with her—after all, even she had tried forcing him to stay back. Maybe Winter had managed to escape and had returned to the plane.

She also noticed the tenuousness of Tems's relationship with these other men. They'd definitely had arguments before. She filed the bit of knowledge away.

"Well, Syd," Tems said to her. "What do we do now?"

Sydney didn't move. Didn't even blink.

Tems sighed when she remained still and silent. "There's not a very good reason for us to keep you alive," he said. "You know this. So I want you to think very hard about how cooperative you want to be, and whether or not you want to go home."

"Do *you* want to go home?" Sydney asked him.

Tems smiled. "Turning everything back around into your own questions, huh?" He laughed a little. "Panacea's training really does run deep in us."

"Are you really a Panacea agent?"

He shrugged. "As much as you," he replied. "I just happened to have been recruited first by this faction in the CIA."

This faction. Tems had revealed two things to her: one, that he'd worked for the CIA before he ever even stepped foot inside Panacea's headquarters, and two, that the CIA he was working for was a rogue cell.

In a flash, Sydney thought of the Orange Alerts that had gone off at Panacea last year, of Sauda and Niall's whispers and frustrations.

"You've been a double agent since the beginning?" she said through clenched teeth.

He nodded.

She pictured them both at the graduation ceremony, saw herself laughing at his joke about marrying their work.

It's all part of this job, isn't it?

"Why did you kill Niall?" she said hoarsely.

He narrowed his eyes at her, and for a second, she saw pain in his gaze. "Do you think," he said, "that Panacea's hands are clean? Do you think my friend would have died that night in Stockholm, had Niall not meddled in our affairs?"

Sydney swallowed hard. What happened in Stockholm had run deeper than she'd guessed, had involved Niall and some conflict between him and Tems.

"Revenge, then?" she managed to say.

"Let's call it karma," Tems snapped. "He deserved it."

"*Why?*" she snapped back.

"If you don't want her dead," the eldest man interrupted, "then what do you want to do with her?"

Tems stood up, crossed his arms, and regarded her. "I think we can help each other out. I could use a recorded conversation from you that corroborates our story about how everything went down. Can you do that, Syd?"

Sydney wanted to laugh in his face, wanted to scream at him. But she just nodded.

Tems smiled carefully at her, even though she could tell that he didn't believe her. "Very good," he replied. "I think it would be in the best interest of your partner, too."

She realized in a flash that he was doing this for her sake, that he wanted her to answer like this so that the other agents might consider sparing her. Was he trying to warn her that the rogue cell had captured Winter outside? Was his life at stake?

What was going on in Tems's head? They had been trained in the exact same tactics, had done the same exercises and suffered through the same techniques. But Sydney had not been trained to confront a fellow Panacea agent. How the hell was she going to get him to talk? How was she going to get herself out of here?

She needed to talk directly to him, in private, alone. So Sydney looked hesitantly at the other agents, then back at Tems.

"What kind of recorded statement?" she said, loud enough for all of them to hear.

"You need a script?" Tems said.

"You want me to sound believable?" she answered, her lips curling into a snarl. "Then let's talk it out, just you and me, with none of these other shits in the room."

"You're not in a position to bargain, Jackal."

"And yet here you are, asking me for a favor."

Tems glanced over his shoulder at the other agents before nodding at them. "Give us a minute," he replied.

The agent who had been Sydney's attacker shook his head. "No. You're not getting private time."

Sydney watched quietly, noting their dynamic.

"I seem to remember that there was one person vital to the success of this mission," Tems snapped. "And that person is crouched here right now. *Give us a minute.* Or you may not get the war you wanted, after all."

The man looked ready to argue back, but one of the other agents leaned over to him and exchanged a few quiet words that Sydney couldn't pick up. The two discussed it for a second. At last, just when Sydney was starting to think that they wouldn't agree, the agents rose in unison.

"Five minutes," the man said to Tems.

Tems nodded once. Sydney watched as they filed out of the room. When the door closed behind the last of them, she turned back to face Tems. There were a million things she wanted to say to him, a million insults she wanted to throw in his face. But none of that mattered right now. What mattered was completing her mission and getting herself and Winter to safety—what mattered was finding a way to get Tems back to the States under arrest and revealing the rogue cell to Panacea so that the evidence could stop the impending war. So that she could avenge Niall.

She looked at Tems and gave him a grave nod. "You don't have to go down this path," she said.

"I've been on this path since before I arrived at Panacea," Tems replied.

Sydney shook her head. "I don't understand why."

"Why I joined them?"

"Why you wanted Niall dead. What did he do to you?"

Tems looked away at the window, paused for a moment, and then turned back to her. "His name was William Olsson," he said. "No one will ever know that, or that we had been friends, or that he was killed in Stockholm because of me." His lips tightened. "Because of Niall."

Sydney searched his eyes. "What happened?"

"Niall sent me to Stockholm on a mission targeting a terrorist group stationed there. William was my informant. He risked everything to get me the information I needed. By the time you and I met up, he had already riled up the suspicions of the group we were targeting and had gone into hiding. While we were snowed in at the hotel, he was supposed to be smuggled out of the country."

"By who?"

"Niall *promised me* he would be safe and accounted for. He *promised me* they would do their best." He tightened his lips. "Then, at the last minute, the group made a move to Cairo, Egypt. Changed their plans on a dime, because they suspected someone was on to them. Niall was supposed to have sent backup to protect William that night. He didn't. So Will was caught unaware at port. They found him floating near the shore, frozen half-solid, with a dozen gunshot wounds in his body."

Sydney stayed quiet. She tried to remember whether Tems had said anything to her during their hotel stay about his friend, whether his mood had changed. But he'd simply been gone in the morning with her passport, leaving her nothing but a cryptic note.

"So you chased the group to Egypt?" she said.

"Niall ordered me stay in Stockholm, because the main cell was still there. That was my mission. But Will's killers left for Cairo." He narrowed his eyes. "So I went after them."

"Niall wanted you to stay so that they could take down the group, once and for all."

"If he had protected Will, like he promised, I wouldn't have had to abandon my post. If he had kept his promises, I could have kept mine."

"Yours?"

"I promised Will that he would be safe. I gave him my word. And he died."

"Tems," she said quietly, "this is the nature of our work. This is the sacrifice we make, that we're still making at this very moment."

"What's the point of our work if we can't be loyal? If we can't keep our promises?"

"Loyal? You're a double agent!"

"I worked as a double agent to ensure the stability of the world," he snapped. "I did Panacea's bidding when I thought it would benefit the most people. I worked with the rogue cell in the CIA when I thought Panacea needed to be kept in check. But I've never been responsible for the death of a good human."

"That just means you haven't had to make difficult decisions until now," she shot back. "Niall was a good human. Imperfect, but *good*."

"You still think the world of Niall, don't you?" He scowled at her. "Your precious father figure has clouded your judgment."

Had he? Sydney thought of Niall's grumpy exterior, the fear in his eyes whenever she was in danger out in the field, the grief in his words whenever he spoke about missing out on his daughter's life.

"He has a daughter," she went on. "You knew that, didn't you? Quinn. He was about to retire, had been looking forward to this moment for decades so that he could patch things up with her. Now he's gone, because of you."

Tems snorted in disgust. "You mean the daughter he abandoned?"

"Moral purists never stop to examine themselves, do they?" Sydney spat at him. "What makes you so great? Or do you just tear others down because it's secretly fun?"

"I follow my heart." Tems glared at her. "It's that simple."

"Niall was right," she murmured. "You're not cut out to be an agent. It's never simple. You make too many decisions without your head."

"He could have said the same thing about you, Syd. You've made your fair share of rash, emotional decisions." His lips twisted in disgust. "But Niall always favored you more than me, didn't he? You always got passes."

"Is this also about envy, then?" She narrowed her eyes at him. "You resented Niall for demoting you to the Sapphire Cross after Stockholm."

"I resent unfairness. As punishment for honoring a friend's death, I was shipped overseas."

"You didn't honor Will's death. You wasted it. You didn't take down the cell that murdered him. You cut off a finger and left the head."

"I did what I felt everyone deserved," he snapped, then rose to his feet.

Sydney glared at him. "You think Niall deserved death for punishing you?"

He sighed. "Believe what you want, Sydney."

"You don't understand what it means to be an agent, Tems."

He spread his arms. "Don't you ever wonder why you have to give up everything for an agency that doesn't give a shit about you? Do you think Panacea won't sacrifice you someday, when everything comes down to it?"

"We took an oath. That means something to me."

"And you think Panacea always does right by the world?"

"I think they try!" she snapped, teeth clenched. "I think that's all we can ever do!"

"Then maybe they need to try harder," Tems said coldly.

Sydney studied him warily. "You were going to leave the country the instant we arrived back in the States, weren't you? Or maybe you were never planning on getting on board that plane. You were going to abandon me. Just like before."

She finally seemed to hit a nerve at that, because he flinched. He looked at the window to disguise it, then sneered at her. "And you think your famous boy won't leave you behind? Think Winter's going to make you happy?"

Winter. The sound of his name on Tems's lips sent a jolt of rage through her. "I think you shouldn't speak about things you don't understand," she answered. "Or did you not pay attention during that class either?"

He started to rise. "I think we're done here," he said.

"I have one more question for you," she said. "Why do you really want me alive?"

"My beef was with Niall." He fixed his gaze on her. "Not you."

And here, Sydney noticed his expression shift subtly. Past the sneer, past the glare, she could see something that looked like regret. Like he wished there was some other way they could part.

Tems wanted her alive because he didn't want her to die. It was as simple as that.

He scowled and looked away. "Sauda shouldn't have sent you," he muttered under his breath.

It was exactly what he'd said to her on the day she'd first seen him in Winter's hotel suite.

"It's not too late, Tems," she said, her voice soft and quiet now. "Come back with me. Turn yourself in, and wipe your conscience clean."

He laughed dryly. "And go to jail for Niall's sake?"

"You can still help me stop this war. You know this isn't right." She leaned forward in her chair until her restraints made it too painful. "You *know*."

"I know we're done here," he said. "Go on record saying that you were cooperating with us the entire time, that we tried our best to stop the attack on Rosen. That we have no choice but to declare war." He turned his back on her. "Make it easy for yourself . . . and for Winter. Buy yourself some time while I figure out whether it's worth it to keep you alive. Otherwise, I can't do much to protect either of you."

Sydney swallowed her frustration as he went back to the door and opened it. He exchanged some muffled words with those in the hall. As he did, she gingerly twisted her bound hands. Duct tape. She looked around before her eyes settled back on Tems's figure at the door, his hands in his pockets.

Nothing she could use.

The others filed back inside, their eyes flickering suspiciously to her. They didn't sit back down. Instead, they stayed standing by the table as one of them walked over to her. It was the one who had been unhappy with Tems for wanting a private chat.

"You talked sense into her?" he asked Tems.

Tems looked at Sydney. "Ask her yourself," he replied.

The man turned to her. She met his gaze without flinching. Secretly, she gauged her distance from Tems.

"Let's get that statement, then," he told her, pulling out his phone.

Tems had told her to nod along. To go on record vouching for them.

But she had already noted the shaky trust holding Tems and this rogue cell together. Time to take advantage of it.

So Sydney took a deep breath, put her life on the gambling table, and said, "I'll make sure all of you are court marshaled," she said, a snarl rumbling behind her words. "You'll be in jail within a week."

Tems looked sharply at her. The man blinked at her words, then shook his head with a dry laugh.

"Apologies, Mr. Bourton," the man said, taking a step toward her. He pulled a gun out of his jacket pocket.

Panic, rage, and desperation flickered across Tems's face. It was there and gone in the blink of an eye—she had gotten to him, had surprised him. He looked back at the man approaching with the gun, then back at her, then at the man again. His body tensed like a spring.

Sydney gritted her teeth as the man pointed the gun right at her head. She had been in situations like this too many times, but each time, scenes still flashed through her mind—her as a child, joining Panacea, her mother, her home. And this time, Winter.

Come on, Tems, she thought frantically. *Take the bait.* All she needed was to create some chaos, crack the shaky alliance within this group.

"Wait," Tems called out. He lunged toward the man, his hand knocking the man's wrist down before he could fire.

The man gave him a look of indignant surprise. "What the hell?" he grunted.

"A traitor," another snarled.

For once, Tems hesitated. In that space of a second, Sydney heard everything that he was—that in spite of everything, in spite of being a traitor and a killer and a liar . . . he still couldn't bear to watch her die.

The radio spared him from replying. Because in that instant, the static that blared to life on their radios made everyone startle.

"What?" one of the agents said as he picked up the phone.

The answer came in Malay. Through the voice and the static, Sydney could hear a commotion in the background.

"—to get to Jalan Cheras and Ninety-Three, there's a massive crowd—"

"What's going on?"

"—need backup! It's that singer, Winter Young—his car broke down here—"

Winter Young, causing the distraction of a lifetime. Sydney had never been so happy to hear his name in her life.

It was a span of seconds—all the agents' attention turned momentarily away from her and toward the radio. Of Tems looking away.

Seconds was all Sydney needed.

With a single lunge, she kicked against the floor and threw herself straight at the gunman.

32

A Flight to Catch

Tems reacted first, as she expected. In a flash, he was on her, seizing the back of her chair and pulling her away from the man. But Sydney was already moving—twisting her neck back until her teeth found the skin of his arm.

She bit down as hard as she could.

Tems dropped her with the chair, hissing in pain through his teeth. Sydney spun with the chair on her back, then threw herself into him. They crashed to the floor hard enough to break the chair—and suddenly Sydney felt looseness in her limbs as the chair's broken bars slid out from under her arms.

The man pointed his gun at her from the floor.

It was just enough of an awkward angle that he couldn't get a precise shot—so Sydney ducked, putting her bound arms up high in the air and bracing herself.

The bullet shot straight through the tape, grazing her wrist in the process.

Pain shot down her arm in a trail of fire. Sydney swore through her teeth, but forced herself to keep moving, pulling the ripped duct tape apart with the strength of her wrists. Her arms came free.

Blood from the graze smeared against the floor as she ducked low. Tems managed to seize her sleeve and yank her hard toward him, but she slipped out of her jacket like water. Then she turned toward the open window and hurtled out into the night.

She could hear Tems yelling behind her, but she didn't dare look back. Time only existed in seconds now—she could hear it in the pounding of her heart as she sprinted up against the wall, lungs aching, and launched herself over the top. Behind her, an alarm started to blare—and suddenly a spotlight illuminated the ground around her in a blinding flood of white.

She squinted in the glow and ran for the police car that Tems had initially led them both toward. Sure enough, it was still there.

And when she arrived at it, she flung the door open to see that Tems had left the jeep running. He must have spent all his energy dragging her semiconscious form from the car earlier, had completely forgotten about it.

She whispered a thank-you to every god in the world and leapt into the driver's seat. As she revved the engine, she saw the first shapes darting out from the gate.

She didn't wait to see if Tems was one of them. Instead, she slammed her foot down on the gas pedal. The car zoomed forward onto the road with a roar and a scream of rubber against cement.

A bullet pinged against the car's back windshield.

Sydney ducked instinctively. Her eyes darted up to the rearview mirror to see a motorcycle skid onto the road right behind her, followed by two more. The one in the front was Tems—she could see his hair streaming behind him, because he hadn't bothered to throw on a helmet.

Sydney turned her eyes onto the road. Three miles to the airport. She wasn't going to be able to outrun Tems, not in this car, not against a motorcycle, not against a fellow agent who had aced his driving courses—but she could outmuscle him.

Suddenly, she threw the car into reverse. The tires screamed in protest as she spun around until the car faced Tems—then slammed on the brakes.

Tems veered away at the last second before he could collide with her hood. His motorcycle careened off the road and into the grass.

Sydney slammed on the gas pedal and spun the car back around, then forced it onward. She could feel the car struggling from the abuse.

"Steady, girl," she muttered, patting the steering wheel. She flipped on the radio, searching for a channel that might be mentioning the commotion that Winter had stirred up in the city.

It took her just a few seconds to find a station. An explosion of cheering came on, and in the midst of the chaos, she could hear a reporter shouting in Malay over the noise.

"—and we still have no word on whether Mr. Young is in the car or whether he has been safely removed from it. There appears to be some effort in the crowd to make space around the car, but there are too many pushing inward. Look, here come two more police cars! They've got their work cut out for them. The intersection is still closed as a result, and—"

Sydney shook her head. If Winter could make his way back to the airfield, they might have—

Something slammed hard against the back of her car. Sydney was thrown forward against the steering wheel—a second later, she saw the two other police motorcycles fanning out on either side of her, stretching a metal wire between them. Now she could make out the barbs on them. They were going to try to puncture her tires.

She spun the steering wheel and hurtled off the road into the dirt. The car tires protested against the rough terrain.

"Stay together," she pleaded through gritted teeth as she fought to drive back onto the road. The dirt changed suddenly to asphalt again.

Another bullet pinged against the driver's window, sending long cracks up the glass. Sydney only had time to force the car into the second lane before a second bullet hit the window.

It shattered this time. Glass sprayed against Sydney's face as she went.

Now she could see the airfield in the distance, the curve of its roof like a beacon in the night.

She looked in the rearview mirror to see the police motorcycles giving chase. Her jaw tightened. "Come and get me," she snapped.

Then she threw her car back in reverse as hard as she could.

The car slammed into the first motorcycle, then the second. They went flying—the police riders rolled against the pavement as Sydney veered forward again.

The gates leading into the airfield were still thrown open, as if expecting them. Her gaze searched frantically for Winter's jet—for a second, she thought it might have been forced to leave them behind again. But this time, it was still there.

A black motorcycle screeched in front of her. The rider flung himself off the bike as it careened right into her car.

Sydney slammed her foot down, but not fast enough. The motorcycle crashed into windshield.

Her seat belt cut into her chest as the car flipped on its side from the impact. For an instant, all she could see was darkness and stars. Metal screamed and crunched around her. The car jolted to a halt on its side.

Her head swam as she forced her eyes open. Glass shards were everywhere—she was hanging sideways in her seat, the belt the only thing keeping her in position.

Just like Niall, seconds before he died.

Get out, she told herself.

She struggled to unclip her belt. When she did, she fell with a painful thud onto a blanket of glass. The twisted parts of the car seemed to close in around her like the jaws of a beast. Sydney dug her boots against the steering wheel and pulled herself up as hard as she could, reaching for the passenger window that gaped above her.

She pulled herself out of the car's wreckage and slid to the ground. The jet was so close now.

Behind her, she heard the crunch of footsteps on broken glass. She didn't need to look over her shoulder to know that it was Tems.

"Stop," he called.

She didn't. Instead, she broke into a run again. Her lungs screamed for her to stop, but she forced herself onward. Every muscle hurt.

"*Stop*," Tems shouted again. This time, she heard the click of a gun barrel behind her.

Before her, she saw the jet turn on the runway. Was it on? Sure enough, a pilot sat in the cockpit, and he was turning the jet so as to prepare for takeoff. It was headed straight for them.

Sydney slowed to a stop and forced herself to turn around and face Tems. There was blood smeared across his face—his angry grimace told her he'd gotten hurt during the chase, too. He had a gun pointed at her, and his finger rested on the trigger.

His eyes went to the jet. Then back to her. He lifted the gun higher and pushed his finger down slightly on the trigger.

She put her hands up. The jet drew closer.

Tems narrowed his eyes at her. He was going to shoot her, she realized suddenly. So much for wanting her alive.

Just as the thought jolted through her—

A figure barreled out of the darkness and slammed into Tems, knocking him off his feet.

It took her a second to recognize him.

Winter.

33

Showdown

The impact when Winter rammed himself into Tems knocked the breath from him. Both crashed to the ground. The jet's engines roared nearby.

Winter glanced up to where the plane approached them. From the open jetway, he could see Dameon crouched at the entrance, a rope ladder in his hand. He tossed it down. The ladder unfurled, its bottom snapping to a stop right above the ground.

He kicked Tems's gun out of his hands. The weapon spun across the tarmac as Winter shot to his feet and began sprinting toward Sydney.

"*Go!*" he shouted.

She gauged their distance once before turning toward the jet and running for the rope ladder. He glanced over his shoulder to see Tems run for them, too.

Sydney reached the rope ladder and grabbed it. Winter followed close behind her. One of his hands grabbed the ladder, while the other hung back, as if he were having trouble getting a good grip.

Behind him came Tems. Winter glanced up to see Sydney nearly at the top. As Tems lunged toward him, Winter suddenly grabbed the ladder with both hands and jumped up a few rungs. The spotlights from the airport dotted his vision.

He had almost reached the top of the ladder when he suddenly felt a hand yank his ankle down. It was Tems, clawing for him. Winter kicked out with his boot and forced himself up. One arm swung up into the jet.

Then Dameon and Sydney were hauling him up—the jet was increasing in speed—and with a mighty pull, they stumbled inside the cabin.

Winter felt the edge of something metal and sharp against his neck. He stilled as he heard Tems's voice against his ear.

"I'd be careful, if I were you," Tems snapped.

Winter slowly got to his feet as the blade pressed harder. He wanted to swallow, but his throat felt like it was filled with fire. His eyes darted to Dameon, who watched him with a sickened expression—and then to Sydney, whose gaze never left Tems.

"Sit down, Dameon," she said in a steady voice without looking at him.

Dameon did as she said, settling into one of the cabin's seats. The plane sped up more until the roar of its engines filled the air around them. When Winter glanced out the windows, he could see the world speeding by.

Sydney stood in the aisle, each hand gripping the back of a seat. "What do you want us to do, Tems?" she said.

Winter felt the agent's grip tighten around his neck, the blade pressing hard enough now to draw blood. Tems shifted toward the open door of the plane, yanking it closed. The roar from outside turned muted, the engine noise muffled.

"Your cuff," Tems said to Winter.

"What?" he said hoarsely.

"Unlock it. Now."

In a flash, he remembered the explosives on the cuffs of his suit, remembered Niall demonstrating how to remove them.

Tems tightened his grip on the blade. "Nice and slow," he murmured in Winter's ear. "No sudden movements."

Winter gritted his teeth and reached down to the cuff, tapped its edge three times, turned it sideways.

The device came off with a click.

"Activate it," Tems said.

Winter hesitated. Tems pushed the blade harder against his neck. From his seat, Dameon flinched, as if wanting to rush at him.

"Now," Tems snarled.

"Winter," Sydney murmured, giving him a pointed, searing look. "Do it."

Winter tapped the cuff. His fingerprint activated the device, and the sockets of the cuff's skull flashed red in an ominous rhythm.

"Now send a message to Panacea," Tems said to Sydney. "Tell them the pilot is having trouble. Tell Sauda the plane won't climb."

Then, in Winter's periphery, he saw the agent pull something out of his pocket and hold it up.

With a sickening feeling, Winter understood.

Tems *wanted* them to be on the plane. He *wanted* the plane to crash, would use the explosive to disable the jet. If it did, it would make for the perfect excuse to Panacea about what had happened. They had tried to escape the country with Tems in tow; the plane had run into trouble during takeoff on the runway and exploded; the plane had crashed, taking the lives of Winter and Sydney and Dameon—while Tems, most likely, followed an escape plan.

The plane's speed stayed steady, as if the pilot were afraid to take off and too afraid to stop. He must be able to see everything that was happening in here.

Winter closed his eyes for a moment. Somehow, one of his past performances came back to him now—a stunt where he was tied up in midair, dangling arched over the stage as the audience gasped. He had twisted out of a silk rope that had been looped loosely around his neck, had pulled off a stunt that made him look like he defied all laws of gravity.

What is a mission but a performance? Sauda had once said to him.

All of his concentration now homed in on the blade pressed against his neck.

The show must go on, he thought.

Then he threw his head back as hard as he could.

The back of his head collided with Tems's nose. He felt the agent flinch, giving him a slight inch as the blade loosened against his neck. The blinking cufflink dropped from his hands, rolling away and disappearing underneath a row of seats.

Almost instantly, Tems had the knife pressed against his skin again— but Winter was already twisting in his grasp, sliding out like water between rocks.

As he did, he saw Sydney move.

Tems grabbed his arm in a viselike grip and twisted it back. Pain lanced through his muscles—Winter bent with the movement. A lesson from Sydney shot through his head, when she had used his own weight against him and thrown him to the floor.

Tems tightened his hold and pulled up, aiming to break his bone. Winter felt the pressure against his arm. *Now,* he told himself.

When Tems yanked up, he flipped with the motion—channeling all of his momentum in the direction of Tems's movement. The sudden shift in weight threw the agent off balance. Both of them fell backward.

Winter hopped to his feet. But then Tems was on him again. Winter felt a weight hit him hard in the back. He fell forward, collapsing against the floor. The plane veered slightly to one side, as if turning in its run down the curving tarmac, and he felt his body roll with the movement. When he flipped over, he saw Tems standing over him, his eyes flashing with rage, his arm raised, blade in hand.

"Not much of a fighter, are you?" he hissed with a grim smile.

Then he brought the blade down on Winter's chest.

A hand stopped the knife before it could hit him. It was Sydney.

"Oh, but I am," she snarled.

34

You Go, I Go

She was on him like a whirlwind—her hands turned into claws, raking at his eyes. He stumbled backward, momentarily uncoordinated as he squeezed his eyes shut. She slammed him hard into the locked door of the cockpit.

Then he lunged at her again, the knife flashing through the air toward her face. She threw herself to the floor of the aisle and grabbed for his boot. Her hand hooked on the back of his left shoe—she pulled as hard as she could.

On the floor, she saw the cuff, its red lights blinking faster. She had to get rid of it, now.

He was too heavy for her to throw him completely off balance, but it made him stumble, forced him to stop his knife attack for a split second in order to steady himself.

He suddenly held up his hands.

"Syd, stop!" he shouted. *"Stop!"*

Behind her, Winter hesitated—but Sydney just narrowed her eyes at him and held her stance. Her lungs were hurting now.

Tems took a step toward her, his hands still up. "Syd, please," he said. "You don't understand the entire story."

He was playing his mind games with her again. She watched him carefully, bracing herself for the sudden move she knew he would make. Her eyes darted to the floor of the plane. The cuff was about to go off.

Then he lunged for her.

Sydney ducked down—Winter jerked back. As Tems attacked them again, Sydney's eyes darted to the door on the side of the plane, its handle marked with a bold red warning.

DO NOT PULL.

She threw herself at the door, grabbed the handle, and pulled it up with every ounce of strength she had.

"*Hold on!*" she shouted to Winter.

An alarm blared to life all around them, drowning them in sound.

The door flew open.

Their world suddenly turned into a roaring maelstrom—a vacuum of blistering wind from outside slammed into Sydney. The cuff on the floor flew down the aisle.

Her hands clutched the armrest of the nearest seat. Beside her, the gaping door of the plane revealed the runway still zooming by beneath the plane's wheels.

The jet veered sharply to one side.

The flashing cuff flew out of the open hatch.

Tems lost his balance to the strength of the wind. He stumbled backward toward the opening, then twisted around and fell.

Sydney felt a hand close hard around her ankle—then her entire body tugged toward the gaping entrance. Tems had grabbed her leg and was taking her out with him.

Outside the plane came a *boom*—the cuff must have exploded.

The force of it made the plane tilt. The move threw off Tems's grip on Sydney—both of them tumbled across the floor.

She thought she heard Winter shouting her name, but she couldn't look up. All she could do was kick out at Tems, stomping her boot hard against the floor in an attempt to loosen his grip.

For a second, he met her gaze—and in it, she saw a look not of rage or revenge, but of naked fear.

He was afraid of dying, too.

"Get the hell off me," she growled through her teeth, then kicked for his face.

This time, her boot connected perfectly with his jaw. He shuddered—she felt his grip slip and his body go slack.

She didn't know initially why she did it. Perhaps it was years of training to hone her instincts to obey an agent's mantras—perhaps it was the ingrained determination to complete the mission she'd been sent here to do. But as Tems's limp body tumbled toward the plane's open door and the speeding tarmac beyond it, Sydney released her grip on the back of the chair and reached for his falling figure.

"*Sydney!*"

She heard Winter's voice distinctly this time. But everything around her seemed to move slowly now as she lunged for Tems's sleeve and seized the edge of it in her hand.

His weight immediately hit her, yanking her down with him. Her boots hit the wall of the plane next to the door. She threw herself backward until she was flat against the wall, then hung on to his arm with all her might.

She was still slipping.

But she hadn't come all this way to die for Tems, to give her life for a traitor.

Her boots were slipping—she wasn't going to make it if she kept hanging on to Tems. The rope in her mind pulled so tightly that she wanted to scream.

No regrets.

Then she felt Winter's familiar arms lock around her body. Her slip halted abruptly. When she opened her eyes and glanced over, she saw Winter hanging on to her with clenched teeth, a look of fiery determination gleaming in his eyes.

"*Close the goddamn door!*" he yelled.

She pulled with him—

—until they all collapsed against the floor right behind the first row of seats. Sydney glanced back at the door, which was pressed flat against the side of the plane. She wedged one of her boots underneath the handle, then the other, squeezed her eyes shut, then pushed with her legs as hard as she could.

The door creaked against the pressure of the roaring wind. She gave it one last shove.

The door suddenly went up high enough for the wind to catch its other side.

With a slam, it flew shut, its metal handle clanking so loud against the plane's wall that Sydney thought it might break off altogether. She stumbled away from the seats long enough to throw herself against the door, then pumped the handle to seal it into place.

The sudden lack of roaring wind sounded overwhelming in the space. She collapsed against the floor, gasping. Her head swam, and she was only vaguely aware of the sound of the alarm still blaring.

Eventually, she realized the pilot's voice was on the intercom.

"Is everyone alive? Is everyone alive?" he was saying over and over again.

Sydney's mouth felt too dry to respond. All she could do was look over to where Winter was pressed against the jet floor, his gaze going between her and Tems's unconscious form. At the rear of the plane, Dameon finally stirred and hurried up the aisle toward them.

At last, Sydney found her voice. "We're all here," she shouted. "Stop the plane. Stop the plane!"

She could feel the plane steadying to a stop. Through the windows, the lights of fire engines and police cars flashed along either side of the plane, as if guiding it.

Her eyes went back to Winter. He looked pale, and blood stained his arm and face. But he was alive, and right now, that mattered more to Sydney than anything in the world.

"Are you okay?" he murmured.

She held his gaze for a moment. Then she closed her eyes and rested her head against her arm. Her hand stretched out for his, and in the darkness, she felt him take it.

"I will be," she whispered.

Keep Your Heart Open

Once they were debriefed at the Singapore International Airport, once Tems had been cleared for extradition to the United States, once she and Winter were finally back on American soil after catching a new flight, Sydney confirmed several things.

The CIA rogue cell that they—that Tems—had been working with from the beginning of their mission, was behind not only the president's assassination, but had facilitated Niall's murder for Tems. As a result, the CIA itself had exploded into the headlines, with the director resigning in the midst of the scandal and an internal investigation plowing through the agency's ranks. Not a day had passed without the vice president—now the president—addressing the nation to report on the state of international affairs or provide updates about the arrests within the agency as members of the rogue cell were identified.

"He's going to be okay," Sauda told Sydney three weeks later as they sat across from each other in a war room at Panacea's headquarters. The woman nodded at a screen on the wall that was playing a live feed of Winter leaving the FBI's front entrance, his eyes shielded behind large black sunglasses as a crowd of reporters and fans jostled around him. "We've already spoken with both the FBI and President Castillo about him. The news will be reporting on his recovery and the number of postponed concerts he'll need to deal with for the next few months."

Sydney shifted in her seat. The dozens of bruises she'd gained from the chase and final fight at the airport still made her wince.

"I feel like we owe his fans an apology," she replied dryly.

"An apology? All this news around Winter being trapped in Singapore during the president's assassination has practically erased his father's tell-all book from the news. His team should be sending us flowers." Sauda crossed her arms and sighed. "But make no mistake, Sydney. I don't think his cover will last through any more missions with us. Take comfort in the fact that this may be the last time he risks his life for us."

Sydney angled her swivel chair away and pretended not to care. But a hollow in her chest had formed since the day she had separated from Winter, since her life had taken her back to Panacea's headquarters and his life had taken him back into the whirlwind of the spotlight. He seemed like he was doing okay, at least in the news, although she had yet to see him smile for the cameras since his return.

At night, she'd startle awake, still reaching for his hand, still waiting for him to take it. Then she would toss and turn, would sit up in bed, staring at her window in grief and exhaustion until dawn came to burn the darkness away.

No more missions with Winter, at least not with him at her side as a partner. She didn't let herself dwell on it, couldn't bear the thought that she might never see him again. She told herself to be what Sauda suggested— grateful for his safety.

A smaller window on the live feed now showed a CIA agent being led away in cuffs, the latest arrest in the rogue cell scandal.

"War still on?" Sydney asked hesitantly.

Sauda shook her head. "The last intel we were given was that China has backed down after news spilled about the CIA's rogue cell. President

Castillo has gone with the CIA director to China to apologize for the incident and accusations. China is going to introduce sanctions against us, to show their displeasure with the whole incident. There will be years of damage control ahead for us." She looked at Sydney. "But no war."

Sydney sank back in her seat. Suddenly, she felt like everything in her had turned weak, and a curtain of exhaustion draped so heavily on her that she wanted to fall asleep right here in her chair.

"Still," she whispered, almost to herself. "The mission was a failure."

Sauda was quiet for a while. "It could have gone much worse. I think we have the camaraderie between you and Winter to thank."

Camaraderie. A thread of fear shot through her as she met Sauda's searching gaze, as if the woman was reading every thought she had of Winter. Sydney wondered if Sauda had somehow guessed at what had happened between her and Winter during the mission, if something in her demeanor might have given it away. And she wondered if Sauda was thinking of Niall, of the fleeting moments of love in her own life, of future moments that would now never come to pass.

But Sauda just gave her a curt nod.

"The question now is Tems." Sauda laced her fingers together against the table. Grief clouded her features. Niall's name seemed to hover in the air between them, although neither of them had the strength to bring him up.

"What will you do with Tems?" Sydney asked instead.

"I'm hardly the one in control of his fate now," Sauda replied. "The government will make sure he'll never set foot outside of prison again. But they want us to have a conversation with him. He has valuable information about others in the ring he was working with."

"The government needs our help for leverage with him?" Sydney asked.

"I think we both know what leverage will work," Sauda replied gently.

Sydney felt something in her chest twist.

"You do the honors," Sauda went on. "After tomorrow, he's not going to talk to anyone again for a very, very long time. But in spite of all his despicable actions, he cared about you. If there's anything to tell, we have the best chance of him telling you."

Sydney looked away. Tems had lied and cheated, had stolen from the agency more viciously than Sydney ever did. He had taken Niall from her, the only man Sydney had ever seen as a father.

Still. There was some part of her, however small, that felt sorry for him. Even now, perhaps, he believed he'd done it to honor a friend. How strange an emotion love was, how powerful it must be to fuel kindness and hatred and empathy and revenge and grief, all at once.

"Did Niall know?" Sydney asked in the silence that settled between them. "That you loved him?"

Sauda didn't answer. Out of instinct born from years of training, Sydney found her gaze falling on the woman's hands and arms, noted the way she tensed, how her shoulders pulled slightly forward, as if protecting herself. She waited as Sauda stared for a while at the screen.

"No," Sauda said at last. "I never told him. And he never told me. We never uttered a word to each other about how we felt, but it didn't matter. I knew. I could feel it every time we were together in a room, every time we had a late-night chat or shared a laugh or confided in each other. Every time we grieved together over a failed mission, over a lost ally, over his estrangement from his daughter. I don't know how to explain it. But love is something you don't need to explain. When it's there, you just know." She looked at Sydney, and in the woman's eyes, she could see an endless ocean of grief. "We both understood the dangers of our work. We have prepared our entire lives for this ending."

Somehow, Winter's song came back to Sydney now. *You are my meditation. Am I ever yours, too?*

She could feel the pain rising in her chest, could sense the ghost of her mentor in the room. She thought of why Winter chose to leave his heart open, in spite of all that could happen. Her eyes glossed with tears.

"I'm so sorry," she whispered.

Sauda just nodded at her words, swallowed, and looked away.

"I know you understand," she said softly, before walking out of the room.

When Sydney stepped inside his cell in solitary confinement, Tems looked tired, dark circles prominent under his eyes. His skin was pale under the cold wash of fluorescent light. He sat on the ground, because there was no furniture allowed in his room—not even chairs—and regarded her, his head tilted.

"Sauda sent you, did she?" he said.

Sydney felt her rage rise at his words. "Does it matter?" she replied.

Tems sighed, then straightened and looked away from her. "She wants me to tell you everything, because she thinks I care about you."

"Well?" She leaned against the cell door. "Do you?"

She hadn't expected her words to wound him, but she saw a slight wince in his eyes. "What do you want, Syd?" he said tiredly.

She chewed her lip for a moment. "There are others you worked with, aren't there? Those we don't have the names for yet."

He was silent. "You really think I'm going to talk to you," he finally said.

She let out her breath, thought for a minute. "You know, you're not the only person in the world who cared about someone. Niall loved others, too. He had a daughter he cared for, who he'll never see again. He loved Sauda. And whether you want to believe it or not, he worried about your safety when you were out in the field."

Tems let out a sarcastic chuckle at that and turned his head away. "Sure."

"I will never forgive you for what you did," Sydney replied, her face sober. "But I do think you cared. In your own, twisted way." Her voice quieted. "I know that love and anger can make people do the worst things."

He grimaced at her words and leaned back against the wall. "What's this?" he muttered. "A gentler side of Sydney Cossette?"

"I'm giving you a chance to be understood, Tems."

"Ah, well. Thanks for that," he said in disgust.

They sank back into silence. She knelt back down and took a seat on the floor across from him. "You'll live out your life in here. But maybe there will be people alive because of your help. Maybe someone out there will feel gratitude for what you did, even if they don't know who you are. Maybe you'll save someone who was friends with someone else." She crossed her arms. "And if none of those things matter to you, then why are you here at all? Why all the effort to become an agent? Why put yourself through all this?"

He didn't look at her, and in frustration, Sydney looked away, too. Her eyes went to the lone window at the top of his cell. It was barely one square foot in size, the only view of the outside world that he would have, possibly for the rest of his life.

"Back on the plane," Tems said at last.

Her attention returned to him.

"Back on the plane," he repeated, "you could have let go of me. I almost fell through the plane's open hatch and onto the runway. You could have let me die, and you didn't."

She rested her elbows on her knees. "I wanted you to stand trial for what you did," she replied. "I wanted you to know that your actions caused so much pain."

He studied her. "That wasn't the reason," he said. "I saw your face in that moment. You didn't want me to die."

Her lips tightened. "In spite of everything," she said, "I once saw a side of you that opened up and told me your vulnerabilities. That made me laugh, that made me feel like you were my friend. I remembered a version of you that, for a split second, I thought I could be with, if only for fragments of time. That couldn't have all been a hoax. There had to be something real in there."

She thought he would say something sarcastic in response, but he didn't. He looked away from her again. This time, there was something far away in his eyes, something that looked like regret.

"I saved you because I think people are worth saving," she said quietly.

He didn't say anything, turning his gaze instead on a slant of light at the top of his cell's wall, and for a while, Sydney thought he had decided not to speak to her at all.

Then he looked down and sighed. "Alison MacGranger. Neil Wolfe."

Sydney listened carefully as he listed several more names, checking halfway through to make sure that the recording device taped to the back collar of her jacket was functioning.

"Thank you," she said. "If there are discrepancies, we'll be coming back to you. So I hope you said the right names."

He watched her as she rose to her feet. Finally, he said, "It's because of him, isn't it? This new, soft side of you?"

"Who?" she asked.

He nodded at her. "Your fancy boy."

Sydney had stayed calm through their conversation, but at the mention of Winter, she felt the familiar jolt in her heart, the painful tug. "I don't think you understand me," she replied.

"I do. And you would leave all this for him."

It was a dangerous thing for him to suggest, and Sydney noted the purposeful way he'd brought it up, knowing that Panacea was watching.

Still, his words hit something deep and raw in her chest. She wanted to wince, but her expression stayed cool and composed.

"I would do whatever was needed," she said. "As I would for any mission."

Tems stared at her a moment longer. "He's lucky, you know," he said at last. "To have you watching his back."

She snorted. "I'm pretty sure he's never been in more danger than after he began working with me."

"He's lucky," Tems repeated. "I hope he knows that."

She thought of Sauda and the grief in the woman's eyes, thought of all the warnings she'd ever been given about falling in love in this line of work. She thought about whether or not she could bear following in Sauda's shoes.

"I would have stayed with you," Tems said. "If I could."

This was his old charisma coming out again, trying to worm his way back into her heart, telling her things that he didn't mean. Sometimes, people don't change. And once upon a time, she might have believed him, would have thought that he was someone who understood her solely because they had run through the same gauntlets together, had faced the same hardships together.

Now she just straightened and turned toward the cell door. She knew where her heart belonged, and she knew what she wanted to do.

"Goodbye, Tems," she said over her shoulder, and closed the door behind her.

The next night, Sydney found herself parking her rental car in front of a quiet house on an unassuming street in a suburb of Houston, Texas.

This time, Sauda hadn't sent her. Sydney was here on her own, and as she sat in the darkness of the car, she wondered if she was doing the right thing, if she should be opening this wound at all.

She reached into her bag and pulled out Niall's letter, the one he had hoped to give Quinn after his retirement.

Her thumbs glided across the sealed envelope. She'd found it in his desk drawer after helping Sauda sort through stacks of his files, had jotted down Quinn's address from it. Niall's handwriting was painstakingly neat, a contrast to his usual scrawl. The letter was even stamped and ready to go.

When Niall had first mentioned it to her, she had felt a tide of overwhelming envy and resentment, of her futile yearning for the love of a father that she never had. Now, all she felt was grief—and underneath it, a determination to set things right, however much she could, for a man that had been the closest thing to a father she'd ever known.

Now she was here, alone, more nervous than she ever was at the start of any official mission.

Make me proud, kid.

She looked back toward the house. Even now, there was a small part of her that wanted to be selfish, to wallow in her grief at losing Niall, a part of her that wanted to keep this letter for herself. That because Quinn had never known or understood her father, maybe she didn't deserve Niall's love as much as Sydney did.

She wiped tears from her face. She had been in and out of these crying sessions all day—perhaps she would never really be free from them.

What was it that Winter had said in his interview in Honolulu?

Grief is love. It's the price we pay for the gift of someone meaningful in our lives.

She knew Winter would do it, would give the letter to its rightful owner, and that no matter what, he would find a way to absorb the hurt to his open heart.

She wasn't sure if she was as good a person. But she could feel the pull of his influence on her all the same. Tems was right. Winter had changed her, in his own way.

She took a deep breath and composed herself. Then she stepped out of the car.

The only sound in the night was the clip of her boots on the stone walkway up to the house. Sydney rang the doorbell, then took a step back and waited. A few seconds passed, followed by the muffled sound of voices from inside.

Then the door opened, and Sydney found herself looking into the face of a slender young woman that reminded her immediately of Niall. The same soulful eyes, the same thick hair.

It had to be Quinn.

She gave Sydney an uncertain smile. "Can I help you?" she asked.

"I, ah—" Sydney began, her voice hoarse. She held out the letter to Quinn, handing over her heart. "I think this is for you."

Quinn frowned slightly. Behind her, Sydney heard the sound of a man, followed by a baby's cheerful gurgle.

Quinn took the letter, then gave Sydney a questioning look.

"Your father wanted you to have it," Sydney said.

Quinn's expression shifted, morphing from confusion to shock, to pain, then to a wary hope. Her eyes went down to the letter and back up to Sydney.

"Who are you?" she asked.

"A colleague," Sydney said. "And a friend."

When Quinn's hand tightened on the letter, Sydney took another step back. She didn't belong in this moment anymore. "Sorry to interrupt your night," she said politely.

And before Quinn could say anything more to her, she turned around and walked back to her car. Behind her, she could sense the woman standing there, filling with questions she didn't know how to ask, unsure how to handle the tide of emotions that the mention of her father had brought back.

Imperfect. The word echoed in Sydney's mind as she reached her car. When she glanced back at the house, the door had closed.

Imperfect. But we all did the best we could.

Then she got back into the car, took a deep breath, and drove off into the night.

Happiness in Yourself

For a while, Winter thought that Sydney wouldn't get a chance to say farewell at all, that this was the way that Panacea would once again step out of his life. Once he'd flown back to America, he'd been caught up in a media whirlwind, everyone foaming at the mouth for an interview about how he'd been trapped in Singapore during the president's assassination.

In the midst of government upheaval and protests in the streets, in the midst of headlines and his phone ringing off the hook, Winter had waited for word from Sydney.

Nothing.

At night, her figure danced through his dreams. He would lie in bed and reach his hand out, would feel her hand touch his in return, would imagine the warmth of her snuggling close to him, her hair brushing his face. He would dream of her calling on the phone and would try to pick up, only to be met over and over with static on the other end. He would see her on the street and try to say hello, but no matter how loudly he called to her, she wouldn't look back. He would startle awake in bed, heart pounding, her name on the edge of his lips, certain that she must have been here.

But she wasn't. The other side of his bed was always empty and cold.

✦ ✦ ✦

"He's canceling the book."

Winter frowned at Gavi from across the booth tucked into a private corner of the restaurant. It was a late night, and the streets of Santa Monica outside the window were devoid of the tourists that had flocked along the sidewalk earlier in the day. No one else was around except for the waiters, who seemed to give them a respectable distance.

"Are you sure?" Winter asked in a low voice.

Gavi nodded. She was dressed as simply as he'd ever seen her, in an oversized sweater and baggy jeans, her hair tied up in a messy bun—but even so, she looked glamorous, like she was someone destined to be famous. She dipped a fry in ketchup. "Heard it from my publicist friend. You'll probably get the official letter from your legal team soon."

It was strange—after everything that had happened, after losing Niall and nearly their own lives—to concern himself with something like the tell-all book. But Winter felt a rush of relief nevertheless.

"Did he say why?" he asked.

Gavi smiled and lowered her eyes. "You really don't read the news, do you? I leaked a supposedly candid conversation with a friend of mine," she said. "Complaining about how everything in the book is fabricated and entirely false, and about how I could tell because I've been there for so much of it. It caused a bit of backlash online." She licked the fry, then nibbled its edge. "I guess he didn't want to deal with the mounting questions from his publisher in addition to your lawsuit, so he backed down. It's done."

Winter leaned back in his seat. Between the endless coverage about Rosen, he had tried to avoid the clips of his father at the publisher's office, had tried to avoid the tabloids still printing excerpts from the book.

"Thank you," he said to her. "For doing that."

Gavi was quiet for a moment. "I think it's probably the least I could have done."

It was the closest thing he'd ever gotten to an apology from her. Winter gave her a small smile. "True," he said. "But I still appreciate it."

She laughed a little at that, then fell silent. This, at least, was something they were good at—sitting in comfortable silence, each letting the other dwell in their own thoughts. So they did, picking at their food until they were full.

As Winter paid the check and they gathered their things, Gavi asked, "So, how are things with Ashley? You seeing her or what?"

Winter shook his head and kept his voice calm. "It couldn't have gone anywhere. She's not working for me anymore, anyway. I think everything that happened in Singapore was too overwhelming for her."

Gavi made a sympathetic noise. They rose from their booth, then headed toward the back door. As they stepped out into the cool, wet night, Gavi stopped in the parking lot and turned to look at him.

"Hey," she said, then hesitated.

"Hm?" Winter said.

Gavi rarely looked vulnerable, but she did now, her makeup-free face illuminated under the streetlights. "Look." She paused again, sighed in frustration, then went on. "I'm sorry about how things went. Sometimes I don't know why I do these things or let them spiral out of control. I just . . ." She trailed off a bit. "Lies are easier for me than the truth. You know? Sometimes I wish I could live in one."

Winter looked at her and felt that old twinge in his heart. They had always understood each other in this way, at least—they hungered for different sorts of attention, but they were hungry all the same, always afraid in one way or another to lose the eye of the world. When she looked up at him, he saw that fear in her eyes, like she might disappear if she didn't play these games with life.

"I know," he said.

She smiled, wistfully this time. "I know you know," she replied.

"Maybe we can just understand each other, then, and leave it at that," he said. "For old time's sake."

She held a hand out to him. "Maybe," she answered.

He took her hand and shook it. "Take care of yourself, Gavi."

"You too, Winter."

Winter looked on as she got into her car. At some other point in his life, he might have felt the yawning absence of her, might have missed the chaos she always brought with her, however painful it might be. He might have felt that trap close around him again, pulling him back into their endless, fruitless relationship.

But his heart pointed in a different direction now. So he watched her go, until she pulled out of the lot and disappeared around the corner. Then he turned his back.

Later that same night, he got a call from his father.

He woke from a fitful sleep to see the ID on his phone. Hesitated.

The number rang for a while, went silent. Then rang again.

Winter sat there and stared at his father's name. He could imagine the entire conversation, knew that it must be about the book, could see in his mind his father's cold eyes, his cruel face. Even so, everything in him—the once-obedient son, the ashamed child, the lonely boy—screamed to pick it up, to answer in spite of everything, because a son was supposed to pick up for his father.

But this time, he didn't. He stayed there, his hand trembling, his jaw set, and let the phone ring. Let it go silent again. As it did, he thought of Sydney and let the memory of her give him strength.

Sometimes you didn't have to let people back into your life, to absorb all the cruelty of the world. Sometimes you didn't have to open your heart. Sometimes it was okay to just let them go.

So Winter gathered his courage, put his phone away, and let his father go.

A month passed. He still hadn't heard from Sydney.

"You haven't been eating," Dameon told him as they lounged in the living room of Winter's home.

November had arrived in earnest, and a steady rain pelted the windows. Winter looked out at the soaking world and shrugged. "I'm okay," he said.

Dameon gave him a skeptical look. He hadn't asked details about what happened with Panacea after their harrowing flight home, but Winter could see the questions imprinted in his friend's eyes.

"How are *you*?" he asked.

"Well enough." Dameon leaned back on the couch. "I don't know how you deal with all the media these days. I still have nightmares."

"I'm sorry." Winter looked down and ran a hand through his hair. "They've stopped trying to interview you, though. Right?"

"It's quieted down. New phone helped."

"It wasn't supposed to go like this."

"Yeah, I didn't think you expected any of that to happen."

Winter laughed a little, then shook his head as Dameon regarded him with a careful eye.

"How's Sydney?" he asked.

"I have no idea," Winter replied. Dameon might have uncovered some of their secrets, but he wasn't meant to get more, and Winter found himself folding back in again, protecting her as much as he could. "I haven't heard from her since we returned."

Dameon nodded. "So that's why you're not eating."

"I'm eating just fine."

Dameon studied him with a thoughtful expression for a while. Then he leaned forward. "When you first agreed to work with Panacea," he said slowly, "you hadn't met Sydney yet."

He shook his head. "Not yet."

"You risked your life for them. Why would you agree to do something like that?"

Winter turned the question over in his head. It was a very Dameon question, the kind that got under his skin and stayed there, seeking the truth.

"Because they needed me," he decided to say.

Dameon searched his gaze.

"I wanted to be their answer," he explained. "I wanted to do something important, without it being broadcast all over the world. I wanted to do something that no one will ever know about."

Dameon didn't reply to that. Instead, he leaned forward and regarded Winter carefully. "Do you remember," he said, "when we first got together?"

Winter looked at him. They hadn't spoken about their past fling in a long time. "Of course I do," he said.

"Do you remember what you told me one morning, when you couldn't sleep?"

The description was vague, but Winter knew immediately what he meant. He had stayed the night at Dameon's apartment, had woken before dawn and ended up on Dameon's balcony to watch the sunrise.

Something's bothering you, Dameon had said from behind him.

Winter had glanced over his shoulder to see the boy approach, had let him curl an arm around his waist. *Something's always bothering me,* he'd answered.

Dameon hadn't pushed him on it. They'd stood there together as the sky lightened, until the first sliver of orange peeked out from the horizon.

Aren't you happy, Winter? Dameon had asked him then.

Winter had looked on as the sun emerged line by line.

The day I step away from this life, he'd answered, *is the day I'm happy with myself.*

Winter let the memory fade, let himself return Dameon's stare now as he sat on the couch.

"Winter," Dameon said. "You can't live your entire life like this."

"Like what?"

"In this half state of joy." He nodded at the window. "I know you love being onstage—it's like life is literally pouring out of you. I know you need your music like air. And I know you cared deeply about what you did with Panacea. But you've spent your entire life thriving on making others happy. You are always giving yourself away."

Winter looked down at his hands. "I don't know what else to want," he muttered.

"I know what you want." Dameon nodded at him. "I've never seen you more alive than when Sydney's beside you."

Winter looked at him. "I seem to recall being very stressed out when I'm near her," he replied.

Dameon laughed once. "Fair." He sobered. "But there is something so bright about you when you're with her. It's like you can't bear to not see her. Your body is always turned toward her. You're always aware of what she's doing and where she is. And when you're separated from her, you seem like a boat without an anchor. You seem lost. And you know why?"

"Why?"

"Because she makes *you* happy. You, Winter. Nobody else."

"I don't know what to do about it," he said. "She's not someone I can just reach out to."

"Then maybe instead of needing to see her, you need to figure out why it is that she matters so much to you," Dameon said. "Maybe you need to see what it is that she brings out of you, to make you so whole."

She made him whole. It was her, not him. But Winter listened to Dameon nevertheless, trying to accept his friend's words.

"You've got to find happiness in yourself," Dameon replied. "Just you. Or you're going to disappear into the lights."

Winter nodded absently. Happiness in himself. It seemed like an impossible thought, but he hung on to it anyway.

"Maybe someday," he said.

Dameon studied him. Outside, the rain continued.

"Maybe someday," he echoed.

After Dameon left, Winter's house settled back into a lonely silence. He got up, played a little piano, then came back to the couch and stared off into space.

He tried not to think about the fact that he might never see Sydney again.

He was okay with it. He had to be. He would endure this just as he had last time, when he'd walked away from Sydney in London and stepped out of her life for a year. He had no idea how long it would be this time. Maybe another year. Maybe several. The thought of that empty time stretching out in front of him, bleak and mysterious, was more than he could bear.

But he had to bear it if he ever hoped to see her again. And if he didn't, he needed to find a way to live with that.

He could hear the patter of rain against the glass. When he turned to look outside, he saw the trees swaying gently in the wind, their leaves lashing occasionally against the windowpanes. He wondered what Sydney was doing right now, whether she was also in her own home in her own city, staring out at the world. He wondered if she was thinking about him.

He wished he'd had the chance to say a proper goodbye. His last memory was still of her landing at the airport, of her lingering eyes before she was forced to get into her own black car. As if there had been a question on her tongue.

At last, he forced himself out of his stupor and stood up, then walked over to the window with his hands in his pockets. He knew he should get some rest, prepare for his usual marathon of dance practice and meetings the next day. Still, he found himself lingering here, waiting for the rain to change.

It was the faint sound of a knock against his front door that made him tilt his head. He glanced in the direction of the sound, his mind stirring from its trance. Had Dameon forgotten something? No one else had his gated community's entry information.

The knock came again, clearer this time. Winter sighed and walked toward his entryway. As he approached, a premonition tingled in the back of his mind, as if he were drawing closer to something that he knew would happen.

He stood in front of the door for a moment, wondering, before he peeked through the hole.

And saw Sydney standing outside, waiting.

Love Is Falling Anyway

The door opened to reveal Winter with a hesitant smile on his face. It was the most endearingly vulnerable sight that Sydney had ever seen, and she felt a pleasant shiver run down her spine.

"Hello," she said softly.

"How the hell did you get in here?" he replied, glancing down the street. "That gate's ten feet high, and the security guard didn't call me."

A month apart, and those were the first words out of his mouth. Sydney couldn't help the smile that emerged on her lips.

"Don't you know me at all?" she answered, and he laughed.

The only time she'd ever really gotten a chance to take him in was, well, during their night together—and even now, she had the urge to keep her sights trained on his front yard, ever wary of watchful eyes. But they were alone here, and for once, she let herself admire him.

"Let's just say that I'm not supposed to be here," she added. "Can I come in?"

He opened the door wider, and she stepped inside, removing her wet shoes before glancing around. The space was serene and cozy, more modest than she thought a superstar's home would be, filled with clean lines and thick rugs, fluffy couches and tasteful lights.

A beautiful grand piano stood at the far end of the living room, past a fireplace and against a series of glass walls that led to the garden outside. It was there that Winter led them now, facing her as he leaned against the instrument's sleek body with his hands in his pockets.

"Did Sauda send you?" he asked.

She shook her head.

He raised an eyebrow at her. "She's going to kill you if she finds out."

"Yeah, well, I'm always going to be her problem child."

"I'm pretty sure Tems took that title from you." His smile wavered. "What are you doing here?"

They were close enough now that she could feel the slight warmth of his breath against her skin. "I wanted to see you," she said simply.

This time, she thought she could see a shudder of fear run through him, could make out the subtle widening of his eyes, as if he couldn't quite believe his ears.

"I . . ." he said, his voice hoarse, "I can't see you. It's too risky."

"I know," she replied. "And yet here I am." Then she felt the fear, too, and her eyes lowered. "Please don't turn me away," she whispered.

When she looked up at him again, the fear in his eyes was gone, replaced by something gentler. "How long do you have?" he murmured.

"Not long." She looked out the window again, then back at him. "I have to be on a flight tomorrow morning."

He studied her face for answers. She didn't know if he found them, but after another pause, he reached his hand out and took hers, letting their fingers intertwine loosely. His skin felt warm, leaving her palm tingling.

He glanced toward the stairs. "Follow me," he whispered.

She did so without a word as he led her up the steps and along a narrow hall that opened into a large, lush suite of a bedroom, one with the same long windows overlooking the private courtyard. The rain sounded more subdued up here, the echo hollow against his roof. It was just enough noise that, if they whispered, it was as if they weren't speaking at all.

Here, he turned toward her and moved closer. She took a step back until she could feel the glass behind her. His eyes were locked on hers now, and in those dark irises, she could catch reflections of the storm outside.

"I can't promise you anything," she whispered.

He nodded, but his gaze never broke from hers. "I know," he whispered back.

Sydney felt a familiar panic rising once more. "I can't say that I love you, and I can't be here when you need me. I can't cheer for you when you accomplish something great. I can't accept any gifts from you, and I can't give you anything in return. I can't tell you when I'm in trouble. I won't even have a phone number you can dial, not unless you want to risk Sauda finding out about us." She swallowed. Sydney had been in a thousand situations that should frighten anyone, but this moment scared her more than any of them. "I know I shouldn't be here, Winter. I can't give you anything real."

"Then let's not make each other promises we can't keep," he replied. He reached out to run his fingers through her hair, and she leaned into his embrace, savoring the warmth of his skin as if she might never feel it again.

"What *can* we keep?" she murmured.

He lowered his head toward hers, his eyes turned shyly down. When his lips brushed against her cheek, she felt herself lean instinctively forward. Her eyes fluttered closed. He planted soft kisses at the edges of her lips, then kissed her fully. His lips were so soft, the taste of him so sweet. Vaguely, she could feel him sliding her jacket from her shoulders, and shivered at the feeling of his fingers running against the fabric of her shirt.

"Here's a promise I can give to you," he whispered in her ear. "I promise that, when you need me, you can always find me."

He kissed her, and she kissed him back, tugging the collar of his shirt loose, hinting for more, afraid for more, cherishing this little slice of time.

"If you find yourself feeling alone," he whispered, "I promise I'll come to you."

Would he ever brush against her skin again?

Would she ever get to touch his lips again?

He pulled away just enough to meet her gaze. His hand touched her chin, tilting it up gently. "And someday," he murmured, "in some future, when I'm no longer wanted on a stage, and when you no longer want to be a secret agent . . . let's say that, if you aren't trying to find someone else, I promise I'll come find you." His lips brushed hers again. "I promise I'm yours."

A future where Winter stepped away from the spotlight and she stepped out of the shadows. Sydney closed her eyes, felt his hands run along her back, and let herself imagine the possibility. It sounded like a scene from a far, far future, one where they'd both grown old—but a possible one, one that could exist.

"It's a promise," she said softly.

His hand grasped hers and brought it up to his chest, where she could feel the faint rhythm of his heart. His breaths were shallow, and his eyes were still closed, as if savoring some sacred thing. He leaned his forehead against hers. Locks of black hair fell across his face.

"I don't love you," he murmured.

"I don't love you, too," she whispered back.

Later, when he was asleep beside her, she would rise in the dark and slip her clothes on without a sound, would disappear from his room along with the last traces of night. When he woke up alone and unsurprised, she would already be on a plane, staring down at the approaching landscape of a different city. She didn't know when they would see each other again. She didn't know whether their feelings for each other would remain the same. There were a million things she couldn't begin to know.

But perhaps there was beauty in not knowing. Maybe that was its own form of love, the faith of coming together even when you couldn't see the path in front of you, when you had no idea whether joy or heartbreak would await you further down the road of life, when you had nothing but a guiding light in the distance to yearn for.

Maybe love was not knowing and going ahead anyway.

So this time, when he kissed her, she wrapped her arms around his neck.

And let herself fall.

MISSION LOG

AGENT A: "And here are his most recent files."

AGENT B: "Thank you, ma'am."

AGENT A: "You'll notice I highlighted some areas involving ▇▇▇▇▇▇ and the Jackal. I'll need you to scrub any mentions of them from those reports. Make sure we keep them both clean."

AGENT B: "I'll have it done by the end of the week."

AGENT A: "Excellent. What is it?"

AGENT B: "Nothing. That is—I just wanted to extend my condolences to you, ma'am. I know you worked with ▇▇ for a long time."

AGENT A: "Yes. Well. It's the price we pay in this job, isn't it?"

AGENT B: "Yes. I know I have big shoes to fill."

AGENT A: "You were sent to us with high praise. You'll do fine. I hope you stay with us for a long time."

AGENT B: "Thank you, ma'am. And as for the Jackal . . . shall I follow up with her about ▇▇▇▇▇▇▇?"

AGENT A: "Give her a few weeks off. She deserves some peace, at least temporarily."

AGENT B: "Yes, ma'am."

AGENT A: "And don't be surprised if she gives you a hard time. If she tries to bite your head off, it just means she's feeling herself again."

AGENT B: "Always good to know. And, ma'am?"

AGENT A: "Yes?"

AGENT B: "About ███████. Shall I retire his file?"

AGENT B: "Ma'am?"

AGENT A: "Yes . . . I'm thinking."

AGENT B: "It seems unlikely to me that we'll call on him again. Besides, I hear he's taking a brief hiatus from his public career. Lessens his value as an asset."

AGENT A: "No, keep it open."

AGENT B: "Even after everything?"

AGENT A: "Especially after everything."

AGENT B: "That impressive, huh?"

AGENT A: "Let's just say there's some of his brother in him. We may not call on him for a while, but then again, our line of business is unpredictable, isn't it?"

AGENT B: "An understatement. Very well, ma'am. I can change the marker on his file later, if we decide otherwise."

AGENT A: "Good. And let's keep this conversation between us."

AGENT B: "Will do, ma'am. Loyalty to a secret."

AGENT A: "Loyalty to a secret."

Acknowledgments

So much of writing this book and *Stars and Smoke* was about bringing myself and others joy during the pandemic, a time that still haunts us today. Sometimes, when I think back on the origins of this story, all I can see is myself in a fog, wondering if we could ever return to our lives, if I would ever meet readers again, if we would ever find our way back. I write my happiest books during the most turbulent times, and I needed the support of others more than ever to make this story possible.

All my gratitude to Kristin Nelson, my agent going on fifteen(!) years, and the NLA team for always championing this series and sticking by me; and to my incredible, kind, courageous editors and friends, Jen Besser and Kate Meltzer, for guiding me through these books and holding my hand. You work so, so, so hard behind the scenes, and you are so dedicated to both the craft and the creatives. I am forever lucky to build stories with you both.

Our team at Macmillan Children's and Fierce Reads is an absolute dream. To the wonderful Emilia Sowersby, Ana Deboo, Kathy Wielgosz, Jennifer Healey, Melissa Zar, Teresa Farraiolo, Leigh Ann Higgins, John Nora, Molly Brouillette, Kelsey Marrujo, and Tatiana Merced-Zarou— thank you from the bottom of my heart for everything that you do, from untangling travel snafus to working endless hours on a campaign to suggesting brilliant edits to catching all of my inconsistencies and repetitive word choices in copyedits, and so much more. I love working with you all.

If anyone needs proof that art belongs in the hands of real, human artists, they can find it in the covers for *Icon and Inferno* and *Stars and Smoke*. Both are some of my all-time favorites, thanks to the incredible work of Aurora Parlagreco, Xiao Tong, and Jessica Cruickshank—what an honor it is to have your talent and creativity illuminating these books. Thank you so much for making them shine.

The relationship between writers and readers exists because of booksellers, librarians, teachers, and the countless people who strive to put books on shelves and in the hands of those who want and need them. Thank you so, so much for what you do, against all odds.

My deepest love and gratitude to my friends and family, for filling my life with joy. Most of all, to my husband, Primo Gallanosa, and to our little boy, who has changed us in the best of ways. It is such a privilege to walk through life with you both.

Of course, the reason I can do this at all is because of you. Thank you, my readers. There are truly no words to convey how grateful I am for all of you. Thank you for being here, for your kind words and support, and for your companionship. I hope I can share stories with you for a long time to come.

 x

© Bradford Rogne

MARIE LU is the number one *New York Times* bestselling author of the Legend series, the Young Elites trilogy, the Warcross series, *Batman: Nightwalker*, *The Kingdom of Back*, and the Skyhunter duology. She graduated from the University of Southern California and jumped into the video game industry, where she worked as an artist. Now a full-time writer, she spends her spare hours reading, drawing and playing games. She lives in Los Angeles with her illustrator/author husband, Primo Gallanosa, and their son.

marielu.com
Follow her on Instagram and TikTok:
@marieluthewriter

Sydney and Winter's first adventure:

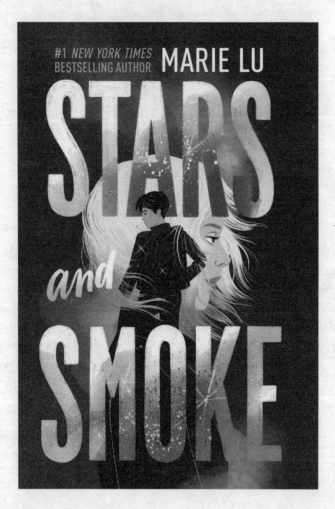